MY BROTHER'S
KEEPER

MY BROTHER'S KEEPER

A THRILLER

VAUGHN C. HARDACKER

Skyhorse Publishing

First Edition

This is a work of fiction. Names, characters, places, and incidents are either the products of the author's imagination or used fictitiously.

Skyhorse Publishing books may be purchased in bulk at special discounts for sales promotion, corporate gifts, fund-raising, or educational purposes. Special editions can also be created to specifications. For details, contact the Special Sales Department, Skyhorse Publishing, Inc., 307 West 36th Street, 11th Floor, New York, NY 10018 or info@skyhorsepublishing.com.

Skyhorse® and Skyhorse Publishing® are registered trademarks of Skyhorse Publishing, Inc.®, a Delaware corporation.

Visit our website at www.skyhorsepublishing.com.

10 9 8 7 6 5 4 3 2 1

Library of Congress Cataloging-in-Publication Data
Names: Hardacker, Vaughn C., author.
Title: My brother's keeper : a novel / Vaughn C. Hardacker.
Description: First Edition. | New York : Skyhorse Publishing, [2019] |
   Includes bibliographical references and index. |
Identifiers: LCCN 2019004387 (print) | LCCN 2019006413 (ebook) | ISBN
   9781510718531 (ebook) | ISBN 9781510718524 (pbk. : alk. paper)
Subjects: LCSH: Murder--Investigation--Fiction. | GSAFD: Mystery fiction.
Classification: LCC PS3608.A72518 (ebook) | LCC PS3608.A72518 M9 2019 (print)
   | DDC 813/.6--dc23
LC record available at https://lccn.loc.gov/2019004387

Cover design by Erin Seaward-Hiatt
Cover illustration and photograph: iStockphoto

Printed in the United States of America

MY BROTHER'S KEEPER

To Connie and Jane

Then the Lord said to Cain, "Where is Abel your brother?"
He said, "I do not know. Am I my brother's keeper?"

—*Genesis, Chapter 4, Verse 9*

O! my offense is rank, it smells to heaven;
It hath the primal eldest curse upon 't;
A brother's murder!

—*William Shakespeare,* Hamlet, *Act III, Scene iii*

1

Four men and a woman huddled in the road, their conversation heated. Rockingham County Sheriff Earl "Buck" Buchanan towered over the two crime scene technicians as he drove home a point by thrusting his right index finger at Kate Toussaint, the solitary woman and deputy chief medical examiner. A gust of wind threw leaves into the air and carried most of their conversation away from the solitary figure standing off to the side, staring at a frozen puddle. Blood had mixed with the pale white ice, resembling strawberry swirl ice cream. Like Buck, Kate was pointing. But her finger pointed at the only person there who was not in an official position. The man felt as if she were aiming a loaded pistol between his eyes. During a lull in the wind, her voice became audible: "Why's Ed Traynor here?"

Hearing them argue, Traynor decided the best way to play things was to be discrete and opted to stay back and wait until one of the combatants motioned him closer. Buck said something in a muted voice.

Although Ed was unable to distinguish Buck's words, he did hear Kate when she distinctly said, "He can do it at the morgue—" Her voice sounded loud and carried in the early morning quiet. Three crows flew overhead and their raucous *CAW CAW* drowned the rest of her speech. Traynor knew that if Kate held her ground, this was as close as he'd get to the tarpaulin-covered body lying in the center of the lane. From his years on the New Hampshire State Police, he knew that while the crime scene may belong to the police, from the instant Kate arrived on site, the body belonged to her. However, Buck was adamant; he bent forward, pushing his ruddy face as close to Kate's as he could without burning her with the stubby cigar he had clenched tightly in his teeth.

Traynor resisted smiling. He and Kate had been a couple once, and he knew her very well. She was not the sort of woman who would be intimidated . . . quite the contrary; she was the type who would attack. "I want him to see the body now—before it leaves the crime scene," Buck's volume increased. "Hell, Kate, the man was a state police homicide detective for ten years! Besides, if the vic is who we think it is he can make a positive ID."

That got Traynor's attention. Since he had gotten Buck's call at 4:40 that morning, asking him to come to the narrow, wooded lane in remote Fremont, it had been eating at him all morning.

Kate said, "I don't give a damn, Buck. He is *not* a cop any longer. He is a private investigator and has no business being here. But, you do whatever you want, Buck—you always have." She threw her hands up in frustration and walked away.

Buchanan had not changed since he and Traynor served together on the state police. As was his usual M.O., he had used his substantial size to get his way. Nevertheless, Traynor knew that if Buck thought he had intimidated Kate and won, he had a big surprise coming. The burly sheriff seemed tentative as he stopped in front of Traynor, his face flushed.

Traynor nodded toward Kate, noting that her eyes still flashed with anger. He said, "Are you sure about this? You could end up owing some favors."

"I know. Kate's a wolverine and like Marines, they fight to the death." Buchanan glanced over his shoulder, studied the deputy chief medical examiner for a few seconds, and then said, "She's still pissed at you for breaking it off with her two years ago." He paused again.

"Well, don't be surprised if this ends up costing you," Traynor said.

"At this point I don't give a damn," Buck said with more fervor that Traynor had heard him display since he'd thrown his hat into the political arena and ran for Rockingham County Sheriff. He glanced off into the trees. "Listen—"

Traynor signaled him to stop. "What's up? You've never before called me to a crime scene."

Buck pulled the cigar out of his mouth and looked at it as if it suddenly tasted foul.

"Come on, man," Traynor pressed him, "you look like you're getting a root canal during a Novocain shortage. Do I know the vic?"

Buck tossed the cigar to the ground and stomped on it before saying, "Yeah, I think it's your brother."

"John?" Traynor struggled not to let shock show on his face.

"You better look for yourself. I haven't seen him in ten years and people change." Buck stepped aside allowing him access to the body.

John, Traynor's only brother, was four years his junior. He was everything Traynor had worked against his entire adult life. Where Ed had chosen law enforcement as his career, John was a petty thief, drug addict, and dealer. Considering their parents, Traynor had to admit that his younger brother had probably turned out closer to what people expected than he had. Their father was a drinker and a brawler and their mother a drinker and a nagger. They had grown up in a family that was self-destructive a long time before TV sitcoms made dysfunctional behavior fashionable and funny.

Buck stepped aside and gave his old friend an unobstructed path to the body. It lay in the bloody ice that Traynor found so mesmerizing. Traynor stared at the tarp and thought: *the least they could have done was take the body out of the ice.*

For the first time in years, Ed Traynor wanted a cigarette. It took all of his willpower to sound calm. "All right, let's get this over with so I can go about my business."

He stared at the menacing tarp and felt resentment build as he recalled the craziness of his childhood. Traynor cursed John. *It is just like him to die like this, dragging me back to places I do not want to go—to places I thought I would never visit again.*

Buck walked around Traynor, stopping beside the covered body. He took care to avoid stepping on the ice and straddled the corpse, squatted down, and reached for the tarp. A gust of wind lifted one side of the canvas and it rose up resembling a cobra poised to strike. Ignoring the violent whipping action, Buck reached out, caught the corner, and pulled it back.

Buck squatted over the body, looked up, and said, "You want to move closer so you can get a closer look at his face?"

The instant Traynor saw the blond hair and the cherry-red birthmark under the left eye, his stomach felt as empty as a hollow tree trunk. "There's no need. It's him."

Buck rocked back on his heels, dropped the tarp, stood up, and looked at the sky again. "Aw shit, Ed. I'm sorry. I thought it was, but I had to be sure."

"You have any idea how long he's been dead?"

"That's hard to say. The weather is too cold for the crime scene techs to determine time of death with any degree of accuracy. Kate will get an estimated T-O-D once she has him opened up." He realized how callous his words sounded and reddened. He looked Traynor in the eye and shifted back into official mode. "He's been here long enough for the blood in his extremities to freeze, and he seems to be in total rigor."

"So that makes it—somewhere between two and twenty-four hours?"

"That sounds about right, give or take; last night was cold enough for a body to start freezing." Buck seemed pensive for a few seconds and then said, "You want a few minutes?"

"Sure, I'd like to get a close look at him. Is it all right to touch him?"

"I don't see a problem, they're finished working the body. Take your time. I'll be with Kate." Buck paused for a second, then reached for another cigar and peeled the wrapper as he walked away.

2

Traynor squatted beside his brother's body. John lay on his side, his right cheek obscured by the milky, white ice. Traynor gently brushed away the thin line of frozen water that stubbornly stuck to John's right cheek, turned the head to the left, and looked at his brother's face. Hoarfrost stuck to the eyebrows and lashes, and his face was a frozen mask that could only be described as a mixture of fright and grief—as if, at the end, he tried to repent, but didn't know how.

Traynor stared at the lifeless eyes and found it hard to remember that in spite of what he'd become as an adult, John had once been a happy little kid. A boy filled with awe at the wonders of life—more importantly, he'd been a kid who worshiped his older brother, the cop.

Traynor leaned forward, parted the frozen hair near John's right temple; the lethal entrance wound was barely discernible—a small hole in the right temple. Years of experience and the size of the wound told

Ed there would be no exit wound on the opposite side. The murder weapon was obviously a small bore and fired a subsonic round—probably a twenty-two caliber, certainly no larger than a twenty-five. The first thing that came to his mind was *professional hit*. Many paid assassins prefer the small twenty-two caliber pistol. It doesn't make a lot of noise and the bullet bangs around inside the skull ripping the brain to shreds. More importantly, there usually isn't enough of the projectile left for a ballistics test to identify the weapon that fired it, and on the outside chance there was anything left, the weapon was usually inexpensive enough to be thrown into the nearest body of water.

Traynor found himself at a loss; for the first time in his life, he was uncertain as to what he should do. Part of him knew that he should grieve. Yet, another part wanted to strike out in rage at John. He glanced at Buck. Kate stood beside him and stared in Traynor's direction, her eyes flashing with anger. Traynor knew that Buck expected him to lose his temper; to rant and rave at John, to vent his frustration at his brother for living a life that led him here—to a violent death on an obscure deserted lane. Traynor often wished his feelings were so cut-and-dry. John was his only brother and he loved him. Nevertheless, the younger of the Traynor boys used and hurt everyone who reached out to him, and that aspect of his personality Ed hated.

The reality of the situation hit him—as hard as hitting the water of the Great Salt Lake after diving off a twenty-foot platform. This wasn't some stranger lying in the ice—it was his brother. For the first time, Ed was at a crime scene where the victim was someone he knew personally. To make matters worse, this time it was a relative, his own flesh and blood. He dropped the canvas, got to his feet, and strode several paces away, hiding his face from Buck and the others.

Ed Traynor had lived in New England for most of his life, leaving only to serve four years as a US Marine, and the last thing a Yankee from New England did was reveal emotion in public. He wanted some time alone—just a few moments. Indignation and rage took control of him; his face felt hot, and his heart began to pound. He knew that more than anything else, he needed to tighten the reins on his anger. Trying to get his wits together, Traynor surveyed the area, studying the leafless trees as they swayed in the wind. It didn't work. Instead, his mind switched channels and he began planning the killer's death. He paused, confused. As a cop, he'd killed two men in the line of duty, but never had he wanted to kill someone intentionally. However, he was resolved that whoever did this was going to pay.

The frozen ground crunched beneath someone's feet, and Ed turned toward the sound. Buck stood a couple of yards away and looked uncomfortable as he reached out, placing his hand on Traynor's arm. "Ed, I wish I could tell you I haven't been expecting this for a long time, but he ran with a rough crowd—this was inevitable, merely a matter of time. John always wanted more out of life than he could get as the son of a . . ." Buck was reluctant to go on.

"Son of a drunken mill worker?" Traynor tried to keep emotion out of his words, but failed.

"Hell, I didn't mean anything, but even in high school, he was completely out of control. Eventually, even the cops who knew you stopped looking the other way and began bringing him in . . . then he got sent away for robbing that convenience store."

Traynor knew that Buck was right and that there was nothing he could say to refute him. It was true: by the time John was sixteen he already had an extensive rap sheet and was well on his way to building a criminal career. It all came to a head when he tried robbing a store and his piece-of-crap partner, a lowlife named Benny Ryan, deserted him. The cops nailed John in the parking lot, still holding the pistol, and it got him a stretch in a state juvenile detention center.

Traynor said, "You don't have to remind me of that—it was the end of his childhood. After his release, his escapades escalated, becoming more serious."

"Doing that time didn't help matters any, that's for sure. It was as if he had earned a Master of Arts degree from the New Hampshire Crime College."

Buck was right. Shortly after John's release, he used contacts he had made in prison to get in with drug dealers and pushers from

Massachusetts. Traynor said, "I warned him that he was dealing with people you didn't screw around with. He laughed, saying he could handle it." Traynor looked at the billowing tarp. Even in death, John was a big man; he was four inches taller than Ed, who was six feet, two inches tall. John spent a lot of time in the gym and had a weight lifter's arms and torso. He, too, suffered from the family curse of having a quick temper and only his size kept him from getting into even more trouble. Traynor looked at the tarp-covered body once again and asked himself: *had John finally run across someone he could not handle?* Traynor's eyes kept moving back and forth between Buck and John's body. "In spite of our differences, I always gave him another chance," he said.

"Well," Buck said, "he just ran out of them."

Rather than console him, his friend's words only served to make Traynor's guilt stronger. Traynor realized that for most of their lives he had ignored John. It was probably the worst thing anyone could have done to a kid with low self-esteem—a kid whose parents ignored him to the point that even negative attention was better than no attention. "I often wonder if many of the things he did were to get people to notice him," Traynor mused.

"Whatever the reason . . . this time, he definitely got someone's attention."

It took a while for Traynor to fight off the belief that John lying dead in a pool of bloody ice was somehow his fault. He asked, "How do you think this went down?" He was relieved when there was no trace of grief in his voice and was thankful for a chance to bury his feelings by reverting to *cop-talk.*

"This has all the markings of a drug hit," Buck said.

Traynor looked around at the rustic setting, a lane in the middle of the New Hampshire woods, not the sort of place one would expect a drug hit to happen. He thought about that for a second and realized no place was immune to drug-related crimes; as a matter of fact, the more remote the site, the more likely it would eventually become a crime scene. "You got any witnesses?"

"Not yet." Buck motioned to the forest surrounding them. "It's almost a quarter mile to Prescott Road. There are houses hidden all through these trees though. I've got some men canvassing the area and asking if anyone heard or saw anything."

"Who found him?"

"A couple of joggers, they come through here every morning on their way to Loon Pond."

"What did he have on him?"

"Not much, want to look at it?"

"Can I?"

"Yeah, we're just waiting for a meat wagon to take him to the morgue." Buck realized how callous he sounded; his face reddened and, once again, looked uncomfortable. Traynor ignored the phrase they'd always used for the ambulances that picked up dead bodies.

Buck called to one of the crime scene technicians, asking them to bring him John's personal effects. The man jogged over and handed him a plastic bag and a pair of latex gloves. Buck, in turn, handed them to Traynor. Allowing him access to John's personal effects was proof of the level of trust that Buck had in his former partner. Like any law enforcement officer, under normal circumstances, Buck would protect the chain of custody of any evidence as a mother bear protects her newborn cubs. Traynor appreciated his confidence, slipped the gloves over his hands, and opened the bag.

The bag contained John's wallet, passport, and an envelope. Traynor opened the wallet first. There was some cash in it, about eighty bucks, eliminating robbery as a motive. He dumped the money into the bag and turned the wallet inside out. There was a business card inside the lining, hidden where a cursory inspection would not find it. The wrinkled and worn card had been in the wallet for quite some time. He glanced at Buck, who now stood with his back to him, speaking with Kate. It looked as if they had patched things up. While they were preoccupied, Traynor read the card. It was from a strip joint just over the Massachusetts line. Traynor knew the place; a low-class club with an even lower clientele.

Like most trained investigators, Traynor took tons of notes over the years, many on the back of his business cards, and out of habit he turned it over. There was a name written in pencil. He put the card back and held the evidence bag against his side with an arm. He didn't think the card would lead him anywhere, but in a murder investigation, you never take anything for granted. One never knew which piece of information would lead to something important. He wrote down the name of the club, The Sexy Fox, and Consuela in his notebook.

The only other thing in the wallet was a picture of John's wife and daughters. When he saw the picture of Jillian, Traynor's knees weakened. *Had anyone informed Jillian about this? If not, who was going to tell her?* He dreaded the thought of performing that onerous task, but knew he was the best person for the job. John had finally gotten the end for which his entire family knew he was destined, leaving his wife alone to raise two beautiful girls.

Traynor doubted that John had either medical or life insurance and was tempted to take the money from the wallet—no matter how small an amount, he knew that Jillian and the girls could use it. Once the police placed the money into evidence it could be months before they got it, if at all. Even in a department under the command of an honest cop like Buck, things have a way of disappearing from the evidence room, especially liquid assets like dope and cash. Traynor decided to talk with Buck. The wallet contained nothing else of any value, and he dumped it back into the bag.

He removed the envelope. Printed on the outside was the name of a travel agency. The address was a mall near John's home in Salem, New Hampshire. He opened it and removed its contents: a single airline ticket. The flight was first class, from Manchester to Buenos Aires, via Chicago. John had laid out some big bucks to fly in luxury. He wondered how he could afford it; first-class tickets on international flights were not cheap. Had John finally made the big score about which he always dreamed? Traynor pondered the first of many questions he knew would have to be answered: *John, what in hell were you into?*

Whatever his plan was, it was evident his family was not part of it. It looked like John was deserting Jillian and the girls. Traynor's face burned. Suddenly, he was aware that, in spite of the cool late-fall weather, sweat had plastered his shirt to his chest. If John had been standing beside him, he would have kicked his ass all the way to Argentina. He put the envelope back in the evidence bag.

Forcing himself to stroll, rather than pace, Traynor approached Buck and the others. While walking, he took deep breaths, calming the raging demon in his chest. By the time he reached them, he was once again in control of his emotions. He handed the evidence bag to Buck and then peeled off the latex gloves. "Will you get me a copy of the autopsy report?" he asked.

Buck nodded.

"Has anyone seen his wife yet?"

"No, I thought you might want to be there when we break the news to her."

"It'll be best if I do it alone. Can you give me a few hours?" Thinking of Jillian and her girls made his voice hard, his diction clipped by anger; she deserved a better husband than John. She had no family left in the state. Her father had passed away three months after her marriage to John, and her mother had moved to Florida within the year.

"Well, considering that she lives in Hillsborough County—I think it'll be a while before anyone can get to her."

For several moments, Traynor stood silent, staring at the barren trees and boulders that were scattered through the woods. Finally, he said, "You need me for anything else?"

"No, tell your sister-in-law that either a state police detective or someone from the Hillsborough County sheriff's office will be by to talk with her. Oh—and give her my best."

"Listen, Buck, Jill works as a waitress and with two girls, money is tight."

Buck looked over his shoulder. He saw that Kate and the others stood beside John's body and took the money out of the bag. He counted it and then gave it to Traynor. "Take the cash. I'll report that I released it to the family." Buck noticed his friend's angry look and put his hand on Traynor's arm, gently restraining him. His big, brown puppy-dog eyes looked concerned when he said, "Eddie, don't, okay?"

Traynor glared at him. "Don't what?"

"Just don't—I know how you can get. I remember the time you lost your cool up north."

Traynor knew the incident to which he referred. The perpetrator had been beating and terrorizing his wife and kids for years. His oldest daughter's aversion to being touched had made Traynor believe that he had been doing worse things than that. In fact, it was for criminal sexual assault on his oldest daughter that the criminal justice system finally sent him up. Traynor lost his cool that day and decided to teach the bastard what being assaulted by someone bigger felt like. For a few years after the perp had gone to prison, Traynor had pleasant dreams about the treatment he was surely receiving. It's no secret how inmates treat child abusers—as far as Traynor was concerned it couldn't happen to a more deserving man.

He turned to Buck and replied, "I'm cool. Keep me in the loop, that's all I ask."

"You got it." He paused. "Remember what I said, okay? Getting crazy and running around kicking ass and taking names could cost you your P.I. ticket." Buck returned to the medical team.

Traynor took a final look at the tarp lying amid a bouquet of gold and red leaves. It felt as if he was abandoning John, leaving him in the hands of strangers yet again. This time, however, he had no choice. Until Kate finished the autopsy, John was property of the state of New Hampshire.

Traynor turned and started walking down the trail to his car. As he breathed in the crisp air, he decided that whether they had gotten along did not matter. John was his brother, and Ed was going to bring his killer down.

3

As Traynor walked back to his car, he decided that it was time he started his own investigation. He saw a house nestled back in the woods, hidden by pines and cedars, and walked off the road, cutting through the trees.

Green mold grew in mangy patches on the cedar shakes that covered the building, the roof of the farmer's front porch that spanned the front sagged in the center, and the boards on the porch were warped and curled. As decrepit as it appeared from a distance, it looked worse up close. Someone had nailed a sign reading *Yeehaw Junction* over the door of the garage, the roof of which looked like it would collapse under the weight of the next snowfall—Traynor thought that it seemed appropriate. The owner had taken advantage of the density of the trees on his property to hide an illegal salvage yard. Rusted hulks of cars, broken appliances, and an old pickup truck with its bed full of garbage and junk littered the property. The detritus had apparently been there for years; everything wore a thick layer of rust.

Ed had one foot on the steps leading to the weathered porch when the door opened with a bang. An overweight man in a filthy T-shirt confronted him. It was just past eight in the morning and Traynor knew that the can of beer in the guy's hand was obviously not his first of the day, nor would it be his last.

"What you want?" His bully attitude did not impress Traynor.

"I'm Ed Traynor, I'm an investigator . . ."

"Cops been here already. I ain't seen or heard nothing."

"I'm not a cop—"

He cut Traynor off mid-sentence. "Then I got nothing to say to you."

His attitude pissed Traynor off. The anger and frustration he had been battling since he first saw his brother's body was ignited, and his bullshit meter flew off the scale. The valve on his internal pressure cooker let go and his pent-up rage cracked through his defenses, releasing a storm of fury. He vaulted up the steps, barreled into the scumbag, and slammed him against the wall. He laid his forearm across the man's throat and pushed forward.

"I got rights . . ." The junkyard owner's voice squeaked.

"I told you, I'm not a cop. You don't have any fucking rights with me."

"I'll sue the shit out of you."

"Go ahead. However, before you do I should warn you that right now I am starting what will be a very shitty day. So bad in fact, that spreading you around the county could turn out to be the high point."

When he swallowed, Traynor felt the man's Adam's apple move beneath his forearm. "You'd better talk to me, because if I think you're holding out, I'll burn off some of my anger. Now let's start over. Did you hear anything last night?"

When Traynor pushed him, the beer fell from his hand, soaking Traynor's right leg. Rather than cool him, the cold liquid fueled his flames. He put more pressure on his forearm. The junkyard owner swallowed hard and, once again, Traynor felt his Adam's apple move. He thought the redneck was about to bawl. Traynor knew his type. He was the neighborhood bully; he had bluffed his way through life with a big front. Eventually, he would come up against someone like Traynor and show his true stripes.

Traynor could have cared less about anything but the task. He wanted to know if this bastard had seen or heard anything and was in no mood to play games with him. As the junk dealer struggled to breathe, his eyes bulged and sweat dripped from his greasy hair. Traynor tightened his grip on the sweat-soaked T-shirt, spun the man around, and pushed him.

The man flailed his arms as he teetered on the edge of the top step, his only support Traynor's grip on his sweaty shirt. Traynor let go of the shirt, punched him in the face, and followed the asshole as he hit the ground. The junk dealer scrambled to his feet, but Traynor was waiting. He hit the man again and watched him backpedal in the direction of a rusted Plymouth. Reaching the car, Traynor placed a leg behind the man and pushed him down. The car's left rear quarter sat on a jack, and, once his captive was on the ground, Traynor reestablished his grip on the shirt and dragged the man until his head was under the rusting chassis. Placing his foot against the jack, he said, "Now asshole, either you talk or I push—"

"ALL RIGHT, SWEET JESUS, DON'T!"

Traynor looked at the man's face and, when his color changed from blue to red, knew he had his full attention. He eased the pressure his foot exerted on the jack.

The junk dealer stared at the metal wheel of the car hovering inches above his face and the pitch of his voice increased to a falsetto. "Last night, around eleven o'clock, a car stopped over by the bike trail. These guys got out—"

"Guys? How many guys?"

"Two got out of the car, but in no time I knew something funny was going on."

"What do you mean funny?"

"They had a third guy in the trunk."

"You saw all this in the dark?"

"Yeah—before it stopped, the car drove by here real slow a couple of times, and I got suspicious. I been having problems with some local kids stealing parts. So, I came outside to check it out. I walked over and hid in some bushes alongside the trail and them guys walked right by me. Like I said, one seemed nervous. The spic—"

"Spic?"

"Yeah, one of the two who was leading the fella from the trunk talked with a Spanish accent. Now, I figured that some real shit was going down. I wanted no part of it and went inside the house—a few minutes later I heard a shot."

"What did you do then?"

"I turned out all the lights, grabbed my shotgun, and hid out back. If those spics saw my lights they might have decided to eliminate any witnesses, and I didn't want to be around if they came calling."

"What about the car?"

"After I heard that shot, I hid. I ain't no hero. But, I did see enough of the car to know it was a 1964 Chevy, a classic. I recognized the taillights, probably an Impala Super Sport."

"You're sure it was a '64 Chevy Super Sport?" John owned one. *Had his killer driven him here in his own car?*

"Well, I'm positive it was a '64 Chevy . . . although I didn't see the inside to tell if it was a Super Sport or not."

As he calmed down, Traynor became aware of the man's body odor. It was strong, an overly ripe smell—similar to rotten fish on a sweltering day. Traynor took a business card from his pocket, wrapped it in a twenty-dollar bill, and stuffed it down the neck of the junk dealer's T-shirt. "That's my card. If you remember anything else, I want a call."

Traynor stepped back, feeling his anger burn out as quickly as it had flared up. "If I were you, I wouldn't stay under there any longer than I had to—that jack doesn't look very stable."

Fully aware he would never hear from him again, Traynor left him there, walked to his car, and got in. It was a forty-five-minute drive to Salem. Time he needed to rehearse what he would say to his sister-in-law.

He gripped the steering wheel so tight his knuckles turned white. Telling Jillian about John was going to be another emotional roller coaster, a chore to which he was not looking forward.

As he sped away, he looked in his rearview mirror. It would not have surprised him to see God standing in the road, accusing him as he had Cain. Apparently, he was going to be his brother's keeper, whether he liked it or not.

4

Traynor pulled into the parking lot of the apartment complex in Salem, New Hampshire, near Rockingham Park Race Track. Twenty years ago, these apartments had been among the best in Salem, and, while still in good shape, they were not luxurious by any measure. For a person who spent his entire life chasing the big score, John did not have much to show for it.

His wife, Jillian, had always been the glue that held their marriage together. She worked full time as a waitress and bore all the responsibility at home. Traynor was sure that even if they could afford a house, she and John would still have lived in apartments; he would have been little, if any, help around a home. John was better suited to living in a place where someone else was accountable for maintenance and yard work. Things between John and Jillian had deteriorated over the past couple of years, and Traynor believed she was finally ready to hand him his walking papers.

He parked in front of the building and shut the motor off. He was hesitant; this would not be easy. He sat with his hands gripping the steering wheel until his fingers began to cramp. He let his mind drift and recalled the day Jill married his brother.

It was a beautiful day for a wedding. A soft, gentle breeze slowly pushed big cumulus clouds across the sky, and the sun warmed the land. Traynor felt that early June was the best time of year in New England; winter's cold and frost were gone, and the heat and humidity of summer had yet to arrive. Wanting to be sure he was not late for the ceremony, Traynor got up at first light and drove to the church early.

He and John hadn't been close since John was arrested as a juvenile delinquent and sentenced to prison. Traynor knew that in these politically correct times, they didn't call kids juvenile delinquents, but youthful offenders. Nevertheless, he surmised that whatever they were called, it meant the same thing; kids so dumb that most of them didn't even know how deep in trouble they were. They believe they're right and everyone else is wrong. John was no exception. Not once in his life had he ever taken responsibility for his actions; he always had someone to blame—in either fact or fiction.

Traynor knew John didn't really want him to be his best man. In fact, he'd been shocked when John asked if he would do it. Traynor accepted—possibly to call his brother's bluff. Someone, most likely Jill, had used their influence and exerted pressure on John; encouragement is not a strong enough word to describe what it took to move John in a given direction. He sure as hell wouldn't have done it on his own. If Traynor were dying of thirst, he doubted that John would cross the street to give him a drink of water. He might do it to taunt him by pouring the water in the gutter. Somewhere, somehow, he and Traynor had lost anything even resembling brotherly love, settling for a long period of sibling hatred. Traynor was certain Jill felt that since both their parents were dead, someone from John's family should be in the wedding. That meant their sister, Maureen, or Traynor had to do something. When Jill considered none of John's friends suitable to serve as his best man, Traynor was most likely her only alternative.

He glanced at his watch. He was ready to kick John's butt, ten minutes to go and still no sign of him. Jill and her father had been inside the church for almost thirty minutes, waiting for the ceremony to start. Traynor could hear the nervous chatter of the bridesmaids primping over each other. It was probable they were checking each other's coiffures and putting final touches on their makeup.

Traynor walked outside the church to see if there was any sign of his brother. His anger increased as he paced back and forth on the steps, trying valiantly not to let his temperament show. Showing a complete disregard for anyone else's feelings was like John. In truth, it had been a long-term behavior pattern for him. He was as mad at himself as he was at his irresponsible younger sibling. He repeatedly asked himself the same question: *Why should I expect anything different?* He stopped pacing and stared up the street, hoping to see John coming. He shook his head knowing that by expecting John to do the right thing, he had once again set himself up.

If John screwed this up, Jill would be devastated. Traynor had never married. In fact, he had had very few long-term relationships with women. However, he remembered how important Maureen's wedding day had been to her, when she got married five years prior. She later explained it to him: for many women, their wedding day is the one day on which they have center stage. It is the beginning of a new life for them. One filled with promises of love, togetherness, and starting their own family, the role their mothers had been preparing them for since they were old enough to put on their first dress. To many young women, their wedding is possibly the most important thing, other than the birth of their children, which would happen in their lives.

A rusted, beat-up Dodge truck pulled over to the curb, and a cloud of white smoke rumbled from the exhaust system, a sure sign of a bad head gasket. John stumbled out of the passenger seat, slammed the door shut, and then leaned in the window. Traynor walked down the steps ready to ream him a new asshole. He was less than five feet away from the pickup when he first detected the unmistakable smell of burnt hemp. He stood behind John, fighting back the urge to grab him by the collar and shake him so hard that his eyeballs clicked. Instead, Traynor stood his ground, shaking with anger, and decided to give John another minute to stop talking with the driver of the car. Benny Ryan sat behind the steering wheel smiling that shit-eating grin dopers get when they are stoned out of their minds. John took a final toke on the joint and passed it to Benny.

Benny waved to Traynor. It was obvious that flaunting his drug use at a state cop amused him. At that moment, more than anything in his life, Traynor wanted to reach in the car and strangle them both. Finally, just as Traynor was losing control, John gave Benny a high five and stumbled away from the car.

Benny, not wanting to lose the chance to show off his disrespect for cops, burned rubber as he pulled away from the church.

John turned with a smirk on his face. There was no way he was able to hide the fact that he was stoned from Jill and her guests. He stumbled and Traynor caught his arm, keeping him from falling.

"Hey *big* brother, how you doing?" John grinned as if there was nothing wrong.

Traynor tightened his grip on his brother's arm, exerting all the pressure he could. John's grin disappeared and he squealed like a pig. Hoping to avoid a scene, Traynor loosened his grip and pulled him closer. He kept his voice low so it would not carry inside the church and said, "Goddamn you, John! Jillian is inside with her family and closest friends. In fact, I think the reason she's marrying you is that she sees some part of you worth redeeming—although I'll be damned if I can think what it might be—and she thinks she can change you, and what do you do? You show up bombed out of your fucking mind! What in hell is the matter with you?"

John pulled free of his grip, grinned again, shrugged his shoulders, and held his hands out to his side, palms out. "Wha' can I say, big bro? I'm just the family fuckup."

His attempt to assuage things with a humorous confession did nothing to cool Traynor down. What it did was piss him off more. He grabbed John again and pulled him closer. John's breath and clothes reeked of marijuana. For Jillian's sake, Traynor hoped no one inside got close enough to smell it—though he knew it was a futile hope. He pushed John away, took a roll of breath mints from his pocket, and gave them to John. "Here, take one of these. Hell, take all of them!"

John teetered back and forth and said in as sarcastic a tone as anyone can when they are stoned, "You wouldn't bust me on my wedding day, would you, big bro?"

"No, but right now I'd like to kick your ass from here to Concord."

"That's my big brother, always wantin' to kick my ass." He pulled his arm free and staggered back a step. Suddenly John morphed, looking like a sad and forlorn small boy. "Why is that, Eddie? How come you always want to beat the hell out of me?"

"Possibly for the same reason that you always seem to do the worst possible fucking thing at the worst possible fucking time! Someone needs to get your attention, you thickheaded ass—and physical force is all you seem to understand." Traynor took his arm and guided him toward the steps. "Now come on, Jill is waiting. Please, for her sake, try not to fuck things up."

"Not to worry. It's a piece of cake."

With Traynor's assistance, John made it to the altar and once they were in place, seemed to straighten up. He hoped that John was not as stoned as he thought he was. He was so busy worrying that his brother would make a shamble of the ceremony, embarrassing Jill and her family, that most of the wedding ceremony seemed to last forever.

Traynor thought it was all over when the presiding priest smelled the aura that surrounded John and looked over the top of his glasses. Obviously, he did not like the situation. Traynor's heart raced for a few seconds but settled down when the clergyman opted not to create a scene in front of his parishioners and their guests. He turned his attention away from the groom and went on with the ceremony. He motioned to the organist. The "Wedding March" started playing, and the procession started down the aisle.

Jill looked regal in her long, flowing white gown, the train spread out behind her as her father led her down the aisle. As he watched her approach, Traynor hoped John appreciated just how lucky he was. Jillian's father, Bill Benton, surely did. He was as proud as any father of the bride could be. Walking his daughter down that aisle was something Bill never thought he would do. He was full of cancer, it was in his liver and his lungs, and his doctors expected him to be dead in less than three months. Bill was another reason why Traynor wanted everything to go well. They had known each other for years, and Traynor had never once heard the man say a mean thing about or do anything malicious to anyone.

Jill stepped beside John, and Traynor saw her eyes narrow appreciably when she saw John's red, blurry, bloodshot eyes and smelled the marijuana. If she had walked out of the church, he, for one, would not have blamed her. Hell, at that time, he probably would have cheered. Instead, he gave her a smile, hoping to reassure her that everything would be all right. Fortunately for everyone concerned, for the remainder of the ceremony it was. The only scare was when John fumbled while getting the ring on her finger.

The reception was another matter. It was an occasion filled with opportunities for John to make an ass of himself. Nevertheless, he survived because everyone was getting drunk and, as the guests' level of sobriety waned, his condition became less noticeable. Traynor wondered if Jill had so much as a clue that she might have taken on a task too daunting even for her.

Traynor made a vow to stay close to them, but not to help John—he wouldn't have appreciated it anyhow.

A group of kids played on the grass common alongside the building, and Traynor stared at them for several seconds before realizing his nieces were among them. When he got out of the car, Julia, John and Jillian's youngest, spotted him and ran forward, shouting, "Uncle Ed!"

She leapt from four feet away and hit him square in the chest. It was a good thing she only weighed about forty pounds or one or both of them would have been hurt. Traynor laughed as he caught the skinny five-year-old bundle of arms, legs, and blond hair. Julia was everyone's darling. Precocious and inquisitive, she was a live wire and always kept everyone around her hopping.

He swung her around and placed her on the ground. Hearing more shouts, he looked up. Carrie, her seven-year-old sister, ran across the parking lot on a collision course with her uncle and sister. Ed had to admit that the one thing John and Jillian did well together was produce beautiful children. Both had their mother's stunning green eyes and clear complexion, and John's wavy golden hair.

Traynor knelt down and gathered them into his arms. They were his treasures, the only kids that ever bonded with him. Over the years, during John's absences, of which there were many, he took them to the amusement park at Canobie Lake, shopping, or to the movies. Sometimes, he had to remind himself that he was their uncle, not their father. Suddenly, he realized that from now on he was most likely going to be the only father they had. He was afraid his face would give away the sadness he suddenly felt for them.

Julia smiled and coyly asked, "Uncle Ed, what's that in there?"

Traynor forced a smile and patted his left jacket pocket. "You mean in this pocket?"

"No, silly, the other one. Do you have something for us in there?" She knew fully well that he always brought them something—Uncle Ed's pockets were always as fruitful as Santa's sack.

He reached inside and took out the candy bars he had bought for them. Once their ritual was complete, they began to chatter, and he held his hands up in surrender and said, "Okay, okay, calm down now. Is Mommy home?"

"Yes," Julia answered, "but she's not in a happy mood. Daddy didn't come home last night and she has to go to work. Are you going to sit us?"

"Whoa, Pumpkin, not so fast. Where's Eileen? I thought your Mom was paying her to watch you girls?"

"Eileen had to go away on vacation and Daddy said he'd watch us. I like it when Daddy's home. He gives me horsey rides," Julia said.

Her face was that of a child still too young to see her father for what he was, and the innocence he saw there made him pause. She looked at John and only saw Daddy. Traynor wished that he could have seen him through a child's eyes. "I need to talk with Mommy. You girls go back and play."

Julia ran off waving the candy, showing her friends the treasure her Uncle Ed had brought. Carrie remained by his side. She was the more perceptive of the girls, but then she was the oldest . . . old enough to realize that her father was not like the fathers of her friends. She reached up, took his hand in hers, then looked at him with her big green eyes, and asked, "Uncle Ed, is something wrong? You look sad."

"I'm okay, Tadpole. I just need to talk with your Mommy in private for a bit. You run along and watch your sister."

For a moment, Traynor believed she was going to push the issue. In that uncanny way kids have, she decided to leave adult problems to the adults. She suddenly jumped up, wrapped her arms around his neck, kissed him on the cheek, and then ran away joining her sister. Traynor swallowed a lump the size of the Old Man of the Mountain and fought back tears.

5

Traynor walked to the apartment building, giving himself a few extra seconds to regain his composure. Entering the foyer, he paused at the mailboxes, reluctant to press the call button beneath the name *Traynor*. With a deep inhalation of chilly air, he pressed the button.

After a few seconds, Jillian's voice said, "Who is it?" The electronic medium of the cheap intercom did not hide the fact that she was angry, and he didn't need a PhD in psychology to know at whom. Trying to keep his voice level, Traynor answered, "Ed." The interior door buzzed and unlocked with a loud click.

It only took a few minutes to climb the stairs to the third floor, and when Traynor approached her door, Jillian stood in the threshold dressed for work. Even in her work clothes, a simple white blouse and black pants, there was an air of elegance about her. Before he was able to say anything, she snapped at him. "Have you seen him?" The angry edge in her voice was sharper than a boning knife.

"Jillian—"

In that uncanny way that women have of sensing bad news, she knew why he was there before he said anything else. She must have read his body language and she backed away, her jaw clenched, and her eyes narrow and hard. The cold, steely look surprised him; it was something he had never seen before. Traynor knew then that she had already turned the corner in her relationship with John. Nobody could ever blame her for finally giving up. On a good day, John was a jerk. The finality of it must have sunk in. When she inhaled, Traynor knew that she was trying to keep her emotions in check. "Something's happened to John."

Traynor knew she was trying as hard as she could to control her anger; her diction was precise, the words clipped with indignation and fury. He stepped inside the apartment, closing the door softly.

That damned lump returned to his throat and he was unable to speak for a couple of seconds. Swallowing hard, Traynor nodded his head. "He's dead—it happened last night. I just left the scene."

"Dead—how did he die?"

"It wasn't an accident."

Her eyes softened and became moist, then the hard set in her jaw loosened—she looked like Jillian again. She took a deep breath, "Oh, damn, Eddie. What are we going to do now?"

Traynor opened his arms, inviting her in. She slid into the protective shell he provided and laid her head against his chest. He savored the feel of her chest pressed against his, the scent of her, and wanted the embrace to go on forever.

After a few seconds, she stepped away and turned to the living room. He followed, guiding her to the couch. She flopped down and buried her face in her hands, trying to conceal her tears. She cried for a few seconds, wiped her eyes and cheeks, and said, "Oh, my God, how will I tell the girls!"

He pulled some tissues from the box that sat on the end table and handed them to her. "The girls don't need to know anything, not until we're ready to tell them, anyway. However, I think you will have to tell them something. When I saw them outside, Carrie was acting as if she already knows something isn't right."

Jillian used a tissue to wipe her eyes and seemed to calm down. Traynor saw her resolve return, replacing the grief.

"How did it happen?"

"It looked like a drug hit."

Her eyes narrowed and anger returned, making them flash. "That stupid bastard! I told him to break it off with those guys!"

Traynor's cop curiosity piqued and he bent toward her. "What guys?" he asked. He realized that his tone sounded official, but was unable to stop himself. He probed, aware he had turned the visit into an investigative interview. "Come on, Jillian, I want the people who did this to pay. John and I were never going to be candidates for a Boy's Town poster, and he wasn't exactly the ideal brother—"

"—or husband," she added.

"Nevertheless, he was my brother and I'm going to do everything I can to find out who did this and make them pay for it."

"He never told me the specifics, but I knew more about his business than he thought. He always had a lot of money for a man who never held a steady job. I've known for years that he was a drug pusher. He said this was going to be his final score. One big payoff and then he'd get out." She snorted. "He was the only one who believed that line of bullshit. I certainly didn't. He was always saying crap like that to convince himself more than anyone else. He used as much of that junk as he sold."

Traynor agreed with her. John was always talking about making a big score. The problem was, all his scores were small, barely producing enough cash to meet his expenses. "You got any coffee?" he asked.

"On the kitchen counter."

"Stay put, I know where everything is." He stood up and walked into the kitchen thinking that John sure got his big payoff this time.

He shook the shiny metal carafe to see how full it was and then poured a cup of coffee. Traynor opened the cupboard looking for sugar and found it behind a set of keys on a round key ring, with the initials *JT* embossed on a large round fob. He pushed the keys aside and took the dispenser out. After he had opened the refrigerator, he turned to Jill and asked, "You want a cup?"

"Yes." She watched—her expression seemed uneasy—as he got a second cup and poured the coffee. Traynor empathized with her. If he had to tell two little girls that they were never going to see their Daddy again, he would be nervous too.

In his cup, he added sugar and half-and-half, and then returned everything to its place. Traynor walked into the living room, gave Jillian her coffee, black as usual, and then sat next to her. "When did you last see John?"

"Yesterday; it was my day off and he stayed around the house until noon. He said he had an important meeting and not to wait up for him, then he left."

"Jillian, think, did John say anything about what he was into, something specific for me to go on? Did he give you any idea who he was meeting?"

"Ed, believe me, if I knew anything, I'd tell you. He didn't tell me anything, not so much as a hint. We know one thing for certain . . . drugs were involved. He was nervous about something. All morning he paced the floor, drank coffee, and chain-smoked. He got on my nerves so bad I wanted to boot him out. But, the girls were excited about having him home for a change. Why, I have no idea. He barely paid attention to them. In fact, it was the first time in almost two weeks he'd been here— all the girls cared about was that Daddy was home." She sipped her coffee, placed the cup on the table. "You probably know things haven't been very good around here. For the last month, I hardly saw him at all. I had no idea where he was or what he was doing. Truthfully, it's been a while since I cared what he did. I finally told him that I couldn't do this anymore—that I was thinking about filing for divorce."

Her proclamation didn't shock him. He had often wondered why she stayed married to John. Still, nobody wants to see a family torn apart. "Was he using a lot? Did he come here strung out?"

"I couldn't swear in court as to the exact amount he was using but I know it was a lot. He had enough sense not to come home when he was high. He knew I wouldn't allow him around the girls when he was high on crack or pot. When he was on a binge, he'd usually stay with Benny Ryan, up in Bow."

Her statement did not require a response, so Traynor nodded. Like all codependents, she was always covering for John.

She sipped the coffee, placed the cup on the table, and leaned back. Jill rubbed her temples, as if trying to massage away a headache. "If it hadn't been for the girls I would have thrown him out last year. He kept promising things were going to get better. He said he was in line for a big payoff. There would be enough money to start that business he's always talked about."

They had heard all about John's dream of his own business, usually when he was in trouble. He was going to open a small convenience store and sell beer, cigarettes, and lottery tickets. Ed had to admit that it was a nice dream—even though they knew John would probably sell more illegal drugs out the back door than he would legitimate goods out the front. He thought about the word, *dream*—wild dream was a more appropriate description. As usual, John had not done his homework. He would never have gotten a license to sell alcohol, not with his record. Either way, making plans and dreaming dreams had never been a problem for John. The one thing he had always been good at was dreaming. Well, now he could dream for eternity.

For a moment, Traynor thought it strange that Jillian had gotten over her anger so quickly. He checked that thought—Jill was different from most people; she was emotionally stronger than many people he knew, including him. It was so like her to mourn and grieve for a man who never gave her anything but hard times and babies—and do it in stoic silence. Traynor took her in his arms, pulling her snug against his chest, and breathed in the clean smell of her.

She inhaled deeply, moved out of his arms, and wiped her eyes with a tissue. "What would I do without you, Eddie? You've always been there for me."

"And I always will be. All you have to do is call." He stood, took out his wallet, and pulled out the money Buck had given him, plus an extra hundred. "John had some cash on him, and Buck and I thought you might need it." He folded the bills and put them in her hand.

She stared at the money and then said, "Thanks, Eddie." She made a halfhearted attempt at a smile. Her eyes were red from crying, and there were dark tracks on her cheeks from her mascara running. His heart wanted to jump out of his chest; even while grieving, he believed that she was beautiful.

Suddenly he realized that he was on dangerous ground. His long-hidden feelings were about to show through, and, in Jill's vulnerable state, things could get out of hand. He stood up. "Do you want me to stay around for a while, maybe help you talk to the girls?"

"No, I've always been the one who had to tell them about the bad things in life. John sure as hell never did." Jill sighed. "I'll have to make all the arrangements."

It dawned on him that she was referring to John's funeral. He had not even thought about that. "It's going to be a few days before we need to worry about that. The state will do an autopsy before releasing the body. "

His heart went out to her, and he made a mental note to call his sister and have her drop by. Maureen lived in Nashua, about twenty miles away, but she would gladly run over and help her sister-in-law with the kids.

He suddenly realized that he had not called Maureen yet, and she probably knew nothing of John's death. She would be distressed. Even though she had been the first to disown him, she still cared about him.

He had started for the door and paused with his hand on the knob as Jill said, "Ed, you know in spite of it all, he idolized you."

"He had a funny way of showing it. He always did the opposite of what I told him to do."

"Sometimes he couldn't help it. You set the mark pretty high—and your parents made sure he knew it."

He stared at her, uncertain what he should say.

"All he ever heard from your folks was 'Eddie this,' or 'Eddie that'... I think he started doing the wild things he did just to get some attention."

"Well, he finally got mine."

Jillian crossed the room, and he took her in his arms again. Her breasts pressed against his chest. He had loved Jill for years and her presence in his arms caused his desire to build. He wondered what sort of man he was to let himself become aroused at a time like this. She turned her face up to his, and he bent down to kiss her. Realizing what he was doing, he backed off and gently pushed her away.

Jillian's face reddened, and she, too, stepped back. He saw her breasts rise and lower as she inhaled deeply. After several intense moments, her breathing became more normal and she regained composure. She said, "Thanks, Eddie. I know how tough it was for you to have to tell me this."

His throat constricted, keeping him from responding. He took her hand, squeezed it, and then walked out of her apartment.

When Traynor got in his car, Julia stopped playing and waved. Now that they had their treats, the girls were reluctant to leave their game. He glanced at the clock on the car's radio and opted for a late lunch before he drove to Maureen's house in Nashua.

He waved as he drove past the girls. Carrie stopped playing and stared at him as he passed. He thought that she looked somber, older than her years, as she stood on the brown grass, raised her hand, and waved to him. He realized that, as young as she was, with John gone, she too would have to be his brother's keeper.

6

Maureen Rose Marx opened the door and seemed shocked to see her brother standing in the threshold. Traynor understood why. He didn't visit Maureen and her family very often. It wasn't because she didn't want him to, but more because he didn't feel comfortable in her impeccable world. She married young, barely nineteen, to a man who worked two jobs and finished a degree in electrical engineering at night and on weekends. David Marx went on to forge a very successful career with a high-tech firm in Massachusetts. He was in every way the antithesis of what John and Ed were like. A personable man, David always treated Traynor well, but for some unknown reason, Traynor always felt uncomfortable as hell around him.

Maureen smiled broadly when she said, "Well, look what the cat dragged in and the dog was afraid to drag out."

"Hi, Sis, how are you?" He immediately knew that his voice was a harbinger of bad news, and she picked up the aura that surrounded him.

"What happened?"

"It's John."

Suddenly, she realized that Traynor was still standing on the porch and stepped aside and motioned him in. She turned away, and Ed saw her shoulders drop in resignation. "What's he done this time?"

"It isn't as much what he did as what was done to him."

"Oh, Eddie, don't you dare tell me . . ."

"Maury, John was murdered last night."

When she spun toward him, her face looked as if it were made of granite. Then he saw the cracks appear as she fought to control her emotions and she began to cry. He took her into his arms and held her tight, feeling her sobs shake her body. It seemed that the only thing he had done all day was hold and console crying women. After a few minutes, she pushed back, extricating herself from his arms. She took his right hand and led him into the living room. Gently, she urged her older brother to the couch and sat as close as a teenage girl on a date.

She inhaled deeply and said, "I don't know why I'm so shocked. We all knew it was bound to happen."

"That doesn't make it any easier. I didn't enjoy identifying his body."

"You saw him?"

"Yeah, Buck called me to make sure it was John."

Maureen jumped to her feet. "Would you like something to drink? I just finished making coffee."

He had no desire for more coffee, but knew she needed something to occupy her while she dealt with her feelings. "Sure."

"Sit there, I'll be right back."

She walked too fast on her way to the kitchen. Traynor disregarded her command and followed her. When he reached her, she was leaning over the sink, tears pouring down her face and her shoulders racked with sobs. He took her into his arms again, led her back into the living room, and guided her to the couch.

Another few minutes passed before she regained her composure yet again. "I'm sorry, Eddie. I don't know why I'm so upset after all he put the family through."

"Maury, he was still our baby brother."

She reached across him, pulled a tissue from a box on the end table, and blew her nose. She crumpled the used tissue in a tight fist and said, "How are you handling this?"

"Truthfully?"

"Of course, truthfully."

"I feel responsible, guilty. I keep wondering if there was something I could have done to change the way John turned out."

"That was always your problem, Eddie. You thought you had to be a hero for John and me."

He leaned back and rested his head on the back of the couch. He kept his eyes glued on the ceiling and said, "I felt responsible. The old man and old woman were not exactly model parents."

"There's only one problem with that."

He sat forward and looked at her. "Which is?"

"Have you ever thought that maybe, just maybe, it would have been better for John and me if you'd been a little less protective?"

"No."

"In that regard, you were worse than any father ever was. My girl-friends worried that their fathers wouldn't like their boyfriends. I had to worry that you'd beat up any guy who got even an inch out of line with me. By my senior year, I could hardly get a date."

He could not resist smiling. "Was I that bad?"

She smiled. It was an odd contrast with her tear-filled red eyes. "Worse; I'm downplaying it."

He sighed. "I had no idea I was that intimidating. I just worried about you two. I didn't want you to have to deal with the old man's drunken rages."

She put her hand on his shoulder. "Ed, you overlooked a couple of things."

"Which I'm certain you are now going to tell me."

"Yup, first, sometimes, by doing that which we think is best in the short term, we do long-term damage. That was where you messed up with John. I often wonder whether or not he'd have gotten so out of control if you'd made him face up to his responsibilities. Every time he screwed up, you came riding in like the Lone Ranger and bailed him out."

He could not refute the wisdom of her words, so he sat quietly and listened.

"Secondly, and this is about me, there were times when all I wanted was someone to talk to."

"That's not fair. I always listened to you."

"Did you?" She lightly brushed the side of his head. "If I came to you with a problem, before I finished telling you about it you were off trying to handle it for me."

He felt his face heat. "I was trying to help."

"All I wanted was validation, Ed. I was a young woman, I needed someone to empathize with me, not be my knight in shining armor."

"Was I that bad?"

She kissed him on the cheek. "In some ways; but, I knew one thing. If I ever got into real trouble, my big brother would travel through the fires of hell to rescue me."

Suddenly, he felt better, much better. He found himself on an emotional roller coaster again and swallowed a lump the size of a twenty-pound turkey. Finally, Ed took her hand and said, "You alone today?"

She nodded. "Dave's out in Silicon Valley this week, and the kids are in school."

"You going to be all right?"

"Of course I am. I'm assuming you've already seen Jill."

"Yes, I came straight here from there."

"She's the one who needs support right now. I'll call her. She'll need someone to help her make arrangements and everything."

He grinned. "Old habits die hard."

"You can't bail him out of this one, Eddie."

"No, but I sure as hell can nail whoever did it to him."

He kissed her on the forehead and walked to the door. As he opened it, Maureen called to him. He stopped and looked at her.

"Don't hide from us, okay? Come and visit occasionally. We're all each other has now."

"You have Dave and the kids."

"Yes, I do, and you know what I mean."

"Yeah, I think I do."

7

Traynor decided to go by The Sexy Fox to see if he could find Consuela.

Even though he had been in law enforcement in New Hampshire and The Fox was across the border in Tyngsboro, Massachusetts, Traynor knew about it. It had a reputation for being a place where cheap women and not-so-cheap nose candy were readily available. Like most strip clubs, the mob controlled The Fox. It had been a hot bed of illicit sex and dope for years, and the business naturally linked itself to some bad people—like the Escobars, the biggest drug lords in New England. Massachusetts cops had busted The Fox so many times that a raid on it did not even rate coverage by the news media anymore.

Now that he had fulfilled his duty to the family, Traynor felt useful for the first time since he had stood over John's body. The investigation was finally underway. He felt like a bear that had risen from hibernation, hungry and ready for action. He was out of limbo and back in his element.

A flashing neon sign, the figure of a well-endowed female fox performing lewd gyrations that was sure to make curious kids ask their parents embarrassing questions, marked the entrance to the club. It was so graphic Traynor could not believe that the city had not made them tear it down. Then again, in most small towns, a monthly check to someone on the city council can fix any problem, and if nothing else it would get the authorities to leave you alone.

It was three in the afternoon and already the parking lot was half-full—Traynor knew he was being optimistic. Experience led him to believe that when people drank in the middle of the day, they were either celebrating or trying to forget. Since World War II, New England, and the Boston area in particular, thrived on high-tech employment. However, the current shit-sandwich the banks were in, NAFTA, and outsourcing had taken a heavy toll. The economy in Massachusetts and southern New Hampshire had been on shaky ground for a couple of years and it seemed that once gasoline hit the magical four-buck-a-gallon mark, the bottom fell out overnight. A similar situation occurred in the early 1990s. It brought a famous quote attributed to Yogi Berra to mind: "It's déjà vu all over again." There was no doubt in his mind that The Sexy Fox was full of people drinking to forget.

Traynor got out of his car and darted across the unpaved lot. The sun was dropping toward the horizon, and the wind blew in from the northwest. Traynor hunched forward, pushing against it. New Englanders call that frigid northwesterly wind The Montreal Express and all he wanted at that moment was to get out of it. He trotted to the door.

He knew what to expect and was not disappointed. The moment he entered the dump, Traynor knew he was in enemy territory. It took all of two seconds for everyone in the joint to ID him as a cop, and no one was happy to see him. He had to be cautious because if things got out of control, he would be on his own with no backup.

He opened his notebook and stared at her name. Consuela did not sound cheap; if anything, he thought it was somewhat exotic. Typical cop questions raced through his mind. *Was she some stripper John met while on a drug binge? Was she rich? Possibly she was not a stripper at all; maybe she ran the joint?* He considered possibilities more ominous too. She may have been John's connection to the Colombians. When it comes to curiosity, cops are right up there with cats, and his was aroused. Traynor wanted to talk with Consuela as soon as possible—even if it meant walking into the sort of place he had previously only visited professionally.

The warm air felt like a furnace after the freezing wind outside, and Traynor opened his coat while paying the ten-dollar cover. Upon entering the dark interior, the stale odor of cigarette smoke, unwashed bodies, and spilled booze assailed him. He thought it was a cornucopia of smells with the allure of week-old roadkill . . . definitely John's type of place.

Traynor slid onto an empty stool at the bar and studied the dimly lit interior. In defiance of the Massachusetts state law prohibiting smoking in public places, a thick cloud of cigarette and cigar smoke hung in the room. Through the fog, he saw that the layout was typical of most of the strip clubs he'd ever been in. The center of the room housed a bar, positioned so every stool offered an unobstructed view of the stage that jutted from the back wall. Its surface bore so many cigarette burns, nicks, and scars that it resembled the face of the loser in a knife fight. Just sitting against it, a customer risked getting splinters.

Two men sat at the side of the bar nearest the entrance, guarding the exit like a pair of Doberman pinschers. Normally he wouldn't have paid them a lot of attention, but one of them had grungy hair, that shade of white with a yellow tint that resembles the nicotine stains on a chain-smoker's fingers. He sat next to a man who, at some time or another, had been on the wrong end of the aforementioned knife fight. A jagged scar ran across the left side of his face. They both appeared to be alert and ready to attack on command as they studied Traynor, but said nothing. He, in turn, decided to pay them no mind.

The circular stage that occupied the far wall filled half of what was not bar. Small tables butted up to the edge, each with three chairs along the sides not abutting the stage. The tables were spaced as close together as possible. In fact, when the joint was full, customers would be touching elbows. Not that the clientele cared, the packed accommodations allowed more degenerates to be close enough to reach up and shove their hard-earned welfare and unemployment dollars into a dancer's garter. Men occupied most of the tables bordering the stage. Other than their initial inspection, they ignored Traynor; most had things that were more urgent on their minds, like the slender redhead who was gyrating onstage. Traynor glanced at her and dismissed her from his mind. Her breasts looked harder than the White Mountain granite of which New Hampshire was so proud and were a major turnoff to him. Beads of sweat flew off the stripper's surgically enhanced boobs as she bumped and grinded to hard rock music. The lighting was minimal, intentionally dimmed—in good light, the dancer would most likely look old enough to be someone's great-grandmother. In these places the dancers working the day shift, when things were slow, were seldom top-of-the-line acts. Her skin seemed phosphorescent as she labored mechanically to keep her lewd movements timed to the music's pulsing beat.

The bartender slid along the bar and stopped before Traynor. He wore a dirty sleeveless shirt with a faded picture of Jerry Garcia stretched across his stomach. His gut was several sizes too large for the shirt, and his hairy paunch drooped over his belt buckle. He sported a full beard of matted dark whiskers, which made him resemble the caricature of the deceased Grateful Dead singer on his shirt and contained enough gray to make him look ten years older than he would if he were clean-shaven. A cigarette stuck out of his maw and drooped toward his chin, with a good inch of ash hanging from the end. He placed his hands on the bar and the stench of stale sweat filled the air around him. "Whatcha havin'?" he asked.

Watching the cigarette ash, Traynor decided against ordering anything that came in a glass. "I'll have a Smuttynose . . . in a bottle."

The bartender ignored the sarcasm. "I got Bud on tap, warm Bud in the bottle, or cold Bud in the bottle. Which one you want?"

"With all those choices, it's hard to decide. I guess I'll have the cold bottle."

He grunted and walked away. Traynor watched him pull a beer from a cooler and waddle back. He half expected him to pop the cap off with his teeth. When he slammed the beer down in front of Traynor and twisted the cap off with his right hand, Traynor breathed easier. When he grabbed the ten Traynor had laid on the scarred bar, the cigarette ash lost its precarious perch, bounced off his gut, smearing a gray swath across Jerry's whiskered face, and tumbled to the floor. He rubbed the residue, grinding it into Jerry's face, and blew a cloud of smoke at Traynor before shuffling to the cash register. He rang up the beer, came back, and put three dollars and ten cents on the bar.

"A beer costs six-ninety?" Traynor asked.

"You must be from New Hampshire—it's six-fifteen plus tax."

Traynor rolled his eyes. "It's no wonder people from Massachusetts shop in beautiful, tax-free New Hampshire."

The barman stared, his eyes squinting against the stream of cigarette smoke that rolled across his face. "Have you been in here before? You look familiar. I've seen you someplace."

"Nope, but I've been in a hundred joints just like this. You may have confused me with my brother . . . he hangs out in here a lot. His name's John, John Traynor."

The bartender paused for a second and then shrugged. "Can't say I do, but then I can't say I don't." He turned and looked at one of the watchdogs.

Out of the corner of his eye, Traynor saw the white-haired bouncer stiffen and take a cell phone out of his jacket pocket. He didn't know if he'd heard John's name or if he had the phone on vibrate and got a call. For whatever reason, the guy flipped the phone open and walked outside.

Traynor grabbed the overpriced beer and went off in hunt of a table, preferably one away from the bar and stage. He found one along the wall, close enough to see what was happening throughout the room and on the stage, but far enough away that he would not have to worry about getting into a conversation with the idiots encircling it. Before he could get comfortable, a bleached blond with black roots stood beside the table. Even in the dim light, he could see she was heavily made-up and her hair had an oily and dirty dullness from hours in the caustic cigarette-smoke-filled atmosphere. Up close, she was less attractive than she was at a distance—a long distance. His first impression was that her cosmetologist was either an excited six-year-old who had gotten into Mommy's makeup or one who had spent her career preparing corpses in a funeral parlor. Three or four thick layers of cosmetic buildup hid an old woman's face. The foundation around her mouth had cracked, emphasizing wrinkles as deep as crevasses. She had applied eyeliner so thick it looked like she had used roofing tar, and her cheeks had a thick coating of rouge. She could be the prototype for a new glamour doll—if anyone wanted their daughter to have an action figure of a retired hooker turned exotic dancer.

The stripper was dressed for work, wearing a revealing white gown with a plunging neckline—braless, no surprise there. She sucked on a cigarette that had to be four inches long and when she bent over the table, her gown dropped forward, giving him a good look at her wares.

"Hi, I'm Alana. You want some company?" she asked.

When she spoke, Traynor got another nauseating surprise. Plaque coated her teeth so thick that you couldn't tell where one tooth ended and the next began. Her mouth resembled a jar of mayonnaise that had gone bad, and her breath smelled like a truckload of fish guts on a hot day. He pushed away his dislike of women who willingly denigrate themselves for a bunch of losers and politely said, "Actually, I'm looking for someone."

She slid into the chair across from him, ending her little peep show, and peered at him as if he were a snake in a glass cage. Her eyes got hard, accentuating the cracks in her makeup. "You a cop?" she asked. Her breath hit his face like a cloud of toxic gas.

"I used to be."

She smiled—it made her look even uglier. "I thought you was. I can smell a cop a mile away. What happen, you get thrown out of the cops?"

"I'm retired."

She leaned forward and bent over, getting closer and providing yet another view of her unfettered breasts. "Really?" she said. "You don't look old enough to be retired."

Traynor turned his head, trying to breathe air she had not fouled. "I'm looking for Consuela."

"Hell, she can't treat you as good as I can. Why don'cha buy me a drink and we'll get to know each other. I'll make you forget about Connie."

He would much rather have forgotten about her. "I don't want to forget about Consuela."

She gave him one of those bitchy looks that the directors of porn films seem to think is sexy. "You want a table dance?"

"No, I want to talk to Consuela."

"Look, if you don't buy me a drink or pay ten bucks for a table dance, I can't hang with you. You got it?"

"Good. I'll buy Consuela a drink and pay her to dance for me."

She gave up on him, made a nasty comment about his sexual orientation, and then spun on her heel, heading off in search of easier game. Hoping his voice would carry over the loud music to which the redhead still gyrated, he said, "I'll pay you twenty bucks to point Consuela out to me."

She stopped and turned back. Traynor gripped a twenty-dollar bill between the index and middle fingers of his right hand. To get her attention, he waved it from side to side. She tried to snatch it from his fingers. Before she could get a grip, he retracted the bill, tore it in half, and pushed the smaller of the two pieces down her dress. "You get the other half when you bring Consuela to me."

He was certain that he had moved up to number two on her shit list. As long as there was twenty bucks at stake, he wouldn't be number one. She raised her dress, giving him a flash of her skimpy underwear, pushed the torn twenty into the garter that encircled her thigh, and said, "Don't move." She disappeared behind a curtain next to the stage.

Sipping on the beer, Traynor wondered what he had gotten into. If Alana was indicative of the women who worked here, what would Consuela look like? He stared at the bottle's label, wondering if he should switch to something stronger.

She returned about five minutes later. "Connie's doing the next set. She says for you to stay here and she'll see you when she's done."

"Fair enough, after she sees me you can collect the rest of your finder's fee."

She made one last attempt to convince him she was a better catch than Consuela was. "You sure you don't want me to hang around? I'll give you a good time."

"I'm sure."

"Okay, it's your loss." She stepped back and turned her attention to the room. In seconds, she locked in on a couple of drunken yuppie types who looked like they had spent their entire day pounding down watery drafts at a buck-fifty a pop. In one swift movement, she left Traynor and stalked toward their table like a wolf closing in on a wounded elk. As she approached them her hips swung provocatively and she adjusted her breasts, pumping them with her hands. In a few seconds, she took a ten from them and gave Traynor a look that he knew she thought said, *eat your heart out*. She slid the top of her dress down and glanced over her shoulder to see if he was watching. She smiled at him and then turned toward her clients and began dancing, grinding her hips at the drunks.

The music suddenly ended and the crowd unconsciously adjusted the volume of their voices. Traynor turned his attention from Alana to the stage in time to see the redhead's naked backside disappear through the drapes at the back of the stage.

The stage lights dimmed, a spotlight centered on the curtains at the back of the stage, and a hot salsa tune blared out of the sound system. The curtains separated a few inches and a shapely leg, moving in sync with the music, pushed through. The curtain parted farther, and a sleek arm appeared, followed by a beautiful Hispanic woman. Her long black hair sparkled in the spotlight's harsh glare. Consuela wore a bright red sequined dress that accentuated a figure for which most women would die. When she moved, the dress seemed to pulsate and emit flashes of light. She was good—very good. For a few seconds Traynor considered moving to a table by the stage.

As she progressed through her repertoire of moves, sexual tension in the room intensified, and the air became charged with testosterone. He concentrated on her every move—he decided that he had been wrong, she was better than good. Her athletic dancing and exquisite body kept every customer's attention glued to the stage until her set ended. When she disappeared behind the curtain, the atmosphere changed, and every man in the joint breathed a collective sigh.

Settling back in his seat, Traynor realized how engrossed he had been while watching her. Several questions raced through his mind; paramount among them were: *Why was she working in this dive and not in one of the more exclusive clubs in Boston? She was good enough to be a headliner. What was a woman like this doing messing around with a small-timer like his brother?*

It took her less than twenty minutes to dress and come to his table. She stood several feet away from him, her face a caricature of a suspicious woman. In heavily accented English she said, "You ast to see me?" Her accent told him she had grown up on the island, probably around Ponce—many of the Puerto Ricans who immigrated to the Boston area came from there. He slid a chair out for her, and she sat. The yuppies at the next table suddenly lost all interest in Alana and stared at them. Obviously, they were trying to decide what Traynor had that they did not. He gave them his best *she's with me* grin.

"My name is Ed Traynor." Her eyes opened wide. "I think you're acquainted with my brother, John."

"I not seen Juan in a couple days. He gone out of town on business."

"I'm afraid you won't be seeing him again." She stared at Traynor, as if she was having difficulty comprehending what he had said.

"He's dead," Traynor said.

She cast an unbelieving look at him. "What?"

"He was murdered last night. If you want I can give you the number for the Rockingham County Sheriff, he'll verify it."

She pulled back in shock. Traynor was surprised to see tears well in her eyes and roll down her cheeks. Once again, he tried to understand what a beauty like this saw in John. All his life, John had attracted beautiful women. It was as if he had a special something—but he was damned if he knew what it was. Traynor had always written it off as the allure some females have for the rogues of the species. In every herd, the strongest, most ruthless males get their pick of the females. The rest of the pack, people like him, settle for what is left—or nothing.

She got up, walked to the bar, and spoke to the grungy bartender. Traynor was surprised; either the guy was capable of feelings, or working here had given him an understanding of women, because he seemed genuinely concerned, gave her a compassionate look, and pulled a box of tissues from beneath the bar.

Consuela snatched a handful and returned to the table. She wiped her eyes and blew her nose into one of the tissues. "H-how did it happen?"

"Someone shot him."

She dabbed at the tears that continued to stream down her cheeks. She sniffed. "I told him not to mess around with those guys. But he won't listen to me." Her grief and shock accentuated her Hispanic accent.

"What guys?"

Her look told Traynor that she didn't believe he was ignorant of whom she was talking. She said, "You know . . . them brothers from Colombia, the big-time dealers in Lawrence."

"The Escobar brothers?" Carlo and Eduardo Escobar were not people anyone wanted to trifle with. They dealt ruthlessly with their competition and were lethal to anyone who crossed them. If John had messed with them, he was lucky all he got was a bullet in the head.

She nodded. "He was goin' to make *mucho dinero*—a lot of money. I warn him no one make nothing dealing drugs for those people—not unless they from Colombia. But Juan, he sure he gonna make a killing."

"John told you all that?"

"Why wouldn't he?"

"My brother was not one to talk to just anyone about his business dealings."

"But," she became indignant, "I not just anyone. Juan was my husband."

At a loss for words, Traynor stared at her for several long seconds. After a few moments, he knew that he needed to say something, so he said, "When were you and John married?"

"Last year, right after his divorce."

John and Jillian were definitely on a collision course with a divorce, but as far as Traynor knew, up until sometime last night they were still man and wife.

"He was tired of the bid-nezz he was in. He wanted to make a big score so we can move out of Lawrence and open a business in New Hampshire."

"Let me guess. He was going to buy a convenience store, right?" Obviously, John had shared the same pipe dream with both his spouses.

"*Si*, yes—I was going to stop working here and have many babies." She stopped speaking and looked at him. A quizzical look came over her face. "You not like Juan said you was."

"Oh? What did John say about me?"

"He told me you didn't visit us because you were mad he married a Puerto Rican. He said you was a racist."

Traynor took a business card out of his wallet and laid it on the table in front of her. "A lot of things aren't the way John told you. When was the last time you saw him?"

"He stopped by here, just after midnight three nights ago. Juan was all excited. He said he was going to score some big money that night. I told him not to go. That was last I heard from my husband."

She dabbed her tears and sniffed. Suddenly she sat up, sighed, and said, "Where his body?"

"The medical examiner still has it. It won't be released for a few days yet."

Her shoulders slumped. "What will I do about a funeral? How will I pay for this?"

"We'll deal with that when the time comes," he said to her.

Suddenly, he felt weary, worn out by this conversation, and needed to get away to do some thinking. "Consuela, call me if you need anything or if you come up with something that might help me get John's killer."

On his way out, he nodded at the bartender and noticed that neither Whitey nor Scarface were there. He wondered if they were already on their way to see the Escobars.

It was dark when Traynor walked out of the club. He crossed the parking lot and sat in his car with the engine running, heater set to max, trying to make sense of everything. There was only one thing of which he was certain: his talk with Consuela had removed any doubts he had had about John being lower than whale shit.

Suddenly Alana exploded through the door, her eyes frantically searching the parking lot. Traynor flashed his headlights. She ran over to the car. When she stopped beside it, he rolled the window down and handed her the second half of the twenty. In spite of the cold wind, she hiked her skirt and shoved the bill into her garter. "I thought you was trying to screw me out of my money," she said.

He grinned. "Sweetheart, I'd never screw you."

He was certain that she got the message. As he drove away, he glanced in his rearview mirror and saw her silhouette framed by the mercury lights that lit the parking lot. She held up both hands. If she had not had her middle fingers extended, he would have thought she was praising God. He laughed. Obviously, he had been elevated to number one on her shit list.

8

Forty-five minutes after he left The Sexy Fox, Traynor was in his Portsmouth office. He checked his machine and listened to the sole message. It was from Harry Bright of New England Mutual Life. "Eddie, this is Harry. I'm up against it, man! Do you have anything on the Cartwright case? I have to go to court on this in a couple of days, and you haven't been in touch since Friday. . . . Call me, will you?" The machine beeped, and its mechanical voice said, "Monday, 6:04 p.m."

Traynor cursed his forgetfulness. Unlike what television and the movies depict, private investigators seldom deal with high-profile murder cases; the state police, big city police departments, and the feds do that. The average P.I. mostly checks backgrounds, looks for missing persons, investigates insurance fraud, and works divorces. A modern private detective is just another name for a database hound. There are times when Traynor wondered how anyone made it in this trade before the Internet. According to his accountant, a pension from the state of New Hampshire and business from New England Mutual Life—his best customer—paid the bills.

For the past three days, Billy Cartwright had been his source of revenue. He was suing NEML and their client, a little old woman who had rear-ended him at a stoplight, for whiplash and back injuries. Yesterday, Traynor had put an end to the suit: Billy and his latest flame drove to a remote woods road and had sex—until then Traynor would have sworn that nobody could make love in the back seat of a rusted-out Kia sedan.

He took his digital camera from his desk drawer, plugged the cable into his computer, and transferred the pictures he had taken through the windows of the compact.

He glanced at the wall clock and saw it was after 8:00 p.m. Traynor grinned and thought: *Harry must be up to his butt in snapping crocodiles if he was frantic enough to call after hours.* He usually called during the day when his secretary, Susan, was in the office. Traynor called, got Bright's voice mail, and listened to his message. After the beep, he said, "Harry? Ed. I have what you need. Cartwright is defrauding you. I have pictures and will have Susan scan and send them in the morning." He reached into the top-right-hand drawer of his desk and took out a bottle of Maker's Mark. He poured an inch into his coffee cup and took a drink. The whiskey hit his stomach and reminded him that he had not eaten since noon.

———————

Traynor, Max Thurston, and Charley Giles had a standing date to meet at a local steakhouse every Thursday night at 8:00 p.m. Traynor got to the Klondike Steakhouse in Newington around 8:30 and saw them sitting in a booth along the back wall. Max and Charley were a matched set; if you called Max, you got Charley and vice versa. To look at them you would never think they were as close as they were; they looked as if they lived on opposite ends of the food chain. However, as a team, they were unbeatable.

Max stood at six-three, weighed around two-fifty, and was a physical fitness freak. He was one of the most fearless people Traynor knew and a good man to have around in a pinch. Max had helped him on several assignments, was a superlative bodyguard, and a real asset in a fight.

Charley, on the other hand, was five-ten and weighed as much as Max, if not more. Charley could be the model on a poster advertising a couch potato, but he was as close to a genius with electronics as anyone Traynor knew. If you needed a phone rigged, a computer set up, or access to any type of data, he could do it for you. Traynor had seen him break through computer firewalls most people considered impenetrable. Charley had contacts that could find out anything, about anyone, and do it at any time. He was a one-stop intelligence network.

When he slid into the booth beside Max, Charley was working his way through the biggest porterhouse Traynor had ever seen. "Thought I'd find you yahoos here." He looked at the slab of meat on Charley's plate and asked, "How big is that thing?"

"Fifty ounces," Charley said, without looking up between bites. "If I eat it and all of the trimmings, I get my meal free. It's a promotion they do here."

"Sounds like a safe promotion to me. Nobody can eat all that meat, let alone the salad, potatoes, and bread."

"I can do it." His face showed his determination to succeed.

"Damn, Charley, that's over three pounds of red meat; your cholesterol must be as high as the national debt."

"No sweat, my doctor has me on a statin drug. That's as good as a license to eat red meat. Besides, like I said, I can do it."

"You sound pretty confident," Traynor said as he waved to their server.

"I oughta be . . . I eat one a couple times a week."

The server came by and Traynor ordered a beer and a twelve-ounce rib eye, with salad and vegetables.

"Sorry to hear about John," Max said.

"Thanks. At first I was pretty shook up and then—"

"At first?" Max interrupted him.

"Yeah, I found out some crap today that even I didn't think John was capable of."

"Like what?"

"Like—" The server brought Traynor's beer and salad, and he waited for her to leave before continuing, "—John had two wives."

Charley almost choked on his steak. "Man," he said after he recovered, "two wives! What was he, a Mormon, or just a masochist?"

Traynor motioned for him to keep his voice down. "Yeah, two wives, Jillian and a Puerto Rican stripper named Consuela. She works at The Sexy Fox across the border."

"I know the joint," Max said. "It ain't exactly top-of-the-line."

"You'll get no argument from me about that. However, this woman is not what you would expect. My first impression was that she could be working top-of-the-line clubs. She's beautiful and moves like every man's dream."

"I'll have to check her out," Max said.

Traynor saw Buck walk into the restaurant. Buck looked around for a second and then spied them. Traynor waved, and the sheriff walked over, sliding into the booth beside Charley.

"I wanted to talk with you and figured I'd find you here," Buck said as he helped himself to some bread, tore off a piece, and tossed it into his mouth. True to his nature, Buck got right to the point. "It was a twenty-two," he announced. "They found what was left of the slug in his head."

"A twenty-two . . . that's a woman's gun," Max said.

"Not always," Traynor said. "There were a couple of guys in Boston who were mobbed up and ready to cut a deal with the US Attorney's office. They found them both dead, twenty-twos to the head." He took a drink of his beer. "Some pro hit men prefer a smaller piece—less noise, easier to conceal, and cheaper than a large caliber gun. Why pay eight hundred bucks or more for a piece you're going to use once and then toss?"

Buck ordered a beer and a burger and said, "You see your sister-in-law yet?"

Charley and Max paused, forks suspended in the air. Traynor pretended to look at the female servers in their Royal Canadian Mountie regalia; high-laced black boots, short black skirts, white blouses with black ties, and fancy little red vests. Trying to appear nonchalant he answered, "Yeah, earlier this afternoon."

"How did she take it?"

"Better than I thought she would. But then, she doesn't know about wife number two—"

Buck leaned toward Ed. "What do you mean *wife number two?* Maybe you better fill me in on what the hell you've been up to."

Traynor spent a few minutes telling Buck where he had been and who he'd seen since he left the crime scene and then returned to the subject of his sister-in-law. "As for Jillian, she knew what happened to John was bound to happen . . . eventually. Besides, they weren't getting along that well."

"Yeah," Buck seemed reluctant to say something that he knew he had to say. He decided to throw it on the table. "I got to talk with her."

"Buck, why waste your time? Jillian can't even kill a spider, let alone her husband or any human being."

"You know as well as I do that the spouse or significant other is always a prime suspect."

Traynor knew that he was right, it was routine, but he felt protective of Jillian and wanted to spare her more pain. A thought occurred to him: *What if she knew about Consuela?* Would learning that her husband was a bigamist be enough to push Jillian over the edge?

The funeral was going to be a real mess. It had all the ingredients of a Hollywood plot; two wives, each one living in a different state and each expecting to bury her husband. Traynor pictured the scene when they came face-to-face, and he was certain that they would. It was inevitable. He wondered if he should have John cremated and then split the ashes between Jillian and Consuela without either of them knowing. "Buck, I need a favor."

He chewed a mouthful of bread and swallowed it. "A favor? Sure, as long as it ain't illegal."

"Ask Kate not to release his body to the family for a couple of days."

"Not a problem, she and the medical examiner's office have control anyhow. I'm curious though. Why do you want the body held?"

"I need some time to check out a couple of things."

He pointed his fork at Traynor. "Check some things out? It sounds to me as if you already checked several things out. Ed, I don't know if you've thought about it, but nothing has changed. In most of the state of New Hampshire, the state police run homicide investigations. Unless something has happened that I don't know about, you're retired. I know the vic was your brother, but that doesn't mean the state police are going to let you run around poking your frigging nose into their case."

"I know that, trust me, okay? I only need a couple of days to check some things out."

"All right, Ed, I'll ask Kate if she'll sit on the body—but I doubt she'll wait more than seventy-two hours . . . if you're lucky. The morgue isn't a funeral parlor." Buck turned his attention to Max and Charley. "How you boys been? Keeping out of trouble?"

They nodded their heads, unsure of what direction the conversation was taking.

Buck laughed, reached across the table, and punched Max on the arm. He guffawed and said, "Boring as hell, ain't it!"

Buck left around ten, and Traynor got down to business with Max and Charley. "Okay, guys, I need some help. Max, I need you to check around and see what you can find out about the Escobar brothers. Who's their main man up here, how much stuff are they moving, anything that might link them to John."

"You better believe that if John was involved with those bastards it's no wonder he ended up dead."

"I don't know anything yet, but the Escobars came up when I talked with wife number two."

Max's smile told Traynor that he already knew something. He shook his head and said, "Nah, no way John was involved in that."

"Involved in what?" Traynor asked.

"Did you hear about the gang shooting earlier this week?"

"Yeah, it was in all the papers."

"Well, street talk is it wasn't gangs. It was a rip-off, and somebody took the Escobars for a lot of cash—in the millions."

Traynor sat back and took a few seconds to absorb what he'd just heard. Finally, he said, "Find out anything you can. I need more to go on than street talk. I'd be particularly interested if you can come up with anything about who did that job. I'll see if I can learn where John was that night."

He turned to Charley. "Charley, I need you to do your magic. I want to know anything you can learn about the Escobar business—financials and acquisitions, all that stuff. I'm particularly interested in anything you can learn about how they got as big as they are. Oh yeah, see if you can find documentation of John's marriage to Consuela."

"No sweat," Charley replied. "You want the guest list?"

"I know you're joking, but it would make interesting reading."

"You got a last name on her?"

"No, but he used his own name. When I told her mine, she made an immediate connection."

Traynor grabbed the check and said, "Leave the waitress a twenty for the tip."

"A bit rich, ain't it?" Max said.

Traynor pointed to Charley's empty plate. "Seeing how she's gonna get screwed out of billing for Charley, it's only fair." He looked at Charley. "You say you eat one of them a couple times a week?"

Charley, his mouth full of bread, nodded.

"Keep it up and they'll probably dump that promotion."

Traynor walked to the front and paid the tab. He left the restaurant and headed for his car.

During the hour and a half he had been in the restaurant, the weather had turned lousy. It was raining heavily and the wind had escalated, pushing sheets of glacial sleet and rain across the parking lot. Trying to ward off the cold, Traynor bundled his collar tight around his neck and ran for the Taurus.

He concentrated on getting into his car and out of the elements when he should have been watching his surroundings. One second he was darting between cars, the next he was lying on the wet pavement, too stunned to feel the cold water soaking through his clothes.

An out-of-focus figure leaned over him, blocking out the light. "We want our money." The voice was threatening and had a Hispanic accent. The speaker's breath was rotten, smelling as if he had been drinking the overflow from a leach field.

"I got no idea what you're talking about." Traynor struggled to get up, rolling onto his hands and knees. A fancy black cowboy boot with shiny steel toes buried itself in his side. The kick lifted Traynor and slammed him against the protruding hub of a four-by-four pickup truck wheel. The metal cap rammed into his side and he felt something inside of him let go. He made a grab for the foot as it thundered into his ribs a second time. He felt something else let go in his side and rolled away from the threatening boots. As he dropped onto his face on the wet pavement he got a fleeting glimpse of the asshole wearing them; he had yellow-tinted white hair. He had seen that same hair earlier in the day.

His stomach heaved and he was barely able to rise up before his dinner erupted from his stomach. Whitey cursed, "Jesus Christ, he's puking!" He kicked Traynor again, this time in the stomach. Traynor rolled backward, lying in a puddle of half-frozen water and vomit, and then rolled over on his side. Rain poured onto his face and suddenly he felt cold and began to shake.

Whitey's fancy boots stepped back and his partner squatted beside Traynor. "Your asshole brother ripped us off."

Traynor groaned and mumbled that he had no idea what he was talking about.

Whitey stepped forward and used him for a football again, and lights flashed before Traynor's eyes. The talker grabbed his jacket and pulled him forward. Traynor concentrated on his face—he wanted to remember him. He had a swarthy complexion, marred by teenage acne scars. Remnants of a long knife wound zigzagged across his left cheek from below his mouth to his ear. He had seen him at the club too. It was the Doberman twins. Even through the pain, he resolved that when he met this bozo again, he was going to think that the fight that had given him that scar had been a lover's tryst. Traynor forced his mind to ignore the physical pain and to concentrate on Scarface's words. "Your brother took our money. You got two days to get it back for us. I want my money. ¿*Comprende?* So, Mr. Detective, you better get busy, because we know how to get our hands on you any time we want."

A door slammed and voices came from the steakhouse; Traynor's attackers slouched down, hiding between cars. Scarface leaned close to his ear; his breath made Limburger smell good and hung heavy around him. He whispered, "Two days, *amigo*, and I take action." He pushed Traynor back into the icy puddle, shoved something into his shirt pocket, and stood up.

It hurt like hell to talk—so Traynor didn't. He lay on the wet pavement, closed his eyes, and drifted away.

9

Traynor woke up feeling like a skydiver whose parachute had failed to open. He couldn't remember a time in his life when he had been in more pain than he was at that moment. Instinctively, his first action was to sit up. Lancing pain shot up his side, and flashes of white light streaked before his eyes. He dropped back on the bed and lay still, afraid to move. Memories of the beating returned, and he grew angry; then a cold, resolute desire for revenge replaced his rage. He studied his surroundings. It took him a few seconds to recognize the McIsaacs' guest room. He gingerly touched his side. Heavy bandages and tape encased his ribs, and dark spots were visible where blood had soaked through the gauze.

Traynor did not have many friends. In fact, he could count them on one hand: Buck, Max, Charley, and the McIsaacs. While Buck, Max, and

Charley were good friends, Bob and Susan McIsaac were his surrogate parents.

For several minutes, he laid still, mustering enough courage to get up. Overnight the shock had worn off, and his body felt the full effect of the level of carnage to which Whitey and Scarface had subjected it. Unwilling to move, he listened to the chilly sounds of wind and freezing rain rattling against the windows. He rolled over, hissed from the pain, and then slid off the bed and rested on his knees. He felt as if a runaway truck had run him over, backed up, and done it again. He broke out in a cold sweat.

He tried to get up but any movement sent waves of intense pain through his body. Unable to stand, he stayed on the floor, pulled a blanket off the bed, and used it to cover his lap. He leaned back and rested his head on the edge of the bed. Another spasm of pain racked him, and Traynor let out an involuntary groan and clutched the bedding tightly around his torso. Normally, he would have been embarrassed to have anyone see him in this condition, but not that morning. Humiliation did not enter the scenario—he just wanted the pain to go away.

He must have groaned loud because the door opened and Susan came into the room, holding a steaming cup of coffee. "You up to this?" she asked.

Even though he fought through a wall of hurt, the coffee smelled terrific. Another stab of pain lanced through him. Through clenched teeth, he muttered, "Yeah, I'm just not going to do much ballroom dancing for a few days. How'd I end up here?"

She knelt down and placed the coffee on the floor beside him. "Max and Charley dropped you off last night. By the way, that's a nice picture of your nieces. It's too bad it got wet."

"What picture?"

"There was a picture of John and Jillian's girls in your shirt pocket. They were playing in front of their apartment building."

Traynor recalled Scarface shoving something in his pocket. It was definite that he had not left it as a token of his esteem; rather it was an ominous message—one that he got. Up to this point all he wanted was to pound the shit out of Scarface and Whitey. The picture of the girls changed the game from penny ante to high stakes. He swore that if anything happened to those girls, he was going to put those two assholes in the ground.

Susan left and quietly closed the door, leaving him alone. He sat on the floor and drank the coffee. With superhuman effort, he staggered to his feet, unraveled the tape and bandages from his ribs, and stumbled into the bathroom. He turned on the shower, waited for the water to turn from cold to hot, and stepped in.

He languished in the hot water, feeling it hit his shoulders and then cascade along his ribs, warming and loosening the stressed muscles in his side. He raised his arm, winced in pain, and inspected the damage. His right side was a mess—swollen and puffy from underarm to waist. In a few days, when the bruises had time to age and turn black and yellow, his ribs were going to look ugly. If he was lucky, of which he had his doubts, he had no fractured ribs, nor had the vicious pointed-toe boots punctured any of his vital organs.

Returning from the bedroom, he saw that Susan had put a T-shirt and a pair of slacks on the bed. He stared at the shirt, wondering if he was going to be able to get it over his head. He picked up the tee, gingerly raised his arms, and slid it over his torso, all the while doing his best to avoid touching his side.

Once he was dressed, he picked up the coffee mug and carried it into the kitchen. After he'd eased his body into a chair at the table and gotten settled, Susan took the mug, refilled it, and then placed a newspaper and bottle of aspirin in front of him. "Where's Bob?" Traynor asked.

"He thought you'd need some clothes, so he went over to your place about a half hour ago. I expect him back any time. Are you going to live?"

"Probably, although right now I wouldn't want to bet on how long."

Susan smiled and laid a hand on his shoulder. He tried not to flinch and was not successful. She noticed it and quickly withdrew her hand. It was not easy keeping up his tough guy facade when everything hurt. "Drink your coffee and read the paper until Bob gets home. Are you hungry? I can fix you something."

"No thanks, coffee's fine."

"Okay. I'm going to straighten up before I go to the office."

He looked into her eyes and said, "What would I do without you?"

He saw her concern for his well-being. She tried to cover it up with humor. "You'd probably find someone else to pick up after you. One thing is certain, if Max and Charley keep bringing you here beaten-up and unconscious, I'm going to start billing our insurance company for emergency room services. Speaking of which, you should see a doctor about those ribs. You could have fractures, and those welts worry me."

He scanned the paper, looking for anything about his brother's murder. John had not even rated the first page of the metropolitan section in the *Granite State Daily News*. They had dedicated the front page to reporting the results of the recent election. Murder always takes a back seat to politics, possibly because the victims of the crooks people elect to office outnumber the victims of murderers by a couple million to one.

Traynor spent a half hour reading the paper before a door opened behind him and Bob McIsaac walked into the kitchen carrying an armload of clothing and a cardboard box. He placed the box in an empty chair, draped Traynor's clothes over it, and then poured himself a cup of coffee.

Bob was retired Portsmouth PD. He had been a good cop, solid. Never flamboyant, he had moved steadily up the ranks, but missed making it to the top—those jobs always go to the politicians and shit-house lawyers. Twenty-five years ago, he had taken a young rookie under his wing and in six months taught him more about law enforcement and life on the streets than he could learn in six years of college or a dozen police academies. He did his twenty as a cop and was now near the end of a successful career with a local security firm. It was time, he said, to kick back at his place on Lake Winnipesaukee, do some fishing and boating, just live the good life. For selfish reasons, Traynor hoped he would not rush into it.

Traynor looked at his friend's weathered, wrinkled face and silver hair, and realized that all of his friends were starting to look the way his grandparents looked when he was twenty. They were getting old and maybe it was time to start worrying about how he would keep the office going if Susan retired. Bob sat across from him and sipped his coffee. Traynor knew he was dying to learn what had happened last night, but would not ask. It was Bob's way. As a street cop, he always got the information he was after and most of the time did it so effortlessly that the informant was not aware he or she was giving him what he wanted. "I didn't know what you wanted to wear," he said, "So I brought you a suit, shirt, tie, raincoat, and anything else I thought you could use." He looked out the window at the driving rain. The wind pushed a sheet of water down the street, driving dead leaves and discarded paper ahead of it. "Going to be a lousy day," he said.

Traynor stared out the same window, possibly seeking a melding of their minds. It did not work. Although he would have preferred a pair of jeans and a flannel shirt, he said, "Suit's fine."

"Sorry to hear about John. However, I can't say I was surprised."

"It was bound to happen."

"That doesn't make it any easier to take."

Traynor turned and stared into the aged eyes of his mentor and best friend. "No, it doesn't."

"You got any idea who did it?"

"Everywhere I turn I find someone with a motive to kill him. But the truth of the matter is that I have no suspects so far. The names Carlo and Eduardo Escobar have come up, but I have nothing to indicate a strong enough motive even though it's rumored that they have a wealth of experience with murder." He told Bob what he had learned thus far.

As he talked, Bob said nothing. Nevertheless, Traynor knew his mind was processing the data as he presented it. When he finished, Bob warmed his coffee and said, "I talked with some of the guys last week. There was a shootout on the west side. Inside a car were two bodies: the driver, and a guy lying on the street next to the car. They thought it was weird that the back seat raised and lowered with pneumatic arms. Boys at Manchester PD said they rousted a couple of dealers who identified the car as the Escobar rolling bank—it had been making the rounds, collecting from their pushers. There was a witness, a homeless guy who was rummaging through some dumpsters when it went down. He said that a single man took them out. Whoever the unknown perpetrator was, one of the guys in that car must have known him. The shooter stood beside them for several minutes before shooting. The two guys in the car were armed, but apparently made no effort to defend themselves. State police investigators have no clue who killed the Escobars' people— no description of the shooter—but whoever did it had planned it well. The rip-off went down in an area where there were no security cameras. Rumor is the bank was carrying a lot of cash—as much as three million, maybe more."

Bob sipped his coffee and said, "In summary, what we've got here is a couple of drug kingpins, who may think John ripped them off, two partners who say he ripped them off, and two wives who it seems didn't know about each other—seems like everything is coming in pairs. So, what's your problem?" He smiled. "It isn't like you're dealing with a John Doe or a random drive-by shooting. You've got plenty of places to start looking."

Susan came in and sat between them. She gave Traynor a stern but caring look. "Before you do anything else, I think you should see a doctor."

"I'll think about it," Traynor said. "If I'm still hurting tomorrow, I'll drop by the ER."

He gathered up the clothes Bob had brought and slowly walked into the bedroom. He tried to put a positive spin on things by telling himself that he did not feel as bad as he had when he woke up and that, if nothing else, the hot shower had made the pain tolerable. He would be able to function—as long as he didn't make any sudden moves.

When he was dressed, he carried his overcoat and suit jacket back into the living room. He dropped the overcoat on the couch and made sure he didn't moan, groan, or grimace when he struggled into the jacket.

Before he had it over his arm Bob said, "Wait a minute." Bob draped the jacket over the back of a reclining chair, walked into the kitchen, and came back carrying the box he had laid on the chair. He handed it to Traynor and said, "After last night, I thought you'd better start carrying this."

Traynor opened the box and saw his nine-millimeter Glock inside.

He seldom carried a gun; most of the time his work didn't call for one, but yesterday things had escalated. Who knows, he might not have had his butt pounded into the pavement if he'd been packing. On the other hand, he probably would still have gotten the crap stomped out of him and would most likely have lost an expensive weapon.

He reached inside, removed his shoulder holster, and handed the now-empty box to Bob, who along with Susan stepped aside, no doubt waiting for Traynor to groan in pain when he put the holster on ... once again, he made a concerted effort not to. When he couldn't raise his left arm enough to get the harness over it, Susan helped loop the holster over his shoulder. "I hope you don't need to use that in a hurry," she said.

He glanced at her to make sure she was talking about the pistol.

"Me too," he answered.

She stood with that stern look on her face again.

He took the gun and pulled the slide back, locking it in place, and worked the magazine release with his thumb. The magazine dropped from its home in the pistol's handle, and he caught it with his left hand. It was empty.

Bob turned, reached into the box, and produced a box of ammunition, which he handed over. Traynor loaded the magazine with a full load of bullets and pushed it until it locked into its home in the handle. He released the safety lock with his thumb, letting the slide ride home, injecting the first round into the chamber. He put the pistol in the holster, and struggled into his jacket. He emptied the rest of the ammunition into one of his pockets. Traynor was ready—at least as ready as he would ever be.

He gave Susan a peck on the cheek and started for the door. "Where you going?" she asked.

"I got places to go, people to see." He struggled into his raincoat, grimacing when he shrugged to adjust the coat to fit over his shoulders.

"In your condition? Who do you need to see so bad that you'll risk your health to see them?"

"The Escobars," Traynor replied. "I want to look them in the eye when I ask them if they had any dealings with John."

"Why bother?" Susan said. "Even if they did have some sort of deal with him, they'll deny it."

"I've been a cop long enough that I can tell when I'm being lied to. Besides, sometimes you have to shake a tree to find out who or what is hiding in it."

"Well, I hope you don't mind walking," she said with a snide smile. "You probably don't remember, but your car is still over in Newington."

Susan opened a closet door, took out her coat, put it on, and grabbed her purse. She lifted her keys from the hook where she kept them and dangled them at him. "Come on, I'll drop you and then head into the office." She kissed Bob on the cheek on their way to the door.

10

The Escobar brothers were reputed to be the primary movers of cocaine and heroin in the northeast. After years of trying, law enforcement agencies in every New England state had failed to nail them for so much as a misdemeanor. They were bad people, whom no one should take lightly. Traynor had seen firsthand how they dealt with their opposition.

A few years ago, while they were still NHSP homicide detectives, he and Buck arrived at a warehouse in Derry. They found what was left of a couple of local punks who had tried to cut in on the brothers' business in southern New Hampshire. They paid dearly for it. The Escobars made sure they left a message for anyone with ideas about screwing around on their turf. That was the only reason Traynor could think of for the gruesome mess they found. Somebody had skinned those boys and then hung them from meat hooks like a couple sides of beef. The medical examiner was almost certain that they were alive when the flaying started. Traynor later heard rumors that Carlo did it personally, and he took great pride in making sure that everyone knew the consequences of crossing him.

Traynor braced himself for what he was sure would follow. This wasn't going to be a routine interview. People like Carlo take offense with inquisitive cops, whether they're active or retired; to Escobar, Traynor's current employment status would make no difference.

The Escobar brothers' import/export company was located in a refurbished warehouse on South Union Street in Lawrence, Massachusetts. Traynor parked far out in the lot and again fought the chilling November wind as he walked to the reception area.

He expected to be turned away at the desk with the usual "Do you have an appointment?" However, that turned out not to be the case. The receptionist called a number and announced, "A Mr. Traynor to see Mr. Escobar," and then said, "Please take a seat, Mr. Escobar will see you shortly."

Traynor sat quietly, slightly shocked at how easily he was getting an audience with the biggest drug lord in five states. It was evident to him that one of two things was taking place here: either he was walking into a trap and might never leave this building alive, or he had something Escobar wanted. He waited twenty minutes before Carlo granted him access to his office.

A security guard led him down a long corridor to an elevator. As they walked, Traynor said, "Nice building."

The guard's only reply was a grunt.

Traynor's stoic escort pressed the button on the right side of the elevator door and, when the door opened, stepped aside, motioning for him to enter. Traynor thought the security guard's personality was ideal for someone working for a drug dealer—compared to him, a confessional priest was as loquacious as a witness for the state. The elevator must have served a dual purpose, to transport people as well as freight. The walls were covered with pads similar to those used to protect furniture during a move. The guard pushed the button with the number three on it and turned to face the rear of the elevator, which Ed thought was odd. During the elevator ride, they said nothing, the guard making a point of standing with his back to Traynor the entire time. Ed realized that the man was baiting him, and he became determined not to rise to the bait and continued facing the door through which they had entered. After several seconds, he heard the sound of a door opening behind him. He turned and watched the back wall open to reveal a door he had not noticed. Traynor wondered: *Is there anything in the building that functioned as it appeared?* The guard smirked at him and stepped aside to allow him to precede him off the elevator.

Traynor exited the elevator and walked into a suite that would make the chief executive officer of a Fortune 500 firm drool with envy. He wondered if he should buy coffee stocks, then thought better of it—the money that paid for this place was not from coffee. He wondered what the building would smell like if you eliminated the overwhelming, but pleasant, aroma of processed coffee beans.

A Hispanic beauty, dressed as if she had just stepped off the cover of *Glamour*, rose to greet him. "Mr. Traynor?" she asked.

"Yes."

She handed him a business card, which read: Gisela Martin. When she introduced herself, she pronounced her name *He-sell-ah Mar-teen*.

Traynor shook her hand, taking care not to grip too tight. She wore a bracelet adorned with enough diamonds to get her on the De Beers Christmas Catalog mailing list. He wondered what her status was; surely, she could not afford those clothes and bracelet on a secretary's salary. Her dress was formfitting, and although he wasn't a slave to fashion by any means, Traynor knew expensive when he saw it. She looked more like the personal assistant of a CEO than an office worker. Her hair fell to the small of her back and was so black it shined with a blue sheen. Everything about her, from the abundance of gemstones to her elegant, graceful posture, was exquisite.

"Mr. Escobar will be with you in a moment. Can I get you something to drink, some coffee, or a soft drink, maybe?"

"Do you have Pepsi?"

"I believe we do." She smiled at him and her teeth were brilliant white when contrasted to her tawny skin.

"That'll be fine."

As she led him into an opulent office, her hips swayed, and it was so sensual he wondered if she was intentionally teasing him with a blatant sexual invitation. Once inside the office, she guided him to one of two leather chairs facing a huge mahogany desk. He didn't hear her as she departed.

Traynor sat alone. After several minutes in isolation, he was starting to lose his composure. Where was Escobar? Was allowing him access just a game—a childish way of screwing with him? He made up his mind that if Escobar did not walk in within the next two minutes, he was walking out.

Suddenly he heard the muted sound of a toilet flushing, followed by the barely audible sound of water running. The dark paneling to his left slid open, revealing a door that was virtually invisible to anyone who didn't know it was there. Moments before, while he was studying the office, he'd looked at that wall without having so much as a clue to its existence. Once again, he realized that nothing in the building was as it seemed.

Carlo Escobar stepped into his office, shaking his hands, obviously trying to remove residual moisture. He looked up and smiled. "Mr. Traynor?" He held his right hand forward.

He was not exactly what Traynor had thought he would be. Rather than a tall, romantic Latin American man, he was a short, dark, and swarthy man of obvious mestizo heritage. Carlo would never be able to deny the Indian blood in his veins. Of all his features, the most dominant were his eyes. They were half-closed, half-open, tending to make one believe he was almost asleep, like those of an alligator basking in the sun, lulling you into a false sense of security—until you got close.

Traynor grasped his hand and ignored the wetness from his recent handwashing; at that point, he did not want to slight him. The strength of his hands surprised Traynor. Although they were small, his grip was strong enough to rip open the cans in which he packaged coffee. Ed immediately knew that he needed to learn more about him; it might save his life down the road.

Escobar studied Traynor's bruised face for a few seconds. A malicious smile spread across his face. "Should I ask what the other guy looks like or did you walk into a door?"

"I had a run-in with a couple of goons last night—would you by any chance know anything about that?"

Escobar's visage morphed into something sinister. "I have never in my life met you before; why would I know anything about that?"

Traynor smiled at Escobar and said, "I guess you wouldn't. Why would a *coffee* importer know about a couple of Hispanic toughs?"

Escobar ignored the sarcasm. "I'm afraid that I must cut this short—I have pressing matters to which I must attend. What is it that you want from me?" he asked.

"I'm John Traynor's brother."

Escobar gave no indication he knew anything about whom he spoke. "John Traynor? Does he work for my company?"

"That is why I'm here. I'm a concerned brother looking into John's affairs, and your name and your brother's came up as possibly doing business with him."

"Look into your brother's affairs? That sounds ominous."

"It should—he's dead."

"You have my condolences. Was he ill?"

"No," Traynor said, "he was murdered."

Carlo's eyes narrowed and seemed to glow with anger. "Why do you come to me with this?" His voice remained level as he walked to the desk and leaned against the edge. "Your brother, who I've never heard of, dies, and you immediately seek me out? What is this bullshit, Mr. Traynor?" The expression on his face was as staid as that on a stone bust; the only indication that Traynor was getting to him was that his reptilian eyes narrowed to dangerous slits.

"I've been told he was involved in some sort of business transaction with you and your brother. I also know that the mortality rate among people who do business with you is higher than the national average."

He glared at Traynor. "What are you saying?"

"Mr. Escobar, I've heard of your reputation. You are a successful businessman and not a person with whom anyone should trifle."

Carlo kept his eyes locked on Traynor's and his facial color changed; it went from a flushed pink to an angry red. Traynor knew he was close to exploding.

It was evident that Escobar struggled to maintain his self-control as he said, "If you know so much about me, then you know, as I'm a businessman, I would find the death of anyone who owed me money most unprofitable. Only a fool throws away money. Believe me, Mr. Traynor, if there is one thing I am not, it is a fool. Everything I do is motivated by profit." He leaned slightly forward, emphasizing his point. "So, if I *was* involved with your brother, and I assure you I was not, and he owed me money, I would be very unlikely to harm him." He leaned back, folded his arms across his chest, and smiled. It was not a pleasant smile.

"That may be," Traynor said. "But, I also know a thing or two about business. For instance, I know the value of publicity. If one was in the industry of supplying a certain commodity—let's say a very lucrative, but illegal one—maybe by suffering a small loss, a *company* might actually ensure that other sources of revenue are not, shall we say, delinquent in their payments?"

Escobar walked over to a small service table and took a mango from a platter. He returned to his desk, opened the drawer, and removed a large, bone-handled knife. He pressed a button and a twelve-inch blade snapped open with enough force to make his hand move. The knife blade sparkled in the light from the lamp on his desk as he leaned back and slowly began to peel the fruit.

"Yes, there is benefit to publicity. But, I deal in a legal commodity, Colombian coffee; it's the finest in the world, you know."

The mango's skin curled downward in a single piece as Escobar showed off his prowess with a blade. Traynor was starting to enjoy this game and smiled at him. "Yes, I've heard how good Colombian coffee is—I've also heard about the quality of its cocaine."

The mango skin, along with the smug look on Escobar's face, fell to the floor. The alligator eyes opened fully. "You really have a large pair of *cojones*, Mr. Traynor, but you should be careful to whom you show them." He flipped the knife into the air, caught it by the handle, and placed it on his desk. "They could get cut off."

Before Traynor could comment, the door behind him opened and, expecting an attack from the rear, he turned. Gisela Martin entered the office carrying a crystal goblet filled with ice and cola. She sensed the tension between Carlo and the visitor, hesitated for a second, then regained her composure and approached.

When she placed the crystal goblet on a coaster on the small table beside Traynor's seat, he got a look at her watch, a Rolex. More than ever, he was convinced that Gisela was like the building and not what she seemed. She glanced at him and then at Carlo, but said nothing. When Traynor thanked her for the drink, she nodded and left the room, closing the door softly behind her. The scent of Chanel lingered in her wake.

Escobar noticed that Traynor watched her as she walked away. "She's exquisite."

"Very beautiful," Traynor said. He turned his attention back to Escobar. "Might I inquire what function she performs for you?"

He shrugged. "Gisela is a woman of many talents and she performs many essential tasks for my company. She's my Director of Special Projects." The tension of a few minutes ago was gone from his demeanor and he said, "I'm sorry, but once again I must emphasize that I didn't know your brother. Maybe my brother did. Unfortunately, Eduardo is out of the country, in Colombia buying coffee. If you leave your card I'll have him get in touch with you when he returns next week."

Traynor placed one of his cards on Escobar's desk, took a drink of the soda, and placed the goblet on the shiny surface of the mahogany table. He intentionally missed the coaster and almost smiled when Escobar's eyebrows arched with disapproval. "Well," Traynor said, "I'm sorry to have wasted your time." He offered Escobar his hand in farewell.

Carlo pretended not to notice the hand, reached across him, placed the wet goblet on its coaster, and then walked across the office and opened the door. He stood beside the threshold and said, "The security guard will escort you."

"That's okay. I can find my way."

"I'm sure you can. Still, the building can often be confusing and I wouldn't want you to get lost and waste your time wandering around."

The security guard from downstairs stood by the door. He nodded at Traynor and grunted.

"Where did you find this guy, Carlo? He's a great conversationalist. . ."

Traynor stepped past Escobar, intentionally bumping him into the doorjamb. "Excuse me," he said.

Escobar's eyes got that predatory reptilian look again. "Mr. Traynor?"

"Yes?"

"Out of curiosity, how did your brother die?"

"He was shot in the head."

"So, his death was quick."

Escobar's face remained stoic; as much as Traynor tried to glean a clue to the man's complacency, he saw nothing in his facial expression.

"Have a good life, Mr. Traynor."

"For some reason, I don't think we're finished doing business, Mr. Escobar."

The reptile warned of its presence. "If we meet again, Mr. Traynor, I can assure you it won't be so cordial."

"I'm crushed, Carlo. I thought we were getting along like long-lost buddies. Hell, I was even going to invite you out for a couple of beers, maybe even take in a ball game when the Sox season starts."

11

Gisela Martin was waiting for Traynor when he walked out of the building. She wore a stunning fur coat bundled tight against the gusting northerly wind. The light in the parking lot was not the best; nevertheless, she looked as enticing as she had in the office. She spoke first. "I hope your meeting with Carlo went well."

"It went as well as I expected it would go."

She lit a cigarette and leaned against his Taurus. "Would you like to buy me a drink?"

Traynor's curiosity piqued. She was after something. Beautiful women did not just ask him to have a drink; that only happened in detective novels and in the 1940s and '50s noir B movies that he watched on cable TV. However, he was not about to let the opportunity to find out more about Carlo and his organization pass him by. "I'd love to—your car or mine?"

She glanced at his Taurus, noted the bumps, bruises, and dings in the body. She must have found it lacking in charm. "My car is right over there." She pointed to a metallic candy-apple red Dodge Viper. Tossing the keys to him, she said, "You drive."

"Nice wheels. What does someone have to do to make enough to own one of these?"

He braced himself for a comeback. Instead, she cast him an alluring smile and said, "Whatever one has to."

Traynor walked around the car and opened the passenger door for her. She rewarded him with a flash of her gorgeous legs. The message was obvious, a stunning Hispanic version of *eat your heart out*.

He circled around, got behind the wheel, turned to her, and again she rewarded him with a longer view of her legs. He started to feel like prey sniffing around an enthralling trap. He tried to ignore the bait. "Where to?"

Traynor followed her directions to an upscale restaurant in Andover, near the exclusive Phillips Academy—training ground for rich and famous kids like the Kennedys. The maître d' recognized her on sight and quickly escorted them to a table in a dark, secluded corner. He opened the wine list, handed them each a copy, and then left. When the waiter arrived Gisela said, "I'll have my usual, James."

The waiter turned to Traynor and asked, "And for you, sir?"

"Maker's Mark, neat."

He bowed slightly and disappeared.

"So," Traynor asked, "do you always pick up men in parking lots?"

She smiled. "You are the first in a long time. I must admit that you intrigue me."

"So that's it, huh. I'm intriguing?" He got the distinct feeling she was not lying. Still, he felt like a fly flitting around a Venus flytrap.

"Yes, you are. I know for a fact that Carlo finds you extremely interesting."

She took a cigarette from her purse and held it before her lips. Ever the gentleman, Traynor lit it with her cigarette lighter, which, like everything about her, was expensive. No cheap two-buck disposable lighter for her; this one was a gold Zippo. She inhaled and stared at him. Her eyes pulled him in, closer to the trap. Like the alluring sweet scent of a carnivorous plant, Traynor knew she was trying to lull him into a false sense of security. He fought against the urge to fall under her spell.

"Is that why *he* told you to pick me up?"

She grinned and said, "You underestimate yourself; Carlo didn't tell me anything. I am quite capable of knowing when something—or someone—is a threat."

"He'd have to sell more coffee than Procter & Gamble and General Foods combined to afford that office, not to mention a Director of Special Projects who drives a Viper. Considering the options you have in that baby, it must have cost you close to a hundred thousand dollars."

"More . . . but, let's not go there." Her face softened, but her eyes remained as hard and dark as obsidian. Traynor watched the beautiful, but lethal, flower open its petals, hoping to entice the fly a bit closer; she tried to put him off guard with a smile that was full of sexual invitation. "You interest me, Ed. It's okay if I call you Ed?"

Traynor nodded.

"You walk into Carlo's office showing no fear and engage him in a battle of words. There are only a handful of people with enough courage, or lack of brains, to do that. I might add that many who try do not get the opportunity to brag. I'm not without experience in these matters. I don't believe for a minute that you're just a concerned brother."

"Then who, or what, do you think I am?"

"I think you're who you say you are, John Traynor's brother, but where he was a petty thief and loser, you've got cop written all over you. How does that American saying go? Once a cop, always a cop." With that simple, offhand phrase, Gisela blew Carlo's denial of knowing John. Without a doubt, if she knew of him, so did Escobar.

"Actually, I believe the saying goes: Once a Marine, always a Marine."

She smiled. "Whatever, but as long as we're trading clichés, if the shoe fits, wear it."

Traynor knew it would be stupid to sell her short. Gisela had brains along with more than her share of ambition. He decided to play it straight. "I'm a retired New Hampshire State Police homicide detective. I own my own security and investigation firm now."

"So this isn't some amateur investigation?"

"One thing I'm not is an amateur."

Her eyes roamed across his chest and he realized what was on her mind. "I'm not wired."

She relaxed and decided to entice him further. He felt her shoeless foot gently touch his left ankle. She elevated her foot, stroking his leg softly. "For some strange reason I believe you." She looked over the lip of her glass as she sipped water.

He struggled to maintain his composure as that most private part of his anatomy began to respond to her expert ministrations. He would have sworn before a grand jury that she smiled as she taunted him. In a sultry voice she said, "I hope I won't regret it."

He moved his foot to the side, and her eyes sparkled as she followed it with her teasing foot. He tried to keep things businesslike and said, "Where do you fit into this mess?"

"I'm merely looking out for my interests."

"And just what are your interests, if you don't mind my asking?"

Her foot disappeared and she sat up in her chair. "Early in life, I learned how to get what I want." When she spoke, her mien was as sharp as a glass shard. Her voice, on the other hand, was deceptive, much softer than her face.

Traynor sat silent, studied her, and for an instant saw past the vixen facade. Like everything surrounding the Escobar brothers, she was not what she appeared to be on the surface. It was obvious that beneath her exterior beauty lay an explosive rage, so powerful it was capable of sweeping away anything in its path. He wondered what could have happened in her past to cause such anger.

She noticed that he was studying her and she morphed again, hiding the inner feelings that bubbled so close to the surface. Traynor became convinced that his instincts were accurate. She was no China doll; this woman was capable of doing whatever it took to get anything that she wanted. He did not discount murder.

He decided to get straight to the point. "Look, at the risk of using yet another cliché, let's lay our cards on the table, okay? I know that the Escobars control most of the dope sold in New England. I also make no bones about the fact that my brother was a punk who dealt those drugs, and his wife told me he said he was working on a deal with Carlo and Eduardo."

She leaned back and folded her arms, which emphasized her jutting breasts, and stared at the cigarette smoke that spiraled into the air around her head.

Traynor pushed forward. "Then, like magic, yesterday morning my brother turns up dead in the middle of the woods. John and I never got along . . . we saw life differently."

"I would never have thought of you as the type to engage in sibling rivalry."

"John and I were never rivals; we didn't compete with each other—we had different ideas about what made a worthwhile life. Nevertheless, don't let that fool you into thinking that I won't turn over every leaf and stone in the forest to uncover his killer. I think Carlo knows a lot more about this than he's letting on."

He took a drink of water and settled back. "I also think that if Carlo knows . . . then you most likely know. As a matter of fact, I get the distinct feeling there isn't a hell of a lot that goes on with the Escobars that you don't know."

Their drinks came and she ground out her cigarette. "Your sources are mistaken. Your brother was not working a deal with either of my employers. The fact of the matter is that Carlo and Eduardo suffered a major setback last week, and they are certain your brother was involved."

"Involved . . . in what way?"

"All I can do is guess. Let's just say that keeping your brother alive was more important to Carlo than having him dead—at least for the time being."

"I assumed that in spite of Carlo's denial, he knew John. That being the case, it's also possible that he, and I might add you, knows whether or not John had accomplices. I also believe that if you have that knowledge you won't be giving it to me. For instance, last night I got the shit stomped out of me by two Hispanic goons, and it wouldn't surprise me if Carlo sent them."

"How could Carlo—or I—do that? Until an hour ago we wouldn't have known you if we passed you on the street."

Traynor paused. Her words resonated with truth. However, he was not ready to give her the benefit of the doubt—not yet. "Come on, Gisela, don't yank my chain. Carlo's temper is evident—he almost blew a head gasket when I was in his office. If he thought John had ripped him off, he would have been enraged, madder than a rabid skunk. I wouldn't be surprised if Carlo didn't do John himself. Took him out to the woods and when John wouldn't give him what he wanted, shot him. However, as vicious as Carlo is, he's also smart. So smart that he sent you here for something. What is it?"

She was as cool as a Wall Street analyst discussing a hostile take-over. "Let me reiterate, I'm here on my own. Someone stole a significant sum of money last week, and Carlo believes your brother was involved. If I could recover that money I'm certain Carlo would be more than generous." She took a cigarette from her pack and lit it. "Carlo is being pressured by some . . . shall we call them suppliers? Possibly 'creditors' is an even better word. Regardless, these are very nasty people who have advanced Carlo and Eduardo a great deal of inventory—over two million dollars' worth—and that's before street value. To make the situation worse, Carlo and Eduardo are behind in their payments. These creditors are not the type of businessmen who will allow anyone to be delinquent for long." She drew on the cigarette, and smoke came from her mouth when she spoke. "So, you see, if your brother knew anything about the missing money, Carlo would not want him dead. On the other hand, if your brother was involved in the rip-off, he's put Carlo in a very bad position. Still, he'd be alive, at least until the money was recovered. After that, Carlo would balance the books."

"How significant an amount was this rip-off we're talking about?"

She paused, obviously debating how much she should reveal to him. She exhaled a cloud of smoke and then seemed to come to a decision. "Over three million dollars, cash."

Traynor tried to keep his surprise from showing on his face. He did not succeed. "But, Carlo denies knowing John."

She grinned.

It was obvious to Traynor that she found his feigned ignorance of life among society's dredges humorous and probably an insult to her intelligence. Still she was playing the game and, in a voice more suitable for communicating with a first-grader, she enlightened him. "Of course he denies knowing him. He is a *jefe*, a chief, the boss if you will, and has risen above having to deal with lowly people such as your brother and you. However, knowing your brother and knowing about him are two different things, aren't they?"

"So Carlo did have dealings with him?"

"They had no direct dealings. Your brother was several rungs down the ladder, if he was even on the ladder, and definitely too small for Carlo to bother with. However, he screwed Carlo, and I don't think I have to tell you what a stupid thing that was." She glared at him and angrily ground out her cigarette to emphasize her point. "You don't want Carlo as your enemy. Believe me when I say that I only know of one person who can be a worse enemy than Carlo."

"Really? And who might that be?"

She stood up, glared at him, and looked satisfied—as if the flower had snared the fly.

"I thought you would have figured that out by now." The face of a street-smart, tough woman quickly erased the mirage of the eloquent Hispanic beauty. "Shall we leave?"

Gisela watched Traynor's car turn right on South Union Street, obviously headed for Interstate 495. A gust of wind broke her reverie, and she walked into the building.

Escobar sat at his desk; a bottle of aguardiente and a glass sat in front of him. Gisela walked into his office without knocking on his door. He pointed to the credenza along the wall to his right. They spoke in their native tongue. "Get a glass," he said.

She walked across the room, picked up a glass, and returned to his desk. He motioned to the bottle, and she poured herself a double shot; as was the Colombian custom, they drank the fiery liquor neat. She settled into the same chair that Traynor had occupied a few hours prior. She held her glass up in a toast and said, "¡Salud!"

Escobar raised his glass, and they each drank.

Gisela crossed her legs, giving Carlo a flash of tawny thigh. She lit a cigarette and once again sipped the liquor.

"Did you learn anything?" Carlo inquired.

"He knows nothing. He's just another cop, poking his nose into things to see what he can learn."

"But, his brother *is* dead?"

"Apparently that is true."

He slammed his palm on the desk, leapt to his feet, and yelled, "Where is my fucking money?"

She placed her glass on the table beside her chair, got up, and circled the desk. She pressed her breasts into his back and began kneading his shoulders with her fingers. "We will find your money, my love; that much money will not remain hidden for long."

His head rocked back as her expert ministrations loosened and relaxed his tense muscles. He turned, wrapped his arms around her, and gripped her buttocks, pressing her pelvis against him. "I hope you are right," he said.

Gisela sighed and ground her hips into him, smiling when his right hand dropped to her thigh and raised the hem of her skirt. His hand found its way to her most sensitive parts, and she gave a soft groan. Her head dropped to rest on his shoulder, and she whispered, "When it does, I will be there with our people to bring it to you."

The cell phone on Carlo's desk rang, and he pulled away from her. He looked at the display and answered the call. "¡*Hola!*" He listened for a few seconds and then said, "I will meet you there in fifteen minutes." He broke the connection and tossed the phone on his desk.

"Trouble?" Gisela asked.

"Nothing major, but something I must take care of." He walked to a coat rack near the door to his office and put on a heavy overcoat.

"Do you want me to come with you?"

"No, this is something that you don't want to be involved with."

"Carlo, you be careful."

He nodded and left.

When the elevator door closed behind him, she took her phone out of her bag and hit a speed dial. When the call was established, she said, "He is on his way down. I want to know where he is going and what he does there."

12

Carlo entered the brilliant lights, made even brighter when they reflected off the stainless-steel tables that filled the room. Two of his security guards stood beside the door, and one took the heavy overcoat when Carlo shrugged out of it and handed it to him.

"Where is he?"

"In the back room, *Jefe*."

Carlo nodded and walked to the back room. He saw another guard leaning against the wall of the back room. The man straightened when he saw his boss enter. Carlo motioned for the guards to join him as he entered the room.

Carlo closed the door, locked the dead bolt with a key, and then turned to the man hanging from a steel ceiling beam with his arms chained and extended above his head.

"Carlo—"

Carlo placed a finger across his lips. "Quiet, Eduardo—you always talk too fucking much." He turned to the guards and said, "Take him down and strap him to the altar."

Sweat covered Eduardo Escobar's face and dripped down his naked chest. The guards lowered him to the floor and unlocked his shackles. Before Eduardo could pull free of their grasp, they dragged him to the center of the room where a rectangular table that resembled a sacrificial altar sat. In seconds, they had him strapped to the table and stepped back.

Carlo nodded to the two thugs and dismissed them. "Leave us."

"*Si, Jefe.*" They scrambled out of the room.

Eduardo struggled in vain to escape his bonds, then he looked at his brother. His eyes were wide with fear and followed Carlo's angry figure pacing left to right in front of him.

Carlo suddenly spun, bent over, and slapped Eduardo across the mouth. "Do you have so much as a clue how much you hurt me—hurt the organization?"

"I-I—"

Carlo punched him in the solar plexus. "You don't fucking speak until I tell you to fucking speak. *¿Comprende?*"

Eduardo wheezed and gasped as he tried to regain the air that Carlo's punch had knocked out of him. His hair shined with sweat, and blood ran down the side of his mouth from his brother's slap.

"There is no way the cartel is going to accept that we—*WE*—were ripped off! More than three million you lost. At least those two fuck heads you used had the good sense to get killed—saving me the trouble."

Carlo began pacing again, working himself into a killing frenzy. "The cartel is like Chac; they will demand a sacrifice," he said. He stopped and looked at his brother. "*Now,* you may speak."

"I will get the money back! I know who the one who killed my people and took it is."

Carlo waved his hand as if he were shooing a troublesome fly. "Yeah, yeah, yeah. John Traynor was the asshole." He turned and faced Eduardo. "The *bastardo* went and got himself killed. No one knows what he did with the money! Now, what do you think Treviño is going to do when he learns that?"

Eduardo's head dropped. "I can make it up, I can . . ."

Carlo reached into his back pocket and brought out a knife. He pressed a button and a sharp blade snapped out.

Eduardo heard the snap of the knife opening and his head snapped up. He saw the knife in Carlo's hand and said, "Carlo . . . we are brothers!"

"Half brothers, Eduardo." He stepped forward.

13

The drive to the morgue was torturous; stop-and-go traffic all the way up Route 4 into Concord. The prospect of facing Kate Toussaint did not help matters. He liked Kate, any man with half a brain would, but she had yet to forgive him for getting cold feet and bailing on her. She was attractive, intelligent, and fun, if you looked past her hair-trigger temper. The problem then—and now—was that he loved someone else. He had for years, and for him to try to maintain a relationship with another woman was a waste of energy. He could not begin to think of what it would be like for anyone to try and take the place of the fantasy he had nurtured for years—and now it looked as if there was a chance that it could come true.

Kate sat at her desk when Traynor walked into the office. Her disposition had not changed since he had seen her at the crime scene in Fremont. He tried to keep things low-key and businesslike.

"Morning, Kate."

She did not respond. Instead, she glared at him over the rim of her morning tea. "You look like you kissed a fast freight train."

"It wasn't one of my better nights."

"Let me know who did it. I'd like to send a thank-you card."

Traynor stood patiently and waited for her to get over her snit. Unfortunately, she was in no rush. "Look, Kate, I didn't come here to give you any flack, okay? I know if I was lying on a slab in here, you wouldn't even try and contact my next-of-kin, but we both want the same thing, even if for different reasons. You want a case cleared, and I want to know who whacked my brother and why."

She got up and walked to a file cabinet, opened the top drawer, and withdrew a file. She pulled a copy of the autopsy report from the folder and threw it on the desk in front of him. "I shouldn't be showing you this, but it's common knowledge that what Buck knows, you know. Cause of death was a small caliber bullet. We found fragments in the skull cavity, but not enough for any type of forensic testing."

"Thanks." He picked up the report, read through it to the end. Kate had laid it out succinctly: *Cause of death: gunshot to the head. Manner of death: homicide.* Sometimes seeing what you already knew on an official document puts closure to the event, as if someone in authority has put their seal of approval on your findings. He read the time of death. "You figure he was killed sometime between midnight and 2:00 a.m.?" That coincided with what the junkyard owner had told him.

She nodded.

Before he turned to leave, he said, "Kate, maybe we can have a drink soon? Discuss what happened and why."

She raised her head and said, "Fuck you, Ed. I know why it happened. I got inside the wall you've built around your feelings—when I did that, you got scared. In many ways, you're brave to a fault. Yet in others, the ones that really matter, you're a coward. Now take what you came for and get the hell out of my office."

———————

Traynor's next stop was to visit Benny Ryan, John's usual partner in crime. If anyone knew what John had been up to, it would be Ryan; it was time to find out what he knew. Ryan's place was in Bow, a few miles from the morgue, and immediately after leaving Kate's office Traynor drove there. Sleet slammed against the windshield and he turned the car's heater temperature up, cursing the first storm of what would be another long New England winter. The damp chill played havoc with his injuries, and the face staring back at him in the rearview mirror was difficult to recognize. It was not turning into one of his better mornings. The only thing that seemed to cheer him up was when he told himself that the next time he met up with Scarface and Whitey, he was going to do everything in his power to ensure that the outcome was very different.

He stopped musing about vengeance and concentrated on the wet surface of I-93. As Traynor drove, he thought about John's longtime relationship with Ryan. If John had ripped off someone, Ryan knew about it. Since he was a teenager, whenever John was hip-deep in shit and needed to hide out, he did it at Ryan's house. If he didn't, Ryan knew where he was hiding.

Traynor arrived at the house, a small gray cape with black trim, shortly after noon. The well-cared-for yard surprised him. The lawn and exterior looked well-manicured and the house appeared freshly painted, uncharacteristic of what one usually expected a drug addict's home to be. On the other hand, Ryan, unlike John, had a trade. When he was straight and not out for an easy buck, he was a damned good carpenter. His main malfunction was that an employer couldn't count on him. He'd show up for work on Monday morning and go gangbusters until noon, then he'd do lunch at a bar or smoke some weed and wouldn't return for a couple of weeks, if at all.

The house was quiet. The drawn drapes made it difficult to tell if it was occupied or empty. Ryan's battered and rusted Dodge pickup sat in the driveway. Traynor walked to the side porch and banged on the door. No one answered, but he heard movement inside. He waited a second to see if someone would come to the door. When they did not, he banged again. For a few seconds, the sounds abruptly ceased. Then from the back of the house, he heard the bang of a sliding door slamming against its stops, followed by the sound of someone running.

A stab of pain ripped through his side when he yanked the nine-millimeter out of its holster. Ignoring the stabbing pain that the sudden movement caused, he scrambled down the porch's four steps. When he turned the corner of the building, he saw a person wearing a red and black plaid coat disappear into the woods behind the house.

Seconds later, he heard a motor crank to life and a four-wheel-drive truck flashed through the trees. The pickup bounced along a small wooded lane and skidded onto the public road about a hundred yards beyond the house. Traynor watched the truck fishtail on the wet pavement then slide around, tires spinning, spewing mud into the air, as it fought to develop traction on the road's surface. He watched it pass in front of the house, going too fast to accurately ID the driver through the grime-coated windows. The Chevy Silverado four-by-four was a mud hole on wheels, its exterior so heavily caked with dirt and dried mud that Traynor could not read the numbers on its license plates. He watched the truck disappear and listened to the roar of its motor diminish in the rain. Traynor knew he would never get to his car in time to catch the truck, so he returned to the house and climbed the steps onto a deck attached to the back wall. When the intruder fled, he had left the sliding door open, drapes flapping through the opening. He stepped inside, avoiding the snapping and undulating curtains, and stood in a combination dining room/kitchen and looked around. Someone had trashed the house, leaving drawers pulled out and cupboard doors open. Their contents had been thrown about, littering the floor with papers, food-stuffs, and kitchen utensils. Traynor carefully picked his way through the debris. It was evident that the interloper had searched every conceivable place, looking for whatever it was he sought. Traynor believed that he had scared him off before he found whatever it was. Obviously, someone else also thought Ryan knew something about John's recent business deals.

Pistol still in hand, Traynor walked through the dining area and entered a small living room. To his left was a stairway leading upstairs. He took his time climbing, avoiding using the handrail and leaving fingerprints on it as he stepped softly. As he ascended, he listened for any sound that would indicate he was not alone in the house. At the top of the stairs, Traynor peered into the master bedroom. A pair of bare feet protruded beyond the corner of the bed. Traynor cautiously stepped inside the room and swept his pistol around as he entered. He was not alone . . . yet he was. Other than the body on the floor, the room was empty.

He craned his neck and peered over the bed. Benny Ryan lay on the floor. He wore nothing but a pair of faded jeans. His head twisted to the left in an unnatural angle. Taking care not to disturb the body more than he had to, Traynor placed two fingers on the carotid—no pulse. Ryan was not going to tell him, or anyone for that matter, anything ever again. The room looked like a nor'easter had raged through it. Traynor concluded that Ryan must have put up one hell of a fight, but lost.

In spite of his dislike of him, Traynor felt newfound respect for Ryan. Never before had he shown any sign of having a backbone. Traynor quickly searched the room, finding nothing that would lead him to either Ryan's or John's killer. He slid his pistol back inside his holster and returned to the kitchen.

He used a pen to sift through the debris, looking for anything he could use to cover his hands, even something as rudimentary as a plastic baggie. He was lucky and found a box of latex gloves under the sink, the type someone might use when cooking a batch of crystal meth. As he put a pair of the gloves on, Traynor wondered if Ryan had been cutting drugs recently. The last thing he needed would be to walk around with enough forensic evidence on his body to put him away for ten to twenty years.

There was one door still closed and Traynor opened it. A set of rudimentary wooden stairs led down to the basement. He snapped on the light switch beside the entrance and walked down. The room appeared untouched; his arrival must have scared the killer off before he could complete his search. Many people finish their basement, and Ryan was no different, although it looked as if he hadn't wanted to put a lot of effort or money into the project. The concrete walls were unfinished; obviously Ryan had avoided the labor and cost of framing them by painting the concrete. Traynor figured it must have cost all of a hundred bucks to decorate the entire room. The opposite was true of Ryan's entertainment equipment. In one corner stood an expensive 65-inch Ultra-HDTV, its screen so large that watching it in the small room would be like sitting in the front row of a movie theater. Traynor was a stereo buff, and he estimated that along with the expensive television, Ryan had a couple thousand dollars of electronic entertainment equipment in his home theater. A 250-watt amplifier fed an impressive array of 7.1 surround-sound speakers and a Blu-ray DVD player capable of playing 3-D movies. The equipment was more sophisticated than anyone needed to watch the type of movie Benny seemed to enjoy. He'd filed alphabetically by title an assortment of fantasy and science fiction movies, as well as a wide variety of porno films so extensive that any XXX-rated video store would love to have the collection in its inventory. The only furniture in the room was a recliner and easy chair with worn arms, a small table, a lamp between them, and a small bookcase by the wall. An ashtray filled with burnt marijuana butts and a roach clip sat on the table close to the recliner. It looked as if Benny had not worked for several days.

The room had a false ceiling—it was not elaborate, just some parachute silk stapled to the underside of the floor joists. Along a seam that ran down the center of the room, Traynor saw a section where the fabric hung different from the rest. He reached up, grabbed a handful of material, and yanked it free from the staples securing it to the joists. He had to jump to one side to avoid Ryan's treasure as it cascaded down. The paraphernalia spread around his feet. Traynor looked at a stash of marijuana and cocaine, and some cash—a little over five hundred dollars. He didn't want the police to get sidetracked thinking this was a robbery, so he shoved the dope and money back inside the false ceiling, even though he was tempted to keep the cash for Jill. As he was leaving, his eyes rested on the bookcase, which he realized was something completely out of character for Benny Ryan. Traynor doubted that his brother's frequent partner ever read anything more detailed than the jackets on the porno movies he loved so much. He crossed the room and studied the books on the case's shelves. Ryan's taste appeared to be eclectic—everything from mysteries to westerns and epic fantasy—but it all seemed to have been purchased at garage sales. Traynor doubted that Ryan had read any of them. His eye paused looking at an expensive-looking leather-bound journal. The book was as out of place on that shelf as a rabbi would be on a pilgrimage to Vatican City. Wondering what Ryan could have written, he picked up the journal and thumbed through the pages. It looked like some type of tally book or ledger. Whatever it was, its contents were important enough to encode. To his untrained eye, the book was full of gobbledygook, scrambled words, and random numbers. However, in the hands of a trained cryptographer, the book might give up its secrets. In the back was a crude map with Xs marked, obviously locations where someone had either buried or cached something. The layout looked familiar, but he found nothing to identify precisely where it was. Anything important enough to be encoded piqued his interest. He decided that the encryption made it more than an inventory of Benny's collection of porno films; he kept the journal and walked upstairs.

He used the kitchen phone to place an anonymous call to 9-1-1, reported a possible burglary, gave them the address, and hung up. He felt a tinge of guilt about taking the ledger—after all, he was removing potential evidence from a murder scene—however, he didn't feel bad enough to turn it over to the cops, at least not until he had some time with it.

Traynor walked out of the house, closing the slider behind him. He took the latex gloves off and stuffed them in his pocket; he would dispose of them later. Benny's nearest neighbor was a quarter of a mile in either direction, and he was confident nobody had seen him. He got into his car and was almost a mile down the road before he saw the first police car race by with its lights flashing. He watched it grow smaller in his rearview mirror and wondered how much time he would have before state police homicide detectives shut his investigation down.

14

As Traynor drove toward Salem, he thought about the past twenty-four hours. Instead of a day, it seemed as if a week had passed since he stood beside John's body. He doubted that either Ryan or John had ever been important enough to be on anyone's hit list. John would push drugs, boost cars, and was not above a little breaking and entering, but in Traynor's experience, his younger brother had been less than brave. Traynor never knew him to carry a gun after his armed robbery bust as a teen, and always figured he would detour miles to avoid violence. However, it appeared that this time he had gotten into something big enough to get him killed.

Another thing bothering him was the sophistication of this; he had a hard time believing either John or Ryan had the smarts to rip off the Escobar brothers . . . not to mention a job as violent as the one described by both Bob and Max. Nothing in John's history had heretofore indicated he was capable of such viciousness.

Traynor paused. Then again, greed was a powerful motivator, and anyone could be capable of becoming ferocious if the reward was lucrative enough. He could not shake the feeling that he was missing something though. What he lacked was some little thing that would link John and his killers. He decided that another talk with his sister-in-law—make that *sisters*-in-law—was in order. Now that they had had a day to adjust to the shock of becoming widows, they may have remembered something.

———————

When Jill did not answer his buzz, Traynor pressed several call buttons before someone opened the door allowing him into Jill's building. He scaled the stairs, knocked on her door, and got no answer. He heard a chain rattle, turned, and saw a tiny old woman peering out of the apartment across the hall. "She ain't home."

Traynor said, "I'm her brother-in-law."

"I know who you are. I seen you around here enough. She left a couple hours ago. She was dressed for work."

He couldn't believe it. Why was Jillian at work? Was she so out of touch with reality that she didn't understand the danger of the situation? He dashed down the stairs, burst through the door, and ran into the parking lot. He entered his car, started the motor, and burned rubber as he sped away.

As he drove to the restaurant where his sister-in-law worked, his initial anger at her lack of common sense cooled, replaced by questions. To the best of his knowledge, John had excluded Jillian from his professional life; her seeming ignorance about the danger in which John may have put her and her daughters was proof of that. If he had done something big enough to get him killed, it might also have been enough to place Jill and her girls in jeopardy.

Once inside the restaurant, Traynor asked the host to seat him at one of Jillian's tables. He was reading the menu when she came to take his order. Seeing it was him, she slid into the booth. "Eddie, what happened? You look like a ton of cement dropped on you."

"I feel like it too. A couple of John's former business associates thought I might know about some money. Jillian, you're not going to like what I have to say . . . as a matter of fact, it'll probably scare you."

Her eyes were intense and bored into his. Anyone who did not know her would have assumed there was nothing wrong. He, however, knew her well and saw the hurt and anger she tried so hard to suppress.

He kept his voice low; there was no need to broadcast their private business. "John either owed a bundle to some very bad people, or he stole a lot of money from them . . . possibly both. These people are ruthless, Jill, and they'll do anything to get what they want." He bent forward to emphasize the point. "They might come after you and the girls. Which brings to mind the obvious question, where are the girls?"

"The girls are in school." As soon as she spoke, the color drained out of her face.

"If someone is tracing John's activities, checking out his places and friends, they'll know about you and the girls. Whatever it was that John was involved in, Benny Ryan must have been in on it with him, or at least knew enough for someone to go after him."

"You're speaking about Benny in past tense, as if he isn't around anymore,"

"He isn't."

"Oh, my God, Eddie, what happened?"

"I'm not sure, when I got to his place I scared off some guy in a four-by-four. I found Ryan in his bedroom . . . dead. It looked to me as if he was murdered."

Her face turned ashen. "What can happen next? I never liked Benny. I always thought he was such a bad influence on John, but even he didn't deserve to be murdered. Ed, what in hell was John into?"

"Jill, you got to help me out here. If you know of anyone John was seeing or even places he may have said he was going, I need to know." As he spoke, he realized that Jillian had not a single clue about how violent and dangerous some of the people John had been dealing with were.

"I have no idea what he has been up to lately. I told you, Ed, we haven't exactly been close this past year. He just came and went as he pleased, barely saying anything to me. Hell, the last few months, he rarely came home."

He reached across the table and took her hand in his. "You should keep the girls close for a few days, until I get to the bottom of this."

Jill stared at him for a few seconds, then shrugged her shoulders, and said, "I'll send the girls to my mother's house, in Florida."

Florida was not what he had in mind. He wanted to keep the kids local, where he knew people who could keep an eye on them. "Jill, these guys can pay enough to find out anything they want. They most likely know where you live, and there's a good chance they know your mother's address as well. The Escobars' operation is international, big enough for them to hunt for you anywhere in the world. We need to find a place around here, so I can protect you, a place unknown to any of John's former business associates."

"So, you think it was these Escobars who murdered him?"

"I don't know that for a fact. One thing is certain, if what I'm hearing is true—they had more motive than anyone else. It seems someone ripped them off for a lot of cash, and they believe that John was a part of it, if not behind it."

Her face flushed with anger, and she struggled to keep her voice low. "He never gave me any money. If he ripped off a bunch of hoods, I never saw one damned penny of it. Now you tell me that these people may be coming after me and my girls. . . ."

"All right, all right, all I can do is to try my best to keep them off you, but you have to help. After work, I want you to call Susan. I'll have her find you a safe house for a while, until I can get to the bottom of this." He gave her what he hoped was his best *everything is under control* look and put his hand over hers. He squeezed lightly, hoping to reassure her everything was going to be all right. "Okay?"

She stared at his hand, and he realized she was trying not to cry. She spoke so softly he was barely able to hear, "Okay."

"Can you get off work for a few days?"

"Do I have any choice?"

"Not really, but I promise you that I'm going to clean this mess up quick. Anybody who wants to hurt you or the girls is going to have to come through me. I swear." He hoped that he looked as reassuring as he hoped his words sounded.

She squeezed his hand. "Eddie, I don't know how the girls and I could have done it without you."

"Don't sell yourself short, Jill. You've always been the one that held things together for your kids. You'll get past this too. Hell, you've spent most of your adult life dealing with John and his pipe dreams."

"Yeah," she replied, "John was a dreamer all right, except his dreams always seem to become my nightmares." She sighed then asked, "Eddie, do you ever feel as if you've spent your life cleaning up after John?"

Honestly, he could not say that. If he had, they might have avoided all this. *Maybe*, he thought, *I should have been my brother's keeper—back when it could have made a difference.*

Traynor drove from Jill's apartment to Max and Charley's auto body shop. He walked inside and saw Charley at his desk staring at his computer screen. Charley noticed him from the corner of his eye and said, "What's up?"

Traynor took the journal from his pocket. "I need you to look at something." He placed the book on the desk.

Charley picked it up and leafed through the pages. "Looks like a journal of some sort."

"I only gave it a quick look, just enough to see it's in some type of code."

Charley opened the journal and looked inside the front cover. He said, "Except for this."

"Except for what?"

Charley handed the journal to Traynor. "Look inside the front cover."

He opened the journal and began to read. On the first page, there was a single name, written in pencil and not in code. The name, Robby

McPherson, was familiar to him. Ed knew him from his days patrolling the highways around Laconia. He was another small-timer who wanted to join the big time and always drove four-by-four Chevy trucks. He did a lot of off-road stuff. Traynor recalled that any time he had seen McPherson his vehicle was mud-coated—just like the truck that sped away from Ryan's house. He wondered if McPherson had moved up from petty larceny, minor drug dealing, and car boosting to murder. Traynor decided to drive to Laconia the next morning.

Charley must have seen the lights come on in his head. "You find something?"

"Yeah, I think maybe I did." It looked as if McPherson knew Ryan, and if he did, then odds were he knew John. Was there a connection between the two deaths? The only way he was going to find answers to these questions was to go to the Lakes Region. Before he took a trip to the Laconia area, he needed to poke a stick in a few holes and see what type of varmint scurried out into the light.

15

Traynor returned to The Sexy Fox, where another twenty bucks got Alana to tell him that Consuela had the day off and her address. By the time he parked in front of the run-down triple-decker in Lawrence, Massachusetts, the rain had increased, the semi-frozen drops sounding like rocks hitting his car. Waiting for the downpour to ease, he idled away the time watching bits of garbage float down the street into a sewer drain. After ten minutes, the deluge abated and he entered the triple-decker.

Night comes early in New England in November, and it was twilight at 3:30 p.m. When he walked into the tenement, the hall was unlit and dark. The slumlords who own buildings such as this one were slow at best to fix minor issues. In fact, their renters are lucky if structural problems get fixed, and they know that it is futile to complain about minor repairs such as burned-out lights. This place was no exception. Looking at the dump, Traynor found the mystery of Consuela even more intriguing. With her looks and moves, he was sure that she had to make enough to afford something better than this dump. As he climbed the stairs, Traynor wondered what percentage of her earnings went to support relatives in Puerto Rico . . . or to support John. It would have been just like him to let a woman carry him until he made his big score or opened that store about which he always fantasized.

Consuela's apartment was at the rear of the top floor. He knocked on the door and got no answer. He waited a few seconds, in case someone was inside quietly waiting for him to leave. Hoping to fool them, he walked away and then crept back and stood outside the door, listening for any sign of occupancy. He stood there for five minutes and heard nothing. Once he was certain no one was inside, Traynor returned to the car to wait.

He wanted to minimize the chance of a neighborhood watch person, if such a thing existed in Lawrence, seeing him loitering in front of the building. To avoid any confrontation, he moved his car down the street and parked on the opposite side. He parked about four car-lengths from the apartment house and turned off the Taurus's motor so exhaust spiraling into the cold air would not give away his presence. He slid down in the seat trying to be less visible and tried to relax—he could be waiting for a while.

The car's interior temperature quickly dropped and, in no time, his side began throbbing with dull pulsing pain. Throughout the day, he had popped aspirin every couple of hours—although it did not ease his discomfort much—and he washed down a couple more with a swallow of water from a bottle he had bought earlier.

By five o'clock, it was completely dark and the rain tapered off, turning into a fine mist. Traynor decided to give it up as a lost afternoon. As he reached for the key, a car turned the corner, and he froze in place watching it come toward him. It drifted up the street and stopped in front of Consuela's building, parking in the very spot he had vacated earlier. A man jumped out and opened the passenger door for a woman, who dashed across the sidewalk toward the building. Even with the magazine she used as a makeshift umbrella hiding her face, Consuela was easy to recognize. Her escort slammed the car door and ran after her. They hurried up the steps, stopping under the overhang that sheltered the porch from the rain. He opened the door, a gentleman in an era when many men do not bother. She stepped around him and disappeared into the triple-decker. Her escort paused before entering, looking up and down the street as if he were expecting someone.

When he turned and faced toward his direction, Traynor tensed and studied him with renewed interest; something about him looked familiar. The man took a pack of cigarettes from his pocket and put one in his mouth. When he struck the lighter, Traynor got a good look at him. A scar ran across the right side of his face. Suddenly, Traynor was glad he had waited. He looked at his face in the rearview mirror and saw a smile of satisfaction reflected back.

He gave them enough time to settle in and get comfortable and then walked to the building. Now that night had settled over the area, the passageways were as dark as an abandoned coal mine. He climbed the creaking stairs, staying to the side closest to the wall where the boards were most sturdy. He wanted his approach to be as silent as possible. He stopped outside the door and listened for a few seconds. Inside the apartment, he heard muffled voices speaking in Spanish. He drew his pistol, knocked on the door, and stepped back.

Consuela opened the door as far as the safety chain would allow and peered through the narrow opening. Her face registered surprise when she saw Traynor. She tried to shut the door, but Traynor braced his back against the far wall, ignored the pain in his side, and kicked. His foot hit just below the doorknob, ripping the security chain out of its mooring. The door banged hard against the wall then rebounded toward Traynor. He shouldered it aside and rushed through. The door slammed open with such force it pushed into Consuela and knocked her deeper into the apartment. She backpedaled, arms cartwheeling as she tried to maintain her balance. Traynor bulled his way in, pushing her out of the way. She stumbled over a hassock and fell on her rump. She sat on the floor with her skirt hiked up, exposing her shapely thighs.

Traynor's pistol was in his hand and poised for action. Scarface stood in the middle of the room. If a newspaper had published a picture of the look on his face, it would have had the caption, "WTF." Scarface paused for a brief second, and then reached his right hand inside his black leather jacket. Before he could pull hardware, Traynor slammed him in the mouth with the side of his nine-millimeter. Scarface's hand changed course, going from his coat to his face. He clasped it tightly against his split lips. It was a poor substitute for a bandage, and blood poured through his fingers, dripping onto his shirt. His eyes narrowed with pain and hate. He spit a wad of bloody sputum and a couple of teeth at Traynor, who twisted his torso, avoiding most of the mess. However, Consuela wasn't as lucky. The gory sputum splattered across her blouse. Once again, Scarface reached for the inside of his coat. Traynor pushed the business end of the pistol against his forehead. In a soft voice, he said, "Careful, you wouldn't want to do something stupid, like pull a gun on me—that could be a life-altering decision."

Scarface slowly dropped his hand and tried to lessen the nine-millimeter barrel's pressure against his forehead by arching backward. Traynor pulled the pistol away from his forehead and in a single motion, smacked him with it again, this time across the bridge of his nose. Scarface fell back onto the room's largest piece of furniture, a worn couch, his nose bent to one side, broken. Blood and mucous poured from it and mixed with sputum from his mouth, ruining his fancy tailored shirt. Large drops fell and spotted the couch's white fabric.

Traynor reached under Scarface's coat, took his handgun, and inspected it. It was a shiny silver thirty-eight revolver. Even though someone had ground off the serial number, it was too expensive a piece to be a midnight special, and was the wrong caliber to be the gun used to kill John. He put it in his coat pocket. "Scarface, you make one move, and I'll shoot you."

He turned his attention to Consuela. She sat on the floor, glaring at him while wiping at the blood on her blouse. Her effort was futile; rather than clean the stain, all she accomplished was to smear it deeper into the fabric.

"Consuela," Traynor said, motioning to her with the pistol, "get over here."

She looked like an angry but wary cat as she got up, straightened her skirt, walked to the sofa, and flopped down beside Scarface. She turned his face so she could look at him and inspected the damage. "Are you okay, Humberto?" she asked.

Now Traynor had Scarface's name. "Does Humberto have a last name?" he asked.

When she stared at him, hatred twisted her beautiful face into something ugly. Traynor could feel the heat generated by her wrath. He was not getting off to a good start with his newest sister-in-law. Not that it mattered all that much because he did not give a damn whether she liked him or not.

He kicked Humberto in the kneecap. "What's the rest of your name? *¿Cómo te llamas, Humberto?*"

Humberto glared and tried to look macho for Consuela. Traynor had no patience for his bullshit and hit him again. This time he took careful aim, making sure the bloody pistol hit the already damaged nose. Humberto's head jerked sideways; more blood flew across the room, leaving a trail of droplets on the hardwood floor. Consuela stopped rubbing at the smear across her breasts and cried, "Stop hitting him!"

"Before I whack him again, you might ask him why he and his buddy, the prick with the white hair and fancy cowboy boots, worked me over last night. On the other hand, maybe you already know the answer."

She looked at Traynor, obviously confused, and then turned and said, "Humberto, what did you and Theo do?"

Traynor could not suppress a nasty grin. Now he had Whitey's name too—Theo. It would only be a matter of time before he would even the score with him too.

Humberto ignored her and spit another gory wad at Traynor. It landed square in Traynor's chest and ruined a good shirt. By this time,

Ed had had enough of Humberto's macho crap and, mustering all the force he could, drove his left fist into his ravaged nose. The punch took what little defiance the punk had left out of him. He slumped over, his head in Consuela's lap, wrecking her skirt.

Traynor pulled him upright and twisted his head to one side, admiring the nose job he had given him—it resembled a hot dog that had been steamed until it had split open. "Now," he said, "let's start over. Who the fuck are you, and what went down between you and my brother?"

Humberto said something inaudible. It is not easy to talk with busted teeth and a broken nose. He had his hands clamped over his damaged face, muffling his voice even more.

Traynor said to Consuela, "Go get a wet rag, cold water."

She turned toward the kitchen and he motioned with the pistol. "And don't come back with anything else in your hand—you know, like a knife or something I might mistake for a weapon. I would hate to have to use this; we are family after all."

He heard water running and surveyed the apartment. The furniture was old, but serviceable. A modern HDTV seemed out of place among the secondhand store furnishings. Keeping one eye on Humberto, he opened the door to the bedroom and gave it a cursory look. She had made the bed, and the room was so small it was safe to assume that no one was in there. There was no way to check out the closet without taking his eyes off Humberto, so he took it on faith that it too was unoccupied.

After a few seconds, Consuela appeared holding a wet washcloth. She walked to the couch and bent over, gingerly placing the homemade compress over Humberto's nose and mouth. Traynor relished the sound of him whimpering like a little boy in pain and assumed a position where he could watch both of them closely. It would not have surprised him if she had hidden a weapon somewhere where he could get it.

He turned his attention to Consuela. "What's his full name?"

"It's Humberto Baerga. He's from my home village."

"Really?" This whole caper was starting to look like one big family affair. Traynor turned to him. "What did John do to you, Humberto?"

He pointed a finger at Consuela. "Let him answer, his English was real good last night."

Humberto gingerly took the wet rag from his ruined face. His voice sounded as if he had a bad head cold when he spoke. "John been doing some business with us." He pronounced business *bid-nezz*.

"And who was this *bid-nezz* with?" Traynor mocked him.

"Some guys."

"Humberto, I don't care if you're a friend of the family or not—if you don't start talking to me, I'm going to smack your goddamned nose again. What guys?"

"I don't know, goddamnit! I never seen them before . . . John, he done all the talkin'. I knew that they was connected, though."

"Connected? Like to the Colombian mob?"

Humberto nodded, and his eyes grew large and the skin on his forehead arched, giving his fear away.

Traynor asked, "Did you help John rip off Carlo and Eduardo Escobar?"

He was reluctant to talk and Traynor cocked his arm, once again poised to slap him in the face.

"Don't hit me no more, damn it! Yeah, we ripped Escobar off. John got to them before us and decided that he'd clean up."

"Suppose you tell me what went down?" Traynor was getting tired of having to pull everything out of him. If Consuela had not been there, he would have shoved something long and pointy up his snout.

"I don't know . . . me an' Theo wasn't with him. All I can tell you is that he ripped off the Escobars. Then he cheated Theo and me out of our share."

"Where were you two while John was taking down the Escobars' people?"

"We was late getting there. By the time we did we found the bank with both people in it dead. John and the money was gone."

He glared at Traynor, but his anger was not enough to cover up the fear that was evident there. "We need that money to get away. If Carlo finds out about us, we're dead men."

"How much did he get?"

"I don't know. We never seen it, but I been told it was a lot . . . in the millions."

It was not the first time that amount had come up, and Traynor was impressed. John obviously had more balls than he had given him credit for having. However, three mil is a lot of cash; no wonder Carlo was surprised to learn that John had died. "Specifics, Humberto, I want to know what went down." He raised the nine-millimeter, poised to smack him in the nose again.

"Okay, okay. Shit, man, don't hit me no more. I'll tell you."

Traynor looked at Consuela. "Maybe you ought to get us something to drink."

"All I got is water and some beer."

"Beer's fine. Now, Humberto, let's get down to the important stuff. When did you guys take down the Escobar brothers and what was John's role in this operation?"

"The plan was for me and Theo to wait by the interstate. John was to follow the bank, and he was supposed to call us before stopping it. I already tol' you that I don't know what went down exactly, but John did the hit and kilt the Escobars' people. We ain't seen John or the money since. We looked for him every fuckin' place we knew. Then we hear that he shows up dead and you start nosing around. We thought you knew something, so we decided to see if you was in on it with John."

"Who were the guys in the car?"

"Felipè Munōz and Josè Renaldo, they worked for the Escobars. They'd been picking up cash between Lawrence and Portland. They hadn't made a pickup for a couple weeks, and there was a lot of money coming out of the clubs."

"So John thought he was smart enough to make off with Carlo and Eduardo's profits?"

"No. Even John wasn't that crazy, or so we thought. The plan never was to keep it. We was going to return the loot, collecting a big reward. John was going to contact Carlo and tell him that we found the car with his people dead and took the cash so the fucking cops wouldn't get it. At least that's what he told me and Theo."

"Only he got popped first," Traynor finished for him. He recalled the airline ticket in John's personal effects. There was no way in hell John was after any reward. Traynor was convinced his brother had ripped off everyone and that it had probably been his intention from the outset.

"Yeah, he got popped first."

"Who developed this plan? It seems quite elaborate. You had to have an information source to know the timing of the bank's run. If I think you're holding anything back, I'm going to rap you on the nose again. Do you understand? *¿Entendido?*"

"Like I already tol' you, John met these motherfuckers at the club where Consuela works. The guys was drunk and flashing fat rolls of cash around. Hell, they was stuffing twenties up the girls' asses. Spent money like there was no end to it. One of them told John he worked for the Escobars and they were making a big money run."

Something sounded screwy to Traynor. "Do you think I'm stupid? No one who works for the Escobars would talk business to a stranger."

"The dude was fucked up, drunk on his ass. I think he was trying to make an impression on the women. Whether you believe me or not, man, that's what fucking happened."

"Okay, so this guy was spouting off about a big money pickup. I'll give you the benefit of the doubt on that, go on."

"John, he got real interested in the conversation, and he talked the guy into going outside to smoke some *mafú*—"

"What's *mafú*?" Traynor asked.

"It's what we call marijuana at home," Consuela answered.

"Okay, go on." Traynor turned his attention back to Humberto.

"Once we got him outside, we beat the shit out of him until he told us about the Escobars making a big cash run. The guy wasn't sure exactly when the pickup would take place but he was able to give John three dates. The run was on the second day."

"Where is this guy now?"

"In the woods behind The Fox . . . he got himself dead." Humberto grimaced, and Traynor heard bubbles popping in his nose as he paused for a breath. It was not easy for him to talk with blood and snot pouring down his face.

Ed motioned for Consuela to rinse the towel and freshen it a bit. She returned and sat beside Humberto on the couch and applied the fresh compress to his face. As she ministered to him, Traynor watched Humberto, looking for any sign that he was lying. For most of his life, he had dealt with liars and prided himself on being able to detect a lie the instant he heard it. There was none of the telltale signs of prefabrication, such as shifting eyes, in his face. Humberto was telling him the truth, at least the truth as he saw it. Traynor believed he finally had a motive for John's death.

Still, something did not add up. John had been taken out too quickly, one little slug to the temple. *If someone had three million dollars of mine, I would really work him over trying to find out where it was.* If the Escobar brothers, or Humberto for that matter, had killed him, he should have looked like a couple hundred pounds of extra-lean ground chuck. His execution had been too quick and clean. The Colombians would have had a party with him even if they had gotten their money back. Then there was the murder scene—Traynor doubted they would leave John in a patch of woods. They would want to get as much publicity as possible, to send a message to anyone else who might think they were easy pickings.

The adrenaline generated during his attack dissipated, and Traynor's ribs began to pulse with pain. He reached into his pocket and got out the bottle of aspirin. He shook three into his hand and offered the bottle to Humberto. "Aspirin?"

Humberto turned Traynor down with a malevolent glare. *So much for being Mr. Nice-Guy.*

Something clicked in his brain. He remembered the picture they had left in his pocket. Traynor stood up and said, "I got the picture you left. You better pray nothing happens to those kids. If a car, or anything, should accidentally hit them, I'm coming after you. *¿Entendido?*"

"What kids?" Consuela asked.

"John's daughters."

The shocked look Consuela gave him told Traynor that she had not known about John's other family, let alone the implied threat to hurt Jillian's girls. He wondered if maybe she was not as involved in this as he had first thought.

He saw a confused look on Consuela's face and said, "John used you like he did everyone, Consuela. He didn't divorce his wife; your marriage to him was illegal."

Her eyes widened in shock.

Traynor turned away from her and looked at Humberto. "Am I clear on that?"

Humberto nodded. In spite of the surly look, Traynor knew he got the message.

"Tell your buddy Theo to watch his back, because I'm coming for him too."

He stopped before leaving the apartment. "Did you frigging idiots really think the Escobars would buy your bullshit story? Why would anyone go through all the trouble of killing two of the Escobars' people and then take off leaving the money behind?"

Humberto's complexion paled. "You sayin' John planned to rip us off all along?"

"Kind of looks that way, doesn't it? You two lovebirds have a nice evening." Traynor left the apartment.

Back in the car, Traynor dropped his guard and gave into the pain, which felt worse than before. Adrenaline must have numbed the pain while he was in the apartment; now it came roaring back. He bent over, touching his head to the steering wheel while he waited it out.

Once the pain subsided to a bearable level, he straightened up, took Humberto's revolver from his pocket and put it in the glove box. *You never know when an extra gun may come in handy.* But then again, who knew how many crimes had been committed with it. He decided to dump it into the first river he crossed.

After talking to Humberto, Traynor debated whether he should visit Carlo again. He didn't think it would serve any purpose, except to maybe get him killed, so he got on I-495 north and drove to I-95 and back to Portsmouth. The more he thought about the case, the more it confused him. He had worked many homicides and in virtually every one, he could find a logical reason for the events that took place. However, John's killing was unusual. Just about everyone involved with him had good reason to shoot him in the head: the Escobar brothers were out a lot of money; Humberto and his partner Theo were out their share of the loot; and Consuela was out her share of the money from either John or Humberto—maybe he'd been too hasty in considering her as not being in on the plan. There was one question eating at him more than all the others, though. Was there anyone, other than him, who did not have a reason to kill John?

16

Susan McIsaac invited Traynor to dinner, nothing fancy, just pizza and beer. He got to their house a few minutes after eight. The moment he stepped through their door, the pressure and fatigue of the day seemed to fall from him. Susan hugged him and quickly stepped back when he inhaled sharply as she encircled his battered ribs.

"I'm sorry, Ed, I forgot." She looked concerned, motherly.

"No problem."

"Are you in much pain? Did you go to a doctor, like I told you?"

"Naw, I'll be okay, I just need a couple of days for my ribs to heal."

He knew from her skeptical look that she did not entirely believe him. "How did it go today?"

He thought about his meeting with Consuela and Humberto and

grinned. "Great, just great, it couldn't have worked out better if I'd scripted it."

Dinner went well, and after eating, Susan disappeared into the bedroom and Bob switched on the TV, turning to a local cable news channel. He and Traynor did not say much, just listened to the anchor read the latest headlines. Keeping abreast of what was going on was something Bob took seriously. He did more than just watch the news—he studied it and did not take kindly to idle chatter while doing so; therefore when he watched it, he watched it. When the anchor started recapping the day's stories, Bob aimed the remote at the TV and shut it off.

Susan came out of the bedroom and walked into the kitchen. Traynor heard the refrigerator door open and then close. Susan reappeared and handed him a beer. She placed one on the coffee table in front of Bob and dropped down beside him on the couch. She snuggled close to him. Subconsciously, Bob's hand found hers; no doubt, a habit developed over many years of togetherness.

Traynor watched from his seat across from them. He watched their affectionate touches and became aware of the fact that he had never seen anything like that between his parents. Seeing the McIsaacs' love for each other made him think about Jillian. He had loved her since he first laid eyes on her, but at the time she only saw John. As the years passed, nothing happened to dampen his feelings, which was why he had been unsuccessful in all his relationships.

Susan smiled at him and then gave Traynor a look he knew all too well. She knew something was up with him. Traynor sat back in his chair and sighed.

"Have you learned anything new?" Susan asked.

"I'm not sure. I went to Benny Ryan's place and found what looks like a journal."

"Do you think it might be important?"

"I don't know. I dropped it off with Charley. I think it's in code and there is some sort of map, but until I know what's in it, I won't know if it's important or not."

"So you did look at it."

"Yes, but not in detail. Charley did point out one thing that was not in code—a name that I'm familiar with. I'm going to check it out tomorrow."

They idled the evening away until ten-thirty when Susan announced she had had enough for one day and was going to bed. She gave each of them a peck on the cheek and left. Bob went to the refrigerator and when he came back into the room, he carried two fresh beers. He popped the tops and handed one to Traynor. He dropped into his favorite chair, sipped his beer, and then turned to face the younger man. "How are you doing?"

"I'll be okay. They didn't break anything."

"Cut the crap, Ed. You know what I'm talking about."

Traynor knew very well. "I'm coping."

"You know, he never was your responsibility."

"Not legally, but I've always thought I could've done more. Maybe been there for him more than I was."

Bob swallowed another mouthful of beer and snorted. "Come on, Ed. I know John was your brother but," he glanced over his shoulder to ensure Susan was not within hearing, "he was rotten, never any fucking good."

Traynor did not understand why, but he felt as if he had to defend John. "He never had a chance, Bob."

"Oh?" He seemed skeptical and it showed on his face. "Then why didn't you and Maureen turn out like him? You came from the same gene pool, didn't you? I don't recall you ripping off people, selling drugs, and holding up convenience stores."

"No, but—"

"Stop it, Ed! Goddamn it, stop making excuses for him. You've been carrying his guilt ever since he was sixteen and went to juvie. You are *not* the reason John was the way he was."

Traynor drank his beer. He did not care how rotten John was nor did he give a damn about whether his brother deserved what he got; he was still his brother. He was still the four-year-old kid who wanted to tag along after him. Traynor suffered an attack of angst. Maybe the root of John's problems started back then. Maybe if he had paid some attention to him instead of leaving him behind, he might have turned out different.

"But that's a side issue to what's really on your mind, isn't it?"

Traynor stood up and began pacing around the room. "Yeah, I guess you're right. What's really bothering me is—"

"Jillian," Susan said, completing the sentence.

Traynor had not seen her come back into the room and her voice startled him. She walked over, took his arm, and guided him back to his chair, and then she sat on the arm of Bob's chair. "So," she said, "get it out. Let's hear it."

"It started almost five years ago, when Jillian was pregnant with Julia—at Christmas, to be exact."

Susan said, "Tell me the rest."

"What rest?"

"You know, the part that really scares you. The part where you tell us how you feel. Don't think you'll shock us, not me anyway. I've known you for almost half your life. Do you think I haven't noticed how you act around Jill and her girls? You think you're hard to figure out, but you're not. I can take one look at you and tell how you feel. You've loved her for as long as I can remember."

"Yeah, and now that the road is clear, I can't do anything about it."

"Why can't you?" Bob asked.

"Hell, John isn't even in the ground yet and I'm thinking about marrying his wife! That's goddamned sick!"

"Not as sick as you may think," Susan said. "In some cultures, it happens automatically; it's a custom. When a man dies his brother will take the wife in, even marry her. Besides, who gives a damn what anyone else thinks?"

Bob drained his beer and picked up Ed's can. He shook it and seemed satisfied that it was empty. He went to get each of them a refill, and while he was out Susan tried to reason with Traynor.

"Ed, you're as close to us as if you were our son. Frankly, I've never seen anyone else whip themselves like you whip yourself—especially when John is involved. You set goals for yourself that God couldn't meet, and I think it's depressing you more than you believe."

Bob returned, opened the beers, and slapped a frosty can down on the table beside Traynor. He ignored the spill as the beer foamed out of the can and said, "Ed, you have as much right to happiness as anyone, but as long as you keep carrying John around on your back, you'll never have it. So, my recommendation to you is that you go find his killer and then get on with your life."

Bob picked up his beer and chugged it down. Ed had never seen him drink anything that fast. He crushed the empty can in his hand, walked into the kitchen, threw it into the trash, and belched.

Bob looked at his wife, who was cleaning up the beer he'd spilled and said, "I'm going to bed." He turned to Traynor and asked, "Are you staying here or going home?"

Traynor went home.

17

Gisela Martin entered The Top of The Hub restaurant in Boston's Prudential Tower. When the maître d' approached she said, "I'm to meet Mr. Federico Treviño."

The server led her through the dining room with its breathtaking views of Boston from the fifty-second floor. The sun had set, and the lights of the city reached toward the horizon. They turned to the north, and a panoramic view of the harbor with Logan Airport opened up before her. Two nattily dressed Hispanic men stood as she approached their table.

"Señor Treviño?" she asked.

The taller of the two replied, "Señorita Martin?"

She gave the two men her most alluring smile and sat in the chair that the maître d' slid out for her. She faced the expansive window and saw an airliner depart the runway and turn over the black expanse that she knew to be the Atlantic Ocean, climbing as it went. The host placed a menu in front of her and stepped aside as the wine steward took his place. She smiled at him and said, "I will have whatever the gentleman is having."

Treviño turned to the waiter and said, "*Albariño, Martín Códax, Rías Baixas*, please."

Treviño introduced the second man as Reyes Aguayo, a business associate. He nodded to Gisela and undressed her with his eyes. She immediately dismissed him as being another machismo Hispanic ass. She decided to ignore him and focus her attention on Treviño, who was the true *jefe*. They made small talk until the server brought the wine and dinner orders were placed. Treviño turned the conversation to business with a cursory check to ensure that they could not be overheard and to determine whether any of the other diners appeared to be eavesdropping. "I understand that you have something that we might have a use for, Señorita . . ."

"Please, Gisela."

"Then you must address me as Federico."

She nodded, making a point to ignore the third member of the party. "I have been in the employ of, shall we say, one of your customers? This customer—two brothers, I believe you know of whom I speak—are due to make a substantial payment to you."

Treviño said nothing. His eyes seemed to cut through to her heart, and Gisela knew that she was on dangerous ground and had to be careful. Colombian men were known for taking any slight seriously, especially from a woman. "For several years now, these brothers have been slowly losing control of their business. It is a known fact that it is on very shaky financial ground."

She sensed an increased interest in what she was saying and noted that the men had unconsciously inclined their torsos toward her. She knew she had them when she said, "Recently, there has been an event that will make it very, very improbable that the brothers will be able to meet their obligation to you."

Treviño must have realized that his body language was giving away his interest in what she was saying and he sat back. "Maybe you can be more specific?"

"Last week, the brothers lost a great deal of money." She glanced around and then bent forward. "More than three million dollars. They cannot pay what they owe."

Treviño looked at Aguayo. "Do you know anything of this?"

"I have heard a rumor, but we have not been able to verify it."

"Well," Treviño ordered, "verify it." He turned back to her. "Now, Gisela, tell me what can you do for me, and why we should not deal with you as we will with your employer?"

"I have kept records on every aspect of Carlo's business."

"What can you tell me that Carlo can't?"

"I know who took Carlo's money and how to get it back . . ."

Treviño sat back, and Gisela knew he was undressing her with his eyes. She smiled at him in a manner that she hoped would let him know that she was available for the asking.

They spent the remainder of the dinner discussing their youth and growing up in some of the poorest sections of their home country. After they had coffee, Aguayo excused himself using jet lag as an excuse. When he was gone, Treviño said, "I hope that you don't have plans for the evening . . ."

She smiled at him and asked, "I don't have any plans, perhaps you may?"

He stood, circled the table, and pulled her chair out. "I am certain we can find something to do."

18

Traynor was on the road by seven in the morning. A freezing drizzle fell as he drove along Route 4. In Concord, he picked up I-93 and headed north. By the time he reached the Tilton exit, the precipitation had changed to a heavy rain that slammed against the car so hard that it sounded like he was sitting inside a kettledrum during a percussion instrument concert. Traynor didn't know where Robby lived, but during his tenure as a state police officer, he had met Mildred McPherson several times, usually whenever her wayward boy was up to his ass in trouble. She was a good, hardworking woman; nevertheless, her only son was a loser. Eight-thirty found Traynor sitting in front of Mrs. McPherson's house drinking the last of his coffee. He got out of the Taurus, reached inside, and grabbed his raincoat, which he'd draped over the passenger seat. He put the overcoat on while examining the McPherson residence.

The house was an old cape, built with a steeply sloped roof. It appeared to be structurally sound but in need of some minor repair—one of the shutters hung from a single nail and it was a couple of years past due for a coat of paint. It occurred to Traynor that if Robby came around the place, he was not dirtying his hands with anything as mundane as manual labor.

He bypassed the front door and walked to the side of the house, where he saw a small porch. He had always been of the mind-set that all cape-style houses were designed using the same cookie cutter. He knew which door led to the kitchen and that in New England everyone came and went through the kitchen. He knocked on the door. A woman, whom he estimated to be in her mid-to-late thirties, opened it. He would not describe her as pretty, but she was attractive in the way of a woman who does her best to take care of herself. She looked, for want of a better word, wholesome. Her brown hair was pinned back into a ponytail and she wore a denim skirt and a pullover. "Pardon me," he said, "I'm looking for Mildred McPherson. She used to live here."

"This is her house, but she's not home. She's in the hospital, has been for a few weeks. I'm her daughter, Amanda. Can I help you?"

"My name is Ed Traynor." He handed her one of his cards. "I'm a private investigator from Portsmouth."

Without taking her eyes from the card she said, "What do you want my mother for?"

"Actually, I'm looking for your brother, Robby."

Her face flushed. "What's he done now?"

"I just need to ask him some questions." He decided to stretch the truth a bit. "It's an insurance thing. I've been hired by New England Mutual Life to check into a claim he placed about an accident."

Some of the anger dissipated from her face and she looked skeptical. Still she stepped aside and beckoned him to enter. "Please, come in."

Traynor stepped out of the chilly rain and into the overly warm kitchen. The mixture of cigarette smoke and the aromas of baking bread and fresh coffee brought back memories of his grandmother. She made her own bread right up until she died, and he could not recall a time when there was not a pot of coffee warming on her old stove—she, too, was a smoker. This kitchen, like his grandmother's, was a room in which he would be comfortable spending hours sitting, drinking coffee, and discussing local and national issues.

"Let me take your coat," Amanda offered.

His ribs, though still far from healed, were feeling better than they had the previous day; still he carefully shrugged his shoulders out of the raincoat, trying to remove it without wincing in pain. It was not easy. He saw her stare at the nine-millimeter that rested in its holster just under his left arm.

"Do you always wear a gun when checking an accident claim?"

"Only on cold, rainy days," he tried to put her at ease with a smile. "Truthfully, it's an old habit . . ."

". . . and old habits die slowly," she finished the cliché.

She took his coat, hung it in a closet near the refrigerator, and motioned for him to sit at the kitchen table. She placed a mug on the table in front of him and, without asking, filled it with coffee, then sat across from him and lit a cigarette. "I know you." Smoke drifted from her mouth and nose as she spoke. "You used to be a cop around here."

He tried to recall if he had ever met her, but had no memory of such a meeting. He was glad he did not detect the malice he usually heard when meeting someone who said that they knew him when he was a cop.

"You gave me a ticket once, on Route 3."

Her comment made Traynor wonder if he had any hope of getting information, but he decided to try anyway. "Were you speeding?"

She smiled through the thin cloud of cigarette smoke. "Yeah, but it was what happened after you stopped me that made me mad."

He waited for her to explain.

She sipped from her mug. When she looked at him, her eyes had a mischievous sparkle. "I'd only had my license for a couple of months when you stopped me. When you were walking toward my car, I hiked my skirt up as far as I dared. I thought if I showed off my legs I'd get off with a warning."

He didn't recall that particular stop. However, during his time patrolling the roads, many young women tried to avoid a bad situation using the allusion of proffered sex. Many of them were most likely trying to use their bodies to get their way for the first time in their life. He knew some cops who gave into temptation; he never did. Possibly, because he was afraid of how high the cost would be if he were caught. Traynor had often wondered how one of those young girls would have reacted if he had paid attention to their implied promise and made a pass. He decided that before he left, he would have to ask her.

"You acted as if nothing had happened. You didn't even notice." The corners of her mouth turned down, but the smile in her eyes belied the exaggerated pout.

Traynor knew she was teasing and played along with her by lying. "Don't sell yourself short. I may not remember your face but I vividly recall those legs."

"I doubt that. But I appreciate the lie." She smiled impishly. "You were supposed to let me off with a warning . . ."

He continued to follow her lead and made the obvious assumption as to her age at the time. "Well, if I recall you couldn't have been more than sixteen, seventeen at the most."

She had a pretty smile. "Seventeen, it was the first time my mother had let me use the car at night."

He decided to keep playing the game. "I thought you needed something to make you exercise a bit more caution. If I'd let you off, you might have pulled that little trick with your skirt one time too many. Not everyone in a uniform is of my high moral fiber." He watched her and relaxed when she laughed. She had a nice one; it was natural, not phony like a lot he had heard.

"At the time, I was really pissed off at you. Because of that ticket, Mother yanked my driving privileges for three months. It really put a cramp in my social life."

She leaned back in her chair and rested one arm on the back; the movement emphasized her bust. Traynor realized that she must have been a beauty when she was in her teens.

"Do you have any idea," she said, "what a blow it was to my ego? I will say that even though I'm sure you're lying to make me feel good, it's nice of you to pretend that you did notice." She laughed again. "So, you still haven't answered my question. What's Robby done now?"

"Like I said, I need to find him—"

"About an accident." Her face altered, became serious, and her voice told him she wasn't buying that line.

"Actually, I wasn't entirely truthful about that." He felt as if they had established enough rapport for him to come clean. "I'm investigating a couple of deaths, and Robby may have some information about them."

"That sounds a lot more like my brother. Were these deaths accidental?"

He shook his head. "No, they were murders."

Her eyes widened. "Robby involved with accidental deaths, maybe—but, Robby involved with criminals and murderers. I can't believe that. I know he's not much good for anything and he's wild, but he's never been violent. When it comes right down to it, he's a coward."

"Does he stay here?"

"Off and on, but he never stays more than a day or two. He complains that I rag on him too much. I think it makes him feel guilty about never helping around here. My nagging doesn't do any good though; instead of doing what I need done, he takes off. He hasn't been around since the day before yesterday."

"What does he drive?"

"An old, beat-up Chevy four-by-four, a Silverado. He's probably staying out at the cabin."

"The cabin?"

"Yeah, he and some of the losers he hangs with have a cabin west of here. I believe it's in Andover. What are you driving?"

"A Taurus."

"You'll never get in there without a four-wheel drive and a hell of a lot more road clearance than you have."

"No other way in?"

"You could walk."

"How far a walk is it from where I'd have to leave the car?"

"A mile, mile and a half at most." She looked at his suit. "You aren't exactly dressed for walking in the woods on a cold, rainy day."

She got up and walked to the coffee pot, poured some into her mug, and asked, "Refill?"

"No, thank you."

She opened a drawer and got out a pad and pencil. "I'll write down the directions." She wrote for several seconds and then tore the page off the pad and handed it to him. When he reached across the table and took the paper, she held onto her end and said, "Keep your gun handy."

"I thought you said Robby wasn't violent?"

"He isn't, but if he and his cronies are up there, they're probably smoking whacky tobaccy and they may do something stupid. Hell, some of those guys will do something nuts even if they aren't high or stoned." She released the paper. "These two people who were murdered, who were they?"

"One was my brother, the other was his friend."

"Your brother? I'm sorry."

"Like Robby and his cronies, my brother did a lot of stupid stuff too."

"Do you think Robby did it?"

"My brother, I'm not sure, probably not. As for his friend, I think I saw Robby run out of the house."

She turned her coffee mug between her hands and did not look at him when she said, "Don't you think it's strange that I'm selling out my brother to you?"

"Not really, I know how trying relatives can be. They can push you to the point where you don't care anymore. Since I've been looking into my brother's death, I've had those same feelings."

"That's part of it. Truthfully, I think if Robby keeps on the way he is, he'll end up like your brother. The only way to keep him alive and get him to settle down may be for him to do some time in jail."

She ground her cigarette out in the ashtray, folded her arms across her chest, and leaned back, letting her head roll backward. She stayed that way for a few seconds, staring at the ceiling. Without trying, she impressed him. Amanda McPherson was strong. She had to be to deal with an invalid mother and a brother who spent his life racing down a dead-end street at a hundred miles an hour.

He finished his coffee and stood up. "Thanks for your help. I've met your mother several times over the years, so say hello to her for me."

She turned her head toward him, and he detected a deep sadness. "It wouldn't do any good."

"Oh?"

"Mother has advanced Alzheimer's. The doctors don't expect her to last the year. Next week they'll be moving her to a nursing home; she'll probably stay there the rest of her life—and never know it." She stared over his shoulder at the rain hammering on the window. "Probably have to sell this place to pay the bills . . ." She caught herself and broke the trance.

"I'm sorry." Traynor hoped it did not sound as condescending as it often does when someone does not know what else to say.

"In a way it's a blessing. She can't remember all the bad stuff in her life and, better yet, Robby can't break her heart anymore."

That hit home. Traynor remembered his mother fretting over John. She took all of the blame others poured on her for his failings, and many times even blamed herself, and to a lesser degree her eldest child for not getting the younger on the straight and narrow. Even back then, he knew John was on a collision course with a bad end. Whenever Traynor thought about getting married and having kids, he remembered the worry lines John and he put in their mother's face and the gray they put in her hair. It was enough to make him back off. He didn't have the guts to take on that responsibility.

Traynor read the directions on the paper, then looked at her and said, "That his phone number at the bottom?"

"Nope, mine. Give me a call sometime."

He put the paper into his pocket. "Well, I should be going."

She got his raincoat from the closet and handed it to him. She smiled and said, "Thanks."

He shrugged his shoulders, adjusted his coat, and paused, looking at her. "For what?"

"For you caring enough to lie to me about remembering a silly seventeen-year-old girl doing something stupid."

He nodded and turned to the door, stopping when she said, "You could stop by again if you want. I'm not seventeen anymore."

"I know." He gave her his best smile. If his heart had not belonged to another, he might have taken her up on it.

19

Stepping from the warm kitchen back into the cold rain gave Traynor a jolt. The storm had grown from a steady drizzle into something more akin to a nor'easter. A gale-force wind propelled the rain, which seemed to roll along the street in waves. Traynor turned up his collar and dashed to his car. As soon as he settled into his seat and started the motor, his cell phone rang, startling him. He snatched it off his belt. "This is Ed."

It was Buck and from the tone of his voice, he was not happy. "Eddie, what in hell you been up to?" Buck was a politician; he had to be to keep his job. It was unusual for him to be so blunt. He was the only person Traynor knew that could chew you out and then have you walk away telling everyone what a hell of a nice guy he was. Traynor knew he did not want to be the cause of whatever was eating at him.

"Whoa, Buck," he said. "What's going on?"

"Eldon Burns, up in Merrimack County, has been busting my ass all morning trying to find you. What do you know about Benny Ryan?"

"Not much, other than he was my brother's buddy."

"Besides him being your brother's buddy," he mocked.

Traynor immediately knew from the sarcastic tone that Buck knew he was being evasive, keeping something from him. "He's dead."

"No shit, he's dead. And you were seen driving away from the house."

Damn. He had thought he had gotten out of there unseen. "I didn't do it. He was dead when I got there. I may have spooked the killer."

"Why didn't you stay put?"

"I had other things to do."

"Well, you better call Burns because he's hotter than a half-fucked fox in a forest fire."

"If it helps, I got a good idea who it was that I saw fleeing the scene."

"Tell it to Eldon, it's his jurisdiction."

Buck was more than a little put out, and Traynor tried to appease him. "Hey, it's okay, man."

"You and I know that. However, I'm not so sure the rest of the world is in on the secret. Later."

Traynor referred to the list of frequently used phone numbers in his notebook, dialed the number of the Merrimack County Sheriff's Department, and asked for Burns. He was not looking forward to chatting with him. Burns's vocabulary tended to be words of a single syllable in length and most of them started with F and ended with K. He and Traynor had never swapped Christmas cards, and it was doubtful that they ever would.

"Sheriff Burns."

"Eldon, Ed Traynor."

"No shit. I been looking all over the fucking state for you. You were seen leaving a crime scene. You cross over the fuckin' line?"

"Eldon—"

"I don't want to hear it. I want your fuckin' ass in my office ASAP, or I put out an APB on you."

Traynor heard him mutter, "Fuckup," and then the phone went dead.

Between the rain and traffic, it took Traynor almost an hour to get from the Lakes Region to Concord and the Merrimack County Sheriff's Office. When he walked into the building, his mood sucked. He was, however, not stupid enough to walk into Burns's office with an attitude. It was very likely that he was a person of interest, if not the prime suspect, in a homicide and he could not afford to antagonize anyone—even a mental midget like Eldon Burns. He didn't have enough time at his disposal to spend any of it as a guest of Merrimack County. If he played this wrong, it would be just like Eldon to lock him up and forget about him for forty-eight hours, time he desperately needed if he was to find John's killer.

Burns was a large, balding man and most of his bulk was not muscle. He swiveled around in his desk chair and when Traynor offered to shake hands, he ignored the gesture. He pointed at a chair, commanding Traynor to sit. He felt like a kid called to the principal's office. Burns's chair needed oiling and squealed in protest every time he spun. He finally came to a rest with his feet propped on the desk. "What the fuck you been up to, Ed?"

"You know me, Eldon. I like to keep busy."

"Been fucking around over in Bow is more like it."

Traynor knew that to play dumb wouldn't have bought him anything, so he spoke frankly. "Ryan was dead when I got there."

"No shit? Got anyone to back that up? You know, maybe a little fucking mouse in your hip pocket."

"Nope, but you can bet dollars against donuts that if I was going to off Ryan I wouldn't leave the body for everyone to admire."

Burns dropped his feet to the floor. "So suppose you tell me why you were fucking around over there?"

"Ryan and my brother were business associates."

"Really? Just what type of fucking business would anyone have with an asshole like Ryan?"

"I was trying to get an answer to that very question."

"Did you?"

Traynor did not like the way the conversation was going and struggled to keep his temper in check. He opted to play dumb for a bit and see what shook out. "Did I what?"

"Don't yank my goddamned chain, Eddie. Did you get an answer to your fucking question?"

"No, I did not."

He leaned forward. "Listen, Eddie, there's no way in hell I think you offed the son of a whore, but someone did and you were seen driving away from his fucking house."

"I think I spooked the killer when I got there. Someone ran out the back door, into the woods, and got away. I saw the perp drive out of there in a black Chevy four-by-four. The windows were too filthy for me to ID the driver."

"We found the road and some tracks. You have any idea who the bastard was?"

"I might; you might want to start looking for a punk named Robby McPherson. He's had dealings with Ryan in the past. Last time I saw him he drove a black Chevy four-by-four."

"I'm familiar with the asswipe. Problem is he lives in Belknap fuckin' County, not mine." Traynor noted that in spite of Eldon's lack of jurisdiction he still wrote down Robby's name. "You ain't dicking me around and holding nothing back are you?"

"Like what?"

"I don't know, but whenever I think someone is holding back I get this crazy fuckin' feeling."

"You know what I know, Eldon."

"Okay, get out of here. But, if I find out you're fu—"

Traynor had had his fill of Eldon's gutter language and shut the door on him.

Burns's response to the door slamming was typical for him. Through the door, Traynor heard him shouting words that would get your mouth stuffed with soap if your mother heard you use them. A secretary, whom he had never seen before, glared at the closed door. Traynor wondered how long she would tolerate Eldon's restricted vocabulary. If there was ever a sexual harassment suit looking for a place to happen, it was Eldon Burns.

Traynor was halfway across the office area when he heard Burns's office door open and the sheriff say, "It true what I saw on the police net?"

"That depends on what you saw."

"Someone offed that useless fuckin' brother of yours."

Traynor ignored Burns's assessment of John and replied, "Yeah, night before last."

Burns nodded, leaned against the doorjamb, and peeled the cellophane off one of the cheap cigars he smoked. An acerbic grin was on his face, and he moistened the cigar with his mouth. "It was a matter of goddamned time, you know. The only thing that surprised me was how long it took."

Once again Traynor refused to rise to the bait. "Yeah, well thanks for caring enough to ask."

"Fuck, I could give a shit less—just wanted to make sure they weren't lying to me." Burns's laughter echoed through the room until the closing of his office door cut it off.

Traynor turned to the disgruntled secretary and said, "Your boss is a real humanitarian, isn't he?"

She gave a disapproving look at the closed office door. "Yeah, isn't he?"

"You have a nice rest of your day," Traynor said.

"So long as he stays in his office with the door shut I will."

Back in the car, Traynor called Max. "Let's go hunting."

"Go huntin'? You haven't hunted in ten years—besides, if I know you, you ain't even got a license."

"Yeah, it's been at least that and I got a permit to carry a handgun; to hunt what we're after, that's all I need. I'd still like you to grab a couple of hunting rifles and meet me in Andover, where State Road 11 and Route 4 intersect. Bring your four-by-four."

"We ain't huntin' deer are we?"

"No, we ain't huntin' deer."

"Bear?"

"Nope."

"That only leaves a manhunt. By the way, Charley wants you to call. He's learned some interesting stuff. It looks like John wasn't the only one in way over his head."

Traynor broke off the connection and called Charley. He answered on the first ring. "Eddie?"

"Yeah, what you got?"

"The Escobar brothers."

"What did you learn about them?"

"They got taken for a lot of cash, in the millions."

"So I heard."

"Well, it gets better. They owe a bundle to some really connected and, I might add, bad mothers in the Cartagena cartel."

"I've also been hearing rumors to that effect. How serious is their trouble?"

"My sources say Eduardo hasn't been seen in over a week. Carlo keeps saying that he's out of the country. However, the smart money says someone has him stashed away until Carlo can make good on the debt. Apparently, Carlo is running out of time. My sources tell me an entourage from Cartagena is in Boston looking for Carlo, who, by the way, is nowhere around. Odds are he's back in the home country, somewhere deep in the mountains."

"This leaves Eduardo to be devoured by the wolves—so much for brotherly love."

"I was able to hack into their computers though. Carlo and Eduardo are pretty much insolvent."

"You mean they're broke?"

"I wouldn't say that; they got a lot of property, but nothing liquid. They're cash poor. If you look at their liquid assets, they're so broke if it cost them a nickel to shit they'd have to sell a building. The truth is if they owe the cartel, they're worse than broke. I hope they've paid up their life insurance premiums; their family could be placing a couple of claims real soon."

Traynor listened closely; this was good information, and it put a different light on some things. However, Charley was not finished yet. "They needed two million bucks to pay back their suppliers and the remainder, over a million according to my sources, was their operating cash. Whoever took down their bank may have done what law enforcement has been unable to do for over ten years . . . they could very well have brought down the entire Escobar drug empire in the United States."

The information did not really open any new avenues for Traynor to investigate. However, it possibly gave him another way to look at things; maybe John's execution was an accident. It was another theory and all he seemed to have was theories. "Thanks, Charley; as usual, I owe you."

"Don't hang up," he said. "I ain't through yet. I dug around and got the information you asked for on their history."

Traynor heard Charley's chair creak as he moved.

"Eddie, you had better be careful with these boys; they ain't anyone you want to be fooling around with. Twenty years ago, they were field laborers in the coca fields in Colombia. They moved up the food chain, becoming muscle for one of the bigwigs in the cartels."

"Another nice bunch," Traynor replied.

"But the Pope loves them because they're all good tithe-paying, church-going Catholics. About ten years ago, there was a big turf war down there. Someone close to their boss took him down. Whoever that someone was, he had to be inside the organization and the Escobar brothers were about as inside as anyone could get. In the end, the only people left standing were Carlo and Eduardo."

"Will the wonders never cease?" Traynor said. "I'm not surprised though. I met Carlo the other day. Before it was all over I felt like the host of a reptile show on Animal Planet after a crocodile hunt."

"Carlo is the more dangerous of the two—he'll cut his mother's throat for a dime—however, Eduardo ain't anyone's fool either. He's not as emotional as Carlo, but you still don't want to mess with him. Both of them are so full of testosterone if they could figure out a way to keep from getting bit, they'd get a blow job from a rattlesnake. I found out some interesting stuff on the Martin woman too."

"Oh?" Now Traynor became interested, very interested, in what he had to say.

"Yeah, she's from the same neck of the woods as the brothers. She grew up like most people down there, scratching for a living. Many days, dinner was whatever they scrounged out of the local dump or the dumpster behind a restaurant. She's as ruthless as her bosses. It wouldn't surprise my source if she'd had more people killed than Carlo and Eduardo combined."

"Really?"

"Ed, watch your ass around her. She isn't content being the hired help. Hell, she may even have been the one who did John. She won't hesitate to do anything that will get her what she wants. I'll keep digging to see if I can learn anything else. Talk to you later." He broke the connection.

Traynor did most of his heavy thinking while driving and as he drove along Route 4, he processed everything he had learned so far. What was frustrating was that it was still adding up to nothing. The more he sifted through the garbage, the more rubbish he found. Common sense said someone other than the brothers had killed John . . . and it could very well have been Gisela Martin. He tapped his left hand against the steering wheel. Every time he thought he was making sense of this case, someone added a new variable to the formula. The equation was starting to be as complicated as quantum physics. He was sure of one thing, though—somewhere, someone was sitting on over three million bucks of Carlo and Eduardo Escobar's money.

20

Traynor was sitting in the parking lot of a combination gas station/convenience store drinking a soda and eating a sandwich when Max arrived. He parked beside the Taurus, and Traynor motioned for him to get into the car. Max looked at the sedan and shook his head, motioning for Traynor to get in his Excursion. Traynor had to agree; cramming Max's bulk in the Taurus would be like trying to shove an elephant into a phone booth. Of course, there were not many phone booths around—they were harder to find than old-fashioned gas stations where attendants pumped your gas and you could get your car repaired. Ed climbed into the passenger seat, and Max looked at his suit and raincoat. "You going hunting dressed like that?"

"I got no choice."

"Yeah, you do. I stopped by the office, and Susan took me to your place. I brought you a change of clothes." He motioned to the leather bag sitting on the back seat. "They got a men's room in there?"

"I hope so, or I'm about to upset someone."

Traynor grabbed the valise and stepped out of the truck. As usual, Susan was on top of things. She had sent a pair of jeans, a heavy flannel shirt, wool socks, some hiking boots, and a hunter's camouflage coat. In ten minutes, he was back in the truck with Max who looked at Traynor's outdoorsy appearance with tacit approval. "That's more like it. Let's go hunting—where to?"

Traynor gave him directions to McPherson's cabin.

An hour earlier, the rain had stopped, but as they drove through Salisbury, it started again, turning into a steady downpour as they drove into Andover. They left the highway and took an unnamed dirt road north through some rough terrain. Traynor sat back and listened to the mud and stones banging against the truck's undercarriage. The din was so loud that talking was more of a shouting contest than conversation. Rather than spend his energy on idle chatter, Traynor studied the terrain, and it was evident that Amanda McPherson had been correct about his car—the road was a quagmire, and he would not have made it fifty yards down this muddy track. The brush came out over the road in several places, and he winced as branches dragged along the side of the truck. "Rough on the paint job," he raised his voice to be heard over the clamor.

"Screw it. It's a truck," Max responded. "If I didn't want to go off-road I'd be like you and drive a car."

Traynor shook his head and grinned. He realized that scratches in the paint were no big thing if, like Max, you owned an auto body shop. He thought about the dings and surface rust on his car and decided that when he got a few days he would have to give the Taurus to Max and have him do some minor bodywork on it.

Max took his time so the truck wouldn't lose traction and send them skidding off into the trees, large boulders, and bushes that lined the sides of the lane. The leafless trees and brush made it easy to see into the woods, and the terrain looked torn up. "Something has this place all fucked up?" Traynor commented.

"Assholes on their ATVs," Max said. "When the ground is saturated and soft they chew the shit out of it. It looks as if McPherson and his chums have spent a lot of time in here."

"I didn't think about ATVs," Traynor replied. "We'll have to be careful if we don't want Robby and his butt-buddies to take off cross-country. The last thing we need is to get into a footrace through the woods."

"Especially if we're chasing someone who knows their way around better than us—and you and I don't know anything about this place."

The road turned sharply, and Max stopped the truck. Through the trees, a cabin was visible; there were two big four-by-four trucks parked in front. Max backed up until the cabin was out of their line of sight and parked the Excursion in the middle of the road, effectively creating a roadblock. "Barring any bad luck, we should be able to surprise McPherson and his chums. We should probably walk from here," Max said.

Traynor got out and pulled his collar up against the cold rain. He looked at the low-hanging clouds and estimated that there were two, maybe two and a half, hours of daylight left. Max came around the truck carrying two rifles, a Remington 700 bolt-action rifle in .308 caliber and a semiautomatic Remington .30-06. Both weapons were great deer rifles but also effective against human targets. The model 700 bolt-action was the weapon that Marine Corps armorers modified into the long-time weapon of choice for Marine Scout/Snipers. Max had chosen well. "Which one you want?" he asked.

Traynor took the bolt-action, leaving Max the semiautomatic. "This will do fine." He checked the action and loaded a round into the chamber. "Let's go."

Staying on the road was too risky—they were too exposed and therefore decided to approach through the trees. Traynor entered the woods on the right side of the road as a gust of wind drove through the trees, sending water cascading to the forest floor and soaking him. He turned and saw Max enter on the left and quickly disappear from sight.

The terrain was typical of New England woodlands, a multitude of ravines created by washouts during the spring thaws, small ledges, boulders, and a mixture of evergreen and deciduous trees. The rain had diminished to a soaking mist, which hugged the ground and hung over the cabin like a rolling fog. Traynor glanced at the woods; the rain had soaked everything, saturating the dead leaves and ground and muffling the sound of his steps. It was not long before his clothes were soaked and Traynor felt a numbing chill. Max suddenly reappeared, his wet hair plastered to his forehead. They spaced themselves about twenty meters apart and stayed in view of each other, one on each side of the road.

Max held his right arm up with the fist tightly clenched, the universal infantry signal for halt, and then pointed to the building. It was brown with a black shingled roof, and smoke drifted from the chimney. The rain and damp air kept the smoke close to the ground, where the wind blew it through the trees. The pleasant woodsy smell of burning hardwood reminded Traynor of happier times. Max, however, seemed impervious to the idyllic scene. He moved first, darted across the road, and dropped to his knees beside Traynor. "How you want to do this?"

"I'd give an arm to know what we'll be up against in there."

"Wait here." Max crept forward to the edge of the trees. He stayed out of sight as he circled the cabin and worked his way around to the back of the building. Traynor had always found it unsettling how easily and quietly Max moved through woods and rough terrain; he always expected a man that large to sound like a foraging bear. In fifteen minutes, Max was back at his side. "Two trucks, one with extended cab out front, another truck and three ATVs in the back," he reported.

"Was one a black Chevy Silverado four-by-four?"

"It was."

"So we could have as few as one and possibly eight or nine idiots in there—probably all armed and fucked up on booze and drugs."

Max kept his eyes on the cabin as he said, "We're in the woods, it is hunting season, and they're most likely idiots."

Traynor glared at him, letting him know he did not appreciate his wit. He finally turned his head away from Max, back to the cabin. "So, how we going about it?" he asked.

"You cover the back. I'm going in the front door—hard and fast."

Max grinned and it was not pretty. Traynor was sure he scared little kids when he smiled like that. He raised a thumb and disappeared into the brush.

Once Max was out of sight, Traynor moved forward and waited in the trees across from the cabin. It would take Max a few minutes to get in position, and he used the time to study the building. He squatted among the wet leaves and dripping foliage and surveyed it. It was quite large for a woods cabin, and the site was isolated enough to be ideal for illegal activity. The construction was crude but appeared to be solid. A roofed porch, sporting six white Adirondack-style chairs, ran the entire width of the front. Centered on the porch was a sturdy door with windows flanking it on either side. He hoped the cabin's isolated location would make its occupants feel safe enough that they had not locked the door.

Traynor saw Max appear at the edge of the trees and wave, indicating he was ready. Traynor took a deep breath and ran across the open space. He did not want to alarm whoever was with McPherson, so when he was close to the porch he slowed to a walk, lightly placing his feet on the steps as he climbed the steps. He stopped beside the door, thumbed the rifle's safety so it was ready to fire, and tried the doorknob. It turned easily and, even more surprising, quietly. He was inside before anyone inside knew it.

Four men sat around a table with whiskey glasses and beer bottles in front of them. A table stakes poker game was in progress. If he had not known these men were local hard cases who hung out with McPherson, Traynor would have sworn they were a bunch of executives on a hunting trip. However, the pungent odor of pot dissipated any notion that these people were law-abiding citizens. One thing bothered him though— McPherson was not among them.

Out of the corner of his eye, Traynor saw the door to his right open and a shotgun barrel appear in the opening. Whoever was behind that door pointed the gun at him. He dove to the floor just as the gun roared.

21

His injured ribs slamming into the hardwood floor caused spots to appear in Traynor's eyes, but still he rolled across the floor and fired at the door. The .308 round hit the doorjamb, an inch from the shotgun holder's head, and showered the gunman with wooden splinters.

Traynor scrambled behind a couch and heard a commotion as Max burst through the back door. The cardplayers dove to the floor scattering cards, chips, and booze glasses helter-skelter across the floor. Their hands were up and one of them shouted, "Don't shoot! Jesus Christ—don't shoot!"

Traynor knew Max had the four cardplayers under control so he shouted at the gunman. "I don't want to hurt you, so put down the shotgun and come out here!"

Robby McPherson poked his head out of the bedroom.

"Come all the way out, Robby." Traynor was tired of playing bullshit games with the kid.

McPherson wore a plaid shirt, blue jeans, and hunting boots. His hair hung in sweaty, oily strands below the blaze orange baseball cap he wore with the visor pointing to the rear. Traynor hated it when people wore their hats backward. Robby had not used a razor in several days, but the stubble on his cheeks was still a couple of weeks away from a full beard. His dilated pupils were ample proof that McPherson was on something, and the mucous he wiped from his upper lip told Traynor that whatever it was, he'd inhaled. Even though he was not very stable, the single-shot twenty-gauge shotgun he held never drifted away from Traynor—its barrel looked like an angry black eye.

"Who in hell are you?" he asked.

"My name is Ed Traynor. I'm looking for you."

"Why?"

"We need to talk."

Robby squinted as if he were trying to focus through a thick fog. "I kn-kn-know you," he stammered. "You was . . ." He blinked his eyes a couple of times. "You was out at Benny's yesterday."

"I saw you run out of there."

Robby's face suddenly fell. He looked like a frightened little boy. "I didn't fuck him up, man. He was like that when I got there."

His story sounded familiar. Traynor doubted it sounded any more convincing when he had used it with Buck and Eldon Burns. If Robby did not kill Benny—and he was not convinced of that yet—then who did? All he was sure of was that he had not done it. If Robby was telling the truth, then he was still chasing his tail. "So you just walked in, found Benny, and decided to help yourself to some free stuff?"

"Yeah, man, that's exactly what happened."

"I think you're lying to me, Robby. How many dead men have you seen in your life?"

"You mean outside a funeral home?"

"Yeah, I mean outside a funeral home."

"Just one—Benny."

"And I'm supposed to believe that you didn't panic? You just saw a golden opportunity and took it."

"You can believe what you want. But I didn't shoot Benny. Whoever did was already gone when I got there."

Benny had died of what Traynor believed was a broken neck. He had seen no bullet wounds on the body. He looked closely at Robby to see if he was setting him up. When a person had been a cop as long as he had been, they learn the signs that tell when someone is lying. Robby didn't know what killed Ryan and that convinced Traynor that he was telling the truth. "Who said Benny was shot?"

"Hell, I don't know. I just assumed he was. You sayin' he wasn't?"

"I'm saying he wasn't."

This case was really starting to drive him nuts. Every lead turned into a circle, bringing him back to the same place. Someone, or someones, was killing people off as if they were flies and the more he looked into things the further he seemed to be from the answer.

"Okay. If you're telling me the truth, then you got no reason to be aiming that shotgun at me."

Robby pointed to the .308. "You go first."

Traynor kept his eyes on Robby and said, "Max?"

"Yeah, Eddie."

"If he as much as twitches, kill him."

"It'll be my pleasure."

Robby must not have seen Max. When he heard him speak, he looked surprised and visibly paled. He ventured a quick look in Max's direction; Traynor knew he didn't like what he saw.

Max pointed the .30-06 at Robby's belt buckle. Something in Max's demeanor told Robby that if he made one false move, he would be history. Traynor knew what it was that rattled the kid—it was the hopeful look on Max's face.

Traynor slowly turned away from Robby and leaned his rifle against the wall. The cardplayers sensed the tension ease and relaxed. Ed turned back to Robby. "What's it going to be, Robby? Are you willing to die today? That shotgun is a single-shot and you haven't had time to reload it."

Robby opened the breech of the single-shot and the spent cartridge ejected, landing on the floor with a clatter. He slowly lowered the shotgun and placed it on the floor to his right.

"Let's have a little talk . . . just you and me." Traynor motioned for McPherson to follow him out to the porch.

He heard Max say, "The rest of you fellows can clean up the mess you made and go on with your game, that way no one will get hurt."

They stepped outside, and Traynor waited for Robby to sit in one of the wooden chairs before moving another around so he could face him. Something stung his right leg and he glanced at it. There was a small tear in his jeans and blood seeped down his leg. It tickled as it ran down his calf and into his sock. He realized that a pellet from McPherson's shot must have hit him. He shook his head. "I ought to kick your ass!"

Robby scooted back in his chair. "Hey, I'm sorry, man! But when you came busting in here like the goddamned DEA, I panicked."

Traynor got his temper under control, at least enough to talk. "I'm not a cop, Robby. I'm John Traynor's brother, a private investigator. Two days ago, someone killed John. He and Benny Ryan were tight and ran scams together. Benny turning up dead within a day of John just makes me wonder what in hell is going on. Why were you at Benny's place when I got there?"

"I wanted drugs and some weed. The guys and I been up here for a week and we're running low."

"Why drive all the way to Bow? Surely, someone like you could score around here—you must have a connection to every dealer in New England. Users and addicts always know where to score."

"It was simple. Benny and your brother moved a lot of good shit."

"What type of good shit?"

"You name it, grass, coke, Ritalin. Lately they been pushing a lot of oxy, meth, and bath salts. Nobody up here was handling as much prime stuff as them." He pointed at the cabin's interior. "Those guys can go through a lot of shit in a day."

"So when you got there Benny was already dead?"

"Yeah, I found some grass and helped myself. I was hoping to find some better stuff when you came along and I lit out of there."

"You saw no one?"

"I ain't sure. But, a car with Mass tags on it passed me on my way in. The car slowed down and they eye-fucked me when we passed each other. Looked like a couple of Puerto Ricans in the car."

"That's it? A couple of Puerto Ricans in a car?"

"Yeah, they looked like a couple of guys you wouldn't want to screw around with, you know what I mean?"

"I think I do. Can you remember anything else?"

"Well nothing I'd want to testify to, but I got a real good look at the spic who was driving. He was an ugly bastard . . . had this big fucking scar on his face."

Traynor smiled. Humberto and Theo make another appearance . . . maybe he was closer to some answers than he had thought. Those morons kept popping up throughout this case. Robby was quaking in his boots, too scared to be lying. He had nothing else to tell, and Ed knew it. "Okay, Robby, but if I were you I'd keep my eyes open and a low profile. People who get involved with this thing seem to have a way of getting the shit kicked out of them—or ending up dead."

Robby studied Traynor's face for a second and obviously noted the bruises. "That what happened to you?" In spite of the bravado of his words, his body language told Traynor that Robby got the message.

"Yeah, that's what happened to me. Probably the same two assholes you saw near Benny's place. If I were you, I'd stick close to home for a while. Being isolated in the woods could be stupid. You may want to keep in mind that eventually one of you idiots is going to get shot—dope and guns don't mix. You know where I'm coming from?"

He pondered those words for several seconds then said, "Yeah, being isolated ain't good." Traynor knew the *Just Say No* message either was lost on him or it was more than he could comprehend in his current state of mind.

"You might even do some stuff around the house for your sister."

"You've seen Amanda?"

"Yeah, she could use some help, Robby. She seems to have her hands full taking care of your mother."

Robby stayed in the chair while Traynor stepped inside the cabin, grabbed his rifle, and motioned to Max. As they walked off the porch, he stopped beside Robby and said, "I'll be in touch with you and Amanda from time to time, Robby. Now you get straight and go home tonight, okay?"

Robby looked like he had just been convicted and given a life sentence. He looked as if he wanted to cry when he said, "It ain't the way it seems, man."

Traynor gave him a quizzical look.

"I want to help my sister and all, but it rips me up to see Mom the way she is . . ."

"Your mother is hospitalized now and your sister shouldn't have to bear everything alone. It's time you grew up and faced your responsibilities, Robby."

When Traynor walked away, McPherson raised his right hand in a halfhearted wave and stayed put.

Max and Traynor walked through the rain, taking the road this time rather than tramping through the wet woods. The pellet from the shotgun had lodged in Ed's leg muscle and walking hurt; he started to limp and Max noticed it. "What happened to you?"

"It's nothing."

They got in the truck and Max saw his bloody leg. "Don't tell me it's nothing. You're bleeding all over the fucking place!"

"I took some shot in the leg."

Max reached over and ripped the leg of Traynor's pants open. Blood flowed from two punctures in the leg. Ed's heart skipped at the look on Max's face when he grabbed his hunting knife. "It's not too bad," he said.

Traynor watched Max get out of the truck and walk around to the passenger side. Max held a Buck hunting knife in his right hand and said, "Let's make sure." In no time, the shot was out of Ed's calf. Max took a first aid kit from the glove box and put a compress on it. "When you get back home, you should go to a doctor and get a stitch or two put in that."

"You mean you didn't amputate it?"

Max got behind the wheel, smiled, and mumbled something.

"What was that?"

"I said, Susan's right, you sure can be a baby."

22

November is New Hampshire's monsoon season. When it isn't raining, the skies are cloudy, keeping the sun from warming the ground. Portsmouth was settling in for another stormy night, and Traynor was tired. Since Buck called him to the site of John's murder, he had slept about four hours a night and it was a stretch to call passing out after a major-league ass-kicking sleep. He wanted a hot shower and eight hours.

He stopped by the hospital and had a couple of stitches put in his leg; fortunately Max's crude first aid made it possible for him to report the wound as an accident with a hunting knife. If he had told them it was a gunshot wound, he would have been there until midnight filling out paperwork. The intern who stitched him was either new and didn't recognize the wound for what it was, or he did and decided to keep quiet so he too wouldn't have to do a ton of reports. Although Traynor was certain the young doctor noticed the bruises on his face, he chose to ignore them. Either way, Traynor was happy when the doctor went along with the knife story.

Traynor got home, cooked a burger, and ate it while catching up on the local news. The anchor spent all of two minutes on Benny Ryan and said nothing about John, not that Traynor expected anything more. He put his plates in the dishwasher and returned to the living room. He hoped he would be able to watch the national news undisturbed. He just barely made it through a half hour of the happenings in the world. At six-fifty-five, the phone rang—some telemarketer wanted to sell him a grave plot. He told him that he didn't need one because he was not going: God didn't want him, and the devil was afraid that he'd take over. The telemarketer hung up on him.

He turned the channel over to the Boston Bruins hockey game and watched them roll over the Buffalo Sabres, four to one. It was difficult to concentrate on the game because he kept playing what he had learned thus far through his mind, trying to figure out what he was missing. He was overlooking something and wished he could put a finger on whatever it was. The game ended just after nine-thirty, and he took a hot shower and went to bed, hoping that a good night's sleep would help cut through some of the cobwebs.

Traynor lay on the bed listening to the wind gusting and rain pounding against the window and wondered what had awakened him. The digital clock's cold blue numbers said it was twenty minutes past eleven o'clock, the absolute lack of light in the room said it was p.m.: he'd only been sleeping for about a half hour. He became aware of the phone ringing and vacillated between getting up and ignoring the obnoxious, intrusive sound. Finally, the incessant ringing won and he got up, fumbling around as he tried to bridge the gap between his dream world and the real world. After a couple of seconds, he got out of bed and staggered into the living room looking for the phone. As a matter of principle, he did not keep one next to his bed. He believed there should be at least one place on Earth where he was more than an arm's reach away from everyone else.

He found the telephone on the floor beside the couch, grabbed the receiver, and said, "Yeah, yeah . . ."

"Eddie?"

It was Jillian.

"How are you doing?" he asked.

"Better. I didn't wake you did I?"

"No." He was certain that the sound of his voice told her he was lying. She ignored the obvious and said, "I need a favor."

"Anything, you know that."

"The forecast for tomorrow is sunny and warm. Would you come over and take me and the girls somewhere for the day?"

"Yeah, I'd like that. It might do me some good too." He suddenly believed that some time away from this case would be a definite plus. Maybe getting away for a day would allow his subconscious to work on the information he had gathered thus far. Usually, once he stopped concentrating on a problem, the solution seemed to present itself. He was aware that he was chasing his tail trying to figure out what it was that he was missing and that he had overlooked the link that would unravel the twisted mess this case had become. It was time to let his conscious mind take a break and let the subconscious go to work. "Where would you like to go?" he asked.

"I thought we could drive north. Go to the notches, maybe up to the Flume Gorge and the Old Man of the Mountain."

"The Old Man is gone."

"I know that, but I still like the area. It will mean a lot to me and the girls."

That was an argument against which he had no defense. "I'll pick you up at eight."

As Jillian had prophesied, the morning dawned clear and warm. It was hard to believe that any day now the area would be facing winter's first blast. In New England, the November weather seldom got as good as it was that day, and Traynor wanted to make the most of it. He picked up Jill and the girls and drove north on I-93, past the Lakes Region, into the White Mountains.

When they arrived at the Flume Gorge, they learned that, while the temperature at the gift shop was in the lower sixties, the parts of the gorge the sun couldn't reach were covered with ice and too dangerous for touring. That morning the park service decided to close it for the season, which was a letdown for the girls. Nevertheless, Traynor was not about to let the day be spoiled and told the girls they would drive a few miles farther north and ride the cable car up Cannon Mountain. After that, it was off to Littleton for a visit to Chutters General Store, home of the world's longest candy counter. The vote to adopt his plan was unanimous.

On the way to Cannon Mountain, they stopped at a scenic turnout and looked up at the place where the Old Man of the Mountain had stood. The Old Man was still the official symbol of New Hampshire and, in years past, a great deal of time and money had gone into preserving him from the ravages of erosion. No trip through the notches was complete without stopping and paying respects to the Old Man. On a Saturday morning, May 3, 2003, he finally gave in to the forces of nature and tumbled into the gorge. After a long, hard winter, the stately presence, who had watched over the *Live Free or Die* state for centuries, gave up his precarious perch and became just another pile of rocks.

The cable car ride was fun. The girls chattered excitedly, their noses pressed against the cool glass as they crept upward to the summit of Cannon Mountain. At the top, the girls wanted to walk along the mountain trails. After some discussion, Traynor convinced Jillian that Carrie was old enough to be responsible for her younger sister. Reluctantly, Jill gave them permission.

The adults watched the children dash off and then went into the cafeteria for a cup of coffee. Since her call, Traynor couldn't shake the premonition that Jillian was going to lay some news on him and he was not going to like it.

They sat in the dining room next to a window overlooking the notch. The sky was free of clouds and they could see Maine to the northeast and Vermont to the northwest. Traynor stared down the mountain, hypnotically watching the sun reflect from the surface of Echo Lake. Cars traveled along the highway, some going north, toward Littleton and St. Johnsbury, Vermont, and a heavier stream going south, toward Concord, Manchester, and, ultimately, Boston. As he watched them speed through Franconia Notch, he thought they resembled a line of hungry ants.

Jillian also stared out the window, lost in her own thoughts as she sipped her coffee. Ed let her have some time alone. He pretended that the scenery entranced him while in reality he was waiting for her to speak first. After a few minutes, she sighed and said, "Eddie, I'm going away."

"Going away . . . for how long?"

"I don't know really—a long time, maybe forever."

His heart sank, but he struggled to keep his feelings hidden. "Do you have any place in mind?"

"I'm not sure; Florida, maybe the West Coast. In Florida we can stay with my mother for a while until I get our lives straight."

"Do you have enough money to relocate?"

Jill paused for a few seconds, as if she had not thought about the expense of moving. "I can borrow some from my mother."

"Have you told the girls?"

"Not yet. It's too soon." She took a deep breath and said, "They still don't know about John."

"They don't? What do they think? They haven't seen him in almost a week."

"John pulled this kind of crap all the time. They think this is normal— the way things have always been with their father."

"He wasn't much of a father, was he?"

"He wasn't much of anything. He never had a sense of purpose; with

John everything had to come the easy way or not at all. There were lots of times when I wished he were dead and out of my life." She raised her eyes to his and said, "I probably shouldn't say things like that, should I? Especially now, after what happened to him."

Traynor nodded. "I understand completely. There are times when I get this weird feeling, as if some burden has been lifted from me."

"Yeah, I get that same feeling. Now that he's finally out of my life, I feel lighter."

"Why did you put up with it for so long? You should have walked years ago. Hell, everyone would have understood. I know I would have."

"No doubt you would have. What about my girls—do you think they would have understood?"

He knew she was right. Young kids don't see their parents as people with weaknesses; they see them as gods and remain loyal to them—no matter how flawed they might be. "Is there any way I can change your mind about leaving?"

She stared at him with those eyes—those beautiful deep pools in which he found it so easy to lose himself. She turned away and sipped her coffee. "Eddie, do you remember that Christmas Eve?"

His heart stopped. "Which one was that?" He didn't want her to know that that night had stayed with him.

"You know. The one when John was not home and I'd drunk too much. It's confession time . . ."

He waited, unwilling to verbalize his hopes.

"I wasn't drunk that night."

"Jillian . . ."

"I know how it must make you feel. After all, I'm your brother's widow. Hell, we haven't even buried him yet. You must think I'm lower than—"

"Stop it. Stop right there, Jill." He took her hand in his. "Yes, I remember that night. It's been with me ever since."

She started to say something, but he held his hand up, stopping her. "Why do you think I've never married?"

"I never thought about it." Her voice was barely audible.

"Because every woman I've ever been with had to compete with you—and you set the bar high."

As if on cue, the girls came in the café. They stampeded through the room and grabbed Jillian by the arm, dragging her to the service counter. He watched them crowd around the cash register while Jill paid for a round of hot chocolate. The girls looked like children on a Christmas card, their faces flushed by the brisk mountain air, cheeks rosy and standing out against their hair, which was so blond it looked white. He felt as if his heart were made of fine china, in danger of breaking. Since Carrie first came into this world, he had entertained fantasies of being father to Jillian's kids. Now, that dream was in peril of dying. Suddenly, it seemed as if everyone in his life was either dead or moving on without him.

He did not want his mood to ruin the day for everyone else, so he did his best to shrug off the blue funk. Still, he couldn't help but think that if Jillian left, he was going to miss many things. He would miss seeing the girls grow into gawky teenagers and then beautiful young women. There would be no watching the excitement of first dates, junior and senior proms, and their joyous expectation as they approached their wedding days. He felt empty. These little girls couldn't have meant more to him if he had fathered them—they were his family. He watched them with their mother. As she spoke to her daughters, Jillian squatted so she was at their level, rather than speaking down to them. It was a simple act, but so very meaningful.

If Jillian and the girls went away, he'd be in that place where he'd spent most of his life; alone, adrift, and there would be no one to blame but him. It is not that he lived a hermit's existence; he had friends. Maureen would always be there; so would Bob and Susan, but it wasn't the same. He had never worried about Maureen; her husband and her kids had always been there to fill any gap in her life. He, on the other hand, had nobody. Then he had a revelation, one that ripped through his gut like a Saracen blade—he was sick and tired of being alone.

It made him realize another reason for his anger toward John. All his life, John had thought that Ed had it all together, that everything came easy for his older brother. He couldn't have been any farther from the truth. True, Ed had always held a steady job while John was hustling for money, never knowing when he'd get it. Still, for Ed, something had always been missing. In reality, without even trying, John had had everything Ed ever wanted and he threw it away, as if it was unimportant, disposable. The thing Ed missed most was a family of his own; John, on the other hand, used his for amusement, and then discarded it when he tired of it.

Traynor didn't believe that he had ever hated John, though there were many times when he'd been extremely disappointed in him, but until that moment, he'd never loathed him. Now, it seemed that even from the grave, John was able to reach out and hurt everyone around him.

Jillian returned to her seat. She looked at him and noticed his anger. "You're annoyed with me."

"No, not with you."

"Then, who?"

"It's something I have to work out myself."

Jillian turned and stared out the window again. "Eddie, my moving isn't about you. Okay? I know my leaving with the girls will be hard on you. The Lord only knows it's tough on me too."

He sat quietly.

"He's gone," she said, "you can stop feeling as if you're to blame for the way he turned out."

He'd once read somewhere that life is about choices and their consequences. The same author said that quality of life is how we handle the bad decisions and things that life dumps on us. Ed knew that he and he alone had made his choices. Thus far, he had forgone having his own family. However, that choice only affected him, not two little girls and a mother. John's choices seemed to leave a string of broken people in their wake. His eyes settled on Jill and he saw himself for the liar he was. Nobody makes choices that affect only him or herself. If people are lucky, someone, like Jillian or Susan, will grab onto them and hang with them to the very end, in spite of the carnage they reap. Ed was firm in his belief that John and he didn't deserve women like them.

The café seemed deathly quiet. Suddenly the girls swept across the room, filling the void with excited chatter. He envied them for their idyllic existence.

The rest of the day went perfectly. They drove to Littleton and it cost him almost twenty bucks at the candy counter at Chutters Store. Knowing that his time with the girls might be limited, Ed would have spent ten times that much on each of them.

Traynor began to feel the loss again when he dropped them off at nine-thirty that evening. He knew that he couldn't hold his emotions much longer, so he didn't go upstairs. He stopped in front of Jillian's apartment, and the girls jumped out of the car like the 82nd Airborne parachuting into 1944 France. Jill turned to him, smiled, and said, "Are you going to be all right?"

At that moment, he had no plausible answer, so he took the easy way out and decided to be honest. He told her, "I'll live, Jill. Over the years, I've learned that I'm a survivor. That doesn't mean it hurts any less, just that I'll live through it."

"Why don't you come to dinner tomorrow night, Ed?"

He hesitated, wanting to minimize his pain by saying no, and then said, "What time?"

23

Traynor sat in his living room mulling over the facts of the case as he knew them and in the course of the review, his thoughts once again turned to John.

He had two images of John. The first was the likable, little towheaded kid who wanted nothing more than to be with his big brother, who was twelve years older. The other image was of him as an adult, surly and angry, a man with a grudge against the world and the lousy circumstances he believed life had forced on him. Traynor was at a loss as he tried to reconcile the two. The images were just too divergent.

He walked into the kitchen and gathered a bucket of ice, a bottle of Maker's Mark, and some ginger ale. If he was going to do the sort of thinking that he had to do, alcoholic fortification was in order. He took the phone off-line by disconnecting it from the back of the answering machine. If anyone called, let him or her leave a message.

He tuned the radio to an oldies station, turned off the lights, and flopped down on the couch. He had always done his best thinking while sitting in a dark room listening to the rock and roll of the nineteen fifties and sixties. He was also aware that he had to be careful that he did not allow himself to wallow in the self-deprecating throes of depression and self-pity; that was probably why he never listened to country and western music when he was in these moods.

He mixed a drink and laid back, his head propped against the couch's arm with a small pillow. He breathed deep, emptying his mind, and let the twanging guitar of Duane Eddy roll over him. In a few seconds, his mind drifted, back to the summer John turned sixteen, the summer all his problems seemed to come to a head.

It was hot, the worst July on record. The temperature and humidity index were the same, in the nineties. It had been one of those oppressive, muggy summer days, too miserable for anyone to be more than three feet from his or her air conditioning. Even the sky looked ominous, showing signs that a real whizbang thunderstorm might be in the works. Traynor parked his cruiser in front of the Epping State Police Barracks and walked inside. His uniform stuck to his back, soaked with sweat, and the air conditioning felt good, cooling his torso. It had been one long son-of-a-bitch of a day. He had been patrolling Route 101 all day, trying to keep beach-bound drivers from killing themselves on what was, at that time, the most dangerous stretch of highway in the state. It reminded him of a locally popular country song about a stretch of road in northern Maine; the title was "A Tombstone Every Mile." He had never been on Route 2A through northern Maine's Haynesville Woods, but 101 could easily have served as a model for a song with the same title.

The traffic to Hampton Beach had been heavy all day, and he spent more time outside his air-conditioned cruiser than in it. He was hot, sweaty, and frustrated. The last thing he needed was a message from his father.

A summons from the old man could only mean one of a couple

things: either the old man needed help doing something at his house, or John had pulled some shit. He took the message, quickly read it, and then crumpled it into a ball and threw it across the room. Someone had perched a novelty backboard on the wastebasket and the paper bounced off it, ricocheted straight up in the air, and then dropped through the net—two points. Traynor walked to the drink machine and dropped in a couple of quarters. When the cold bottle dropped into the tray, he grabbed it, popped the cap, and drained half its contents in a single drink. As he swallowed, the carbonation made his eyes water. He stood beside the machine, waiting for the burning to ease. Belching silently, he walked into the office to file his end-of-shift reports.

Buck had worked the desk that day and was monitoring the two-way radios while trying to keep track of a Red Sox game with a small transistor radio. Traynor sat on the edge of the desk and asked, "Who's winning?"

"You mean at Fenway or on the highways and byways?"

"Either."

"The Sox are getting smacked around by the Orioles, 8–3, and the lawbreakers outnumber us ten thousand to one."

"It sounds like we got a better shot at winning than the Sox. Big Papi do anything today?"

"Two hits, a double off the monster and a homer to right field. He's responsible for all the Sox runs."

Traynor chugged down the last of the cola, released another silent belch, and stood up. "If it's quiet, I'll head home."

"You get your message?"

"Yeah, my old man only calls when he needs help around his house or John's in trouble."

"Someone is going to kill that kid someday."

"He does seem to run around asking for someone to kick his ass, doesn't he?"

Traynor decided to wait until he was home to call his father; the last thing he wanted to do was discuss private matters in front of other cops. He got home a half hour later and turned on the window air conditioner mounted in his living room. It sounded as if it would die from overwork as it tried to overcome the stifling heat. The unit was at least a million BTUs shy of being strong enough to cool the apartment. He walked into the bedroom, shedding his clothes as he crossed the room. Before he was ready to talk with the old man, he needed a long shower; he felt like a bucket of overheated guts and probably smelled like one as well. He was so miserable he did not think he could have smiled if someone offered him a free lobster lunch. He turned into the bathroom and stopped before the shower, adjusting the water so it was warm, rather than his usual blistering hot, and stood under the stinging spray, hoping it would wash the sweat away and alleviate the heat that blasted from his body.

He braced an arm against the wall and stood there until the water beating on his skin felt uncomfortable and he was as clean as he was going to be, even though he didn't feel any fresher.

Before he finished toweling off, he was sweating again; he cursed at the undersized air conditioner as if it was to blame for being too small and pulled on a pair of shorts. He knew he was procrastinating and that he had run out of excuses for not calling his father. He opened a cold beer, took a long drink, and then dialed his parents' home. While listening to the phone ring, he made up his mind not to let the old man talk him into getting involved in raising his screwed-up younger brother. His mother answered the phone. As soon as she said, "Hello?" he knew she'd had too many drinks, which was, unfortunately, a common occurrence.

"Ma, it's Ed."

The dam burst and she started crying. "Eddie, what are we going to do?"

"I don't know, Ma. You haven't told me what's wrong yet."

"The police arrested Johnny. They say he tried to rob a convenience store."

He felt his face heat; this time it was from anger, not the weather. All he needed was for word to get out that local cops had arrested his kid brother on a robbery charge. He was so busy visualizing their taunts and jokes that he did not hear what his mother had said and was forced to ask her to repeat part of it. "When did he do this?"

"Last night."

"Why did you wait so long to call me?"

"Your father thought he could deal with it. He didn't want to get you involved if it was something he could handle—it isn't."

"Have you called a lawyer?"

She hesitated. "Called a lawyer? No, we haven't, surely it won't go that far."

"Ma, if they've arrested him for robbery, it's not kid stuff any longer—this time it's serious." He held the phone against his ear with his shoulder and grabbed a pencil and paper. "Where are they holding him?"

"Portsmouth . . . the city police have him."

"All right, Ma, I'm going to hang up now and see what I can find out. Are you okay?"

She said something about his father, but he was already in take-action mode and didn't catch all of it. He told her he would call back as soon as he knew something, and hung up.

He called Ken Brissette, a friend on the Portsmouth PD, and got him on the third try. "Ken? Ed Traynor. How are you doing?"

"I'm okay. I suppose you're calling about your kid brother?"

"Yeah, I heard you guys were holding him."

"We are. They picked him up about two-thirty this morning. This time it's major league, Ed. He was arrested for armed robbery. If I had known he was in here, I would have called you, but I didn't find out until I came to work this afternoon."

"How bad is it? They shoot anyone?"

"No casualties, but the storeowner is raising hell. He wants both of them to go away for a long time."

"Both . . . who was with him?"

"A real douchebag, name of Benny Ryan; he's got a rap sheet. They tried to take down an all-night convenience store on Woodbury Avenue. Stupid if you ask me; the place couldn't have had more than a few hundred bucks."

"Can I see him?"

"Well, they got him on ice but if you get here within the next half hour, I can probably let you have a few minutes."

"I'm on my way."

He made another call, this time to Burt Healy. Burt was one of the best criminal lawyers north of Boston. He and Traynor had been on the opposite side of the fence on more than a few occasions, but they realized that each was only doing his job and they remained friends. He located him at home and filled him in on the particulars, at least as much as he knew. Healy said he would get down to the jail within the next couple of hours. Traynor thanked him and hung up.

He changed into a pair of slacks and a golf shirt, got into his personal vehicle, and drove into Portsmouth. The car was like an oven, and he cursed John for making him go out into the heat again. The Ford had what he called four-seventy air conditioning—all four windows down and drive seventy miles an hour. The speed limit was only fifty-five, so he never got up enough speed for the AC to really kick in. Even with the windows down, he was miserable; the air racing through the car was blistering, and he felt as if he were sitting in front of a blasting heat duct. By the time he got to Portsmouth, he was sopping wet again. He thought about the overmatched window unit in his apartment. If the place did not cool down by the time he got home, he was going to sleep out on the deck that hung over the parking lot. If he was not irritable enough, the thought of paying four-fifty a month in rent to sleep outdoors really pissed him off.

He parked on the street and walked around to the back of the building. Ken met him at the back door. "Hey, man, hot enough for you?"

"If I got any hotter, Smokey the Bear would throw a bucket of water on me."

Ken laughed and led him inside. When he walked into the air-conditioned jail, he felt like he had jumped into the Arctic Ocean. He shivered but thought it felt damned good. He was tempted to ask if they had an empty cell where he could spend the night.

Ken said, "I can only give you about fifteen minutes, Ed. As it is, when the chief finds out I let you in, he'll probably chew on my ass for an hour."

"I'll handle the chief if you'd like."

Ken looked nervous at the prospect of Traynor talking with his former boss. He tried to be tactful and said, "I'd just as soon you didn't."

"He's still pissed because I jumped over to the state police?"

"Yeah, I don't know if he'll ever forgive you. He had high hopes for you."

"Okay, I'll stay away from him if you want. Listen, I called Burt Healy."

"I'll get him right in."

"Thanks."

Ken led him into the familiar bowels of the police station and turned toward the confinement unit. All the cells appeared empty and it was deathly quiet; so quiet that it was eerie. It was a Saturday night and the cellblock, which should have been full of cursing and complaining drunks and addicts, was empty. On this night, it looked as if John had the entire block to himself. Ken opened a cell and stepped aside for him to enter. "Because of his age, we didn't want him in with the usual weekend crowd. We cleaned all the drunks and rabble out of this cellblock. Put them on the other side."

Traynor nodded. He understood that isolating John had nothing to do with him. The last thing the police wanted was Burt Healy screaming at them for putting a minor in with the general population. Traynor had mixed feelings about it. He wondered if maybe a dose of the usual clientele might not scare the shit out of John and be beneficial. However, knowing John, it probably wouldn't have the desired effect. Traynor walked inside the cell.

John sat on the upper half of his bunk and was as far back into the corner as he could get. Ed stood by the door as Ken closed and locked it behind him. It was hard to see John's face in the dark, but his eyes reflected the ambient light, illuminated, and glowed. As Ed approached, he saw a look on his brother's face with which he was familiar. He had seen it on many other faces, a mixture of fear, anger, and defiance. "You okay?" he asked.

John did not answer. His feet made a pedaling motion on the bunk's single wool blanket as he tried to retreat yet farther into his corner.

Ed sat on the foot of the cot. John stared at him and it was obvious that he was struggling not to cry. Ed tried to get him to talk. "John, I'm here to help."

His younger brother snorted in derision. "There's fat fucking chance of that." Ed was surprised at the anger and bitterness of his words.

"I called a lawyer for you."

"You called a lawyer? You mean the state cop couldn't pull a few fucking strings?"

John was scared and fear made him insolent as he lashed out at the very things he hoped would happen. Still, his attitude was getting under Ed's skin. "Do you have any idea how much goddamned trouble you're in? What are you, fifteen?"

"Sixteen, as if you give a damn!"

"John, you used a gun to commit a felony! They can try you as an adult. We're talking prison time here! They aren't going to take you home for the old man to strap—those days ended forever the minute you walked into that store with a gun. You moved up to the big time!"

John jumped to his feet, getting as far away from his older brother as the cell would allow. "So what?"

"I can't help you this time."

He snorted again; it sounded like a bull grunting. "When have you ever helped me before?"

Ed wanted to tell him just how many times he had helped him without his knowing it. Every cop between Portsmouth and Manchester knew John was Ed's brother and, rather than bust him, they either looked the other way or took him home. Suddenly, it dawned on Ed that by letting him slide by with those minor infractions they had inadvertently helped put him in this cell.

"All right, I didn't come here to fight with you. Tell me what happened."

"There ain't nothing to tell. Me and Benny needed some cash and he had a thirty-eight . . . so we decided to rob a store."

"Who used the gun?"

"Benny."

"I was told you were caught holding the gun."

"I didn't have it in the store—Benny did. . . . I didn't touch it until we were outside."

"That may help." Ed stood and paced the cell, idly looking at the empty cells. "Where's this Benny now?"

"I don't know, I haven't seen him since this morning. I guess he got a lawyer to spring him."

"Some friend this Benny is, he gets sprung and leaves you here alone."

"He does as much for me as anybody."

It took all of Ed's willpower to keep from smacking him in the mouth. If he had, it would have cost him his badge. In this cell, John was not his brother, he was an inmate, and Ed was a law enforcement officer, not his brother. If he were to hit him, it would not be two siblings having a squabble, not to the courts—to them it would be police brutality.

Still, Ed's anger took over and he spun on John, pushing him against the wall. His face was within an inch of his brother's and they glared into each other's eyes. Up close, Ed could clearly see the fear John was trying so hard to mask. He decided that it was time to take off the kid gloves and tell him how things were. "All right, little brother, you seem to feel that you've always been on your own, so let me give you some advice. In a few minutes, a friend of mine, who also happens to be a damn good criminal lawyer, will be coming down here. If you're smart, and right now that's very questionable, you'll knock the shit off and act like the scared little boy you are! If you go before a judge with that chip on your shoulder, he's going to ram the law up your ass like it was a flaming dildo! Right now, you're still a first-time offender and they may be lenient. But, if you go into a courtroom acting like a street punk, they'll fuck you so bad it'll take years for you to get un-fucked! Do you understand what I'm telling you? You think you're pretty goddamned tough, well you're lucky; if this cellblock was filled with its usual Saturday night crowd you'd find out you're nowhere near tough enough to survive in jail."

He heard the door to the cell open and released John. He stepped back and saw Ken standing near the cell. Ed felt his face flush. He had no idea how long Ken had been standing there or how much he had heard. Ken looked slightly nervous when he said, "His lawyer's here."

Ed nodded and turned back to John. "You'd better think about what I just told you." He spun on his heel and stomped to the cell's door. "Let me the fuck out of here."

While walking out of the cellblock, Ed asked, "Is the other perp still in custody?"

"Yeah, but he's got priors and is over eighteen so he's in with the general population. Why do you ask?"

"The kid thinks that . . . what's the guy's name?"

"Ryan, Benny Ryan."

"The kid thinks that Ryan made bail . . ."

"You tell him that can't happen until they appear before a judge?"

Traynor grinned. "Nope, it'll do him good to stew over it for a while."

He walked into the waiting area and saw his father. The old man's body language told him all he needed to know about what his father's day had been like. He was both drunk and at wit's end. He was talking to Burt Healy and his head hung dejectedly. The air was ripe with his whiskey breath.

Burt saw Traynor and motioned for him to come over. "You see him?" he asked.

"Yeah."

"Is he all right?" Traynor's father asked. Years of hard work and equally hard drinking had left a bulbous nose full of broken capillaries and deep crevasses in his face.

"Yeah. He's scared and doesn't want it to show and he's trying to act as if he doesn't care what happens to him." He directed his next statement to Burt. "He did it. He told me he and this Benny Ryan robbed the store. Benny had the gun, and John never touched it until after the robbery. At least that's what he says."

"What's his record like?" Burt asked.

"He's been in a few scrapes, nothing serious, kid stuff. The cops knew he was my brother so they'd bring him home rather than bust him. His record with juvenile is clean."

"I'll shoot for first-time offender, probation. Worst case, he might do some time in a juvie center."

"Are you going to plea him?"

"I don't know. I'm going to play on how long they've had him without letting him contact an attorney." He turned to Ed's father. "Mr. Traynor, when did the police first call you?"

At first, Ed's father seemed bewildered by the question. He was so drunk that he swayed on his feet. "I got the call this morning, around five."

"And he had been in custody since when . . . two-thirty or three o'clock?"

Ed's father thought for a few seconds, obviously trying to remember through his drunken haze. Finally, he nodded. "Guess so . . ."

"That's not too bad. What did you do when they called?"

The old man shuffled again and Traynor knew he was not so drunk that he wasn't ashamed of something, even if he had no reason to be.

"Well, Johnny has been putting us through a lot lately. His mother is a nervous wreck because of him. When the police called, I told them, 'He got his ass in jail without my help; let him get his ass out without it!' His mother talked me into calling Eddie. I was too damned mad to come down here, until later."

Traynor knew that too drunk was the more likely reason, but he kept quiet. The old man had enough on his mind without him unleashing his suspicions and resentment.

"Okay," Burt said, "I want you two out of here. Most likely, I won't be able to bail him until Monday." He turned to Ed. "Is he safe in there?"

"Yeah, they got him by himself. They're probably unsure of his status as a juvenile."

"Good, I'll talk with him." He turned to the father. "Mr. Traynor, I'll call you as soon as I know when his preliminary hearing will be."

Ed and his father walked outside, and the old man turned toward the parking lot. "Come on," Ed said, "I'll drop you off. I was going to stop by anyhow."

"I got my car."

"Let it stay here. The last thing we need now is for you to get stopped and arrested on an OUI charge."

"I ain't drunk. I only had a few."

"Dad, knock off the bullshit, okay? This isn't the time for us to debate your state of sobriety." They glared at each other across the hood of Ed's car. "Now get in the goddamned car," Ed ordered.

The old man said nothing the entire ride home. Ed left him alone because he knew what was going through his mind; he was having the same thoughts. Where had it gone wrong? How had he failed John? He knew that if John were to spend even a minute behind bars in either a state prison or a juvenile detention center he could be lost forever. Nothing good ever came out of those places. If anything, he'd come out with a degree from the New Hampshire campus of Crime University. For the first time, Ed noticed how old and frail his old man had become.

Late Sunday afternoon, Burt Healy called and told Traynor that the arraignment was set for Monday morning. Ed got to the courthouse a few minutes before John's arraignment. When he saw who the judge was, he knew John was going to have a rough go. Judge Barbara Wingate had a reputation for being fair, but she was tough, possibly the sternest adjudicator in the court system. If you copped an attitude with her, she'd drop the hammer, crushing you like a bug.

Burt did everything in his power to keep John from dealing one-on-one with Judge Wingate, but it was not good enough. John still found a way to shoot himself in the foot. His surly, give-a-shit attitude as he sat beside his defense lawyer was evident to everyone in the courtroom, especially the judge.

Judge Wingate wasted no time on Benny Ryan, remanding him for trial. He copped a plea and wound up serving five to ten in Concord; with good behavior, he could be back on the street in two to two and a half years. Once the bailiff led Benny away, the judge turned her attention to John, and his attitude really came across. She ripped into him. "John Traynor, young men like you completely baffle me. Your parents and brother have done everything in their power to make you see the dangers of the path you've chosen, yet you persist in getting into trouble."

It was obvious to Ed that she didn't know their parents. If she had there was no way in hell she would have said that.

"It is the opinion of this court that you have gone beyond the point where parental discipline is capable of controlling you. I'm afraid it's time for the state to step in. I can only hope there's still time for you to straighten up and turn your life around." She shuffled some papers on the bench.

"I have taken into consideration the fact you have entered a plea of guilty. Nevertheless, the severity of the charges against you is such that I would be justified in giving you the same prison sentence as your partner, Mr. Ryan. However, this is your first offense and you are still a minor. Therefore, it is the ruling of this court to remand you to the juvenile authorities. You will remain under the supervision of the State of New Hampshire Juvenile Detention Center until such time as the state feels you are fit to be returned to society or reach the age of majority." She slammed her gavel down and adjourned court.

Ed's mother and father clung to each other, crying as the bailiff took John away in handcuffs and ankle chains. Not once during the entire hearing had John looked at them and, as he shuffled by on his way to the paddy wagon, he continued to ignore his family. Ed saw him smirk as he passed. All he could do was shake his head and curse. The judge had actually given him a longer sentence than Ryan. The juvenile authorities could keep John until he was twenty-one and then, if they deemed him as not been rehabilitated, send him to a state prison; regardless, he would likely spend more time in detention than Ryan, who was an adult offender with multiple offenses on his record.

———

John had remained in the detention center until he turned nineteen, by which time, any hope that he would turn his life around was gone. In no time, he had aligned himself with a bunch of drug dealers and hard-core thugs, who proceeded to school him on the skills of their trade. Three years later, the scared kid who walked inside that teenybopper jail came out a hardened criminal.

Their parents never got over it either: their father died a year after the judge sent John away, his overworked liver finally giving out. Their mother lasted a couple of years after that, but she too passed on feeling as if she had somehow failed. With John in a reformatory and her husband dead, she felt she had no reason to go on and, one night in her sleep, she just went away.

―――――――――

When Traynor woke up, Duane Eddy had ceased twanging, and the Doors were playing. Traynor stared into the darkness, fighting against a deep sense of despair. He had no idea how long he laid like that. He turned onto his side and drifted back to sleep.

24

When he woke up, Traynor was stiff from sleeping on the couch, and the stereo was still playing. He looked at the clock; it was three in the morning. The light on his answering machine flashed, and he pushed the playback button. A woman, he was certain that it was Gisela Martin, spoke quickly. "You want to know who did your brother. You come to the old mill in South Lawrence, by the river, tonight, eleven o'clock." The line dropped. Traynor played the message a second time to be sure he heard it right. The machine was an old one that used cassettes; he took out the tape so nothing would happen to it, walked to the bedroom, and flopped on his bed.

He must have drunk more liquor than he thought. Usually, when he woke up in the middle of the night it took a while for him to get back to sleep, but this time it did not—he went under like a dinghy in high seas.

Traynor groaned as he sat up; his ribs still ached, and his thigh throbbed where Max had performed emergency surgery with his hunting knife. He could taste last night's sour mash, and his breath was so ripe that it could strip paint from an army tank. He scrubbed his teeth with a tooth-brush for five minutes, taking it on faith that it helped. A hot shower got him feeling half-human again. He walked into the living room and saw that the phone was still unhooked. He plugged it back into the rear of the answering machine and almost immediately, it rang. The sharp tone of the ringer was like someone shoving a spike through his ears and into his brain. He snatched it off the cradle. It was Susan.

"Do you have any idea what time it is?" When she was angry, Susan was slightly more subtle then a kick to the groin.

He glanced at the digital display on the phone. "Yeah, it's a little after ten."

"I've been calling you since eight-thirty."

"I had the phone unplugged."

She did not say anything, but he could visualize the gears turning in her head. "Are you okay?" Concern took over, cooling her anger.

"I had a long talk with Maker's Mark last night."

"Oh, so you had another one of those nights?" Susan knew his moods and was familiar with his habit of isolating in a dark room with a bottle when he wanted to lower his defenses and deal with something that could be hazardous to his emotional well-being. "Let me guess—lights out, whiskey, and oldies music?"

"You got it."

"Did our talk the other night trigger this?"

"It might have been part of it. This has been building for a while. I needed to do it."

"I know that. For years, you've been carrying John's monkey on your back. It's way past the time when you should hand it back to him."

"It's a bit late, isn't it?"

"No, you aren't giving it to John so much as you're getting it off your back. Think about it a while and it'll begin to make sense. Trust me on this, okay?"

"I will."

"Are you stopping by the office?"

"Do you need me to?"

"Yes, I got a check from NEML and a note thanking you for the great job you did on the Billy Cartwright case."

"Can't you just deposit it?"

She was quiet, and he finally caught on. Of course, she could stamp the check and deposit it if she wanted to. The check was just her excuse to have him stop by so she could look him over. Traynor realized that he would most likely never be able to predict how women operate in any given situation or get used to having someone around who cared about him.

"I'll be there within the hour. Don't go to lunch, it's on me."

"Okay. Oh, we may have a new client."

"That's good."

"Well I don't know if it's our kind of case."

"What do you mean?"

"I'll tell you more when you get in. But it deals with an angry wife, a philandering husband, and a tube of superglue."

A picture immediately came to his mind. "You don't mean . . . no, she didn't?"

Susan laughed. "Yup, she glued it to the top of his leg. She wants us to find the object of his wandering. I guess she's filing for divorce and wants to really cook his goose."

After hanging up with Susan, Traynor called Charley to find out if he'd learned anything new from the journal.

"Charley, Ed."

"I was just about to call you. There's some interesting shit in that journal you dropped off."

"Enlighten me."

"First of all, it's a really simple code, but still a code. I gave it to a friend of mine who's a retired army cryptographer. It took him a couple of hours to break it. There's enough in this to bring down the entire drug organization in New England. But what was most interesting was the crude map in the back."

"What about it?"

"This is just a guess, but it seems to be a map of a landfill in Massachusetts. More to the point, it's where the bodies are buried. . . ."

"You're kidding me."

"I shit you not. If the DEA gets ahold of this they can put the Escobars and half the dealers in New England in jail cells so deep they'd need a generator to see daylight. Anytime you want it you can come get the book."

The implications of what he'd just learned rocked Traynor. If the contents of the journal were as potentially devastating as Charley had said, the journal alone was more than enough motivation for the Escobars to have killed John. It was also more than enough reason for them to take similar action against anyone who was in possession of it.

Traynor spent the rest of the day in the office, catching up on paperwork, and reassuring Susan that he was, in fact, okay.

Traynor got to Jillian's apartment a little after six in the evening. The girls met him at the door and were so excited about something that they were literally running in place. They swarmed around him both chattering at once until he quieted them by raising his hands and saying, "Whoa! Whoa! Let's calm down so I can hear what's happening."

Carrie took the initiative and hushed her sister. "We're going on a sleepover." She announced it with such enthusiasm one would have thought it was some wonderful adventure.

"Oh, when are you doing that?"

"Tonight."

He glanced over her head and his eyes met Jillian's. He gave her a quizzical look; she smiled at him, and said, "All right, girls, let's finish getting your things together. Your Aunt Carla will be here in fifteen minutes."

She turned to him and in a soft, inviting voice said, "I'll only be a few minutes, Ed. Make yourself comfortable. Oh, I hope you don't mind, but I thought that maybe we could go out for dinner."

"That'll be fine."

While they busied themselves with preparations for a night with Jillian's best friend, known as Aunt Carla to the girls, Traynor sat in the living room wistfully trying to come to grips with the reality of their imminent departure from his life. He knew that he was being overly dramatic. Jillian would stay in touch, either by phone or by letter, and he could see them on vacations and such. However, she and the girls would no longer be available whenever he wanted to see them. If Traynor was anything, he was a realist and knew that over time, they would drift apart until they became strangers to one another. As hard as he tried, he couldn't shake the depression that threatened to turn him into an empty shell. He listened to the girls arguing as they bantered with their mother and felt his anger at John return. He had had no right to screw with people's lives this way. Traynor wondered if he would ever stop being mad at his brother.

Jillian came in and flopped beside him on the couch. She leaned against his arm and rested her head on his shoulder. Without a thought, he put his arm around her shoulders. Jill snuggled against him and said, "You must be thinking. I smell wood burning." The use of one of his father's favorite phrases surprised him. "Is John's death still eating at you?"

"That's one thing."

She gave him a questioning look. "Only one?"

"The other thing is you. Don't leave, Jill. For the first time in my life, I feel as if there's hope for us. If you go away, I'm not sure I'll be able to handle the loneliness. I don't expect you to marry me, but I need you and the girls in my life."

She kissed him softly on the lips, but before she could respond, the girls called for her to come to the bedroom. She stood and smiled at him. "We'll talk after dinner."

Dinner was uneventful and the restaurant crowded. They idled away the meal with small talk, both of them obviously hesitant to breach the topic that was really on their minds. He became determined not to be the one to bring it up first.

They returned to the apartment around eight and Jillian dropped her coat on a chair and asked, "Want a beer?"

"Sure."

She returned in a matter of seconds and sat beside him on the couch. She placed two beers on the coffee table and turned to face him. Her breast brushed against his arm and he felt a surge of desire, but rather than excite him, it made him feel guilty.

"So," he said, "have you made up your mind about when you're leaving?"

"I'm not leaving, Eddie. I realized on Cannon Mountain that I want you in my life and the girls' lives. I believe that if anyone can keep us safe, it's you. When I tell the girls about their father it's going to be hard on them . . . to take you out of their life too, could prove to be catastrophic. For most of their lives you've been their only positive male role model. But, I think we need to take this one day at a time and see each other until we iron out our feelings."

Guilt became the furthest thing from his mind. He pulled her closer and kissed her and felt her respond. He was overwhelmed with emotion, felt the warmth of love, and found himself wishing someone had killed John years ago. As quickly as the thought entered his mind, the burn of guilt returned.

He released her and stood up. Traynor realized that if he stayed any longer, things could easily get out of hand and neither of them was ready for that.

"I should leave," he said.

"Ed, I was hoping that you'd stay—"

He placed a finger across her lips. "I can't, Babe, not yet. Not until I bring down John's killer."

She paled. "Do you know who it is?"

"No, but I'm closing in. I have a meet in Lawrence at eleven."

"A meet?"

"I got an anonymous call at three this morning. The caller said that if I want to find John's killer to be in Lawrence at eleven tonight."

"But—"

"Jill, it's too soon. As much as I would love to stay here and make love to you all night, I can't—not yet, not this way."

"I understand."

"Do you really? Honestly, this has nothing to do with you. It's about me, about family responsibility."

"Yes, I do understand. You go do what you have to." She gave him a nervous look and smiled. "But be careful. No more getting beat up in parking lots."

He grinned. "I swear to you, Hon, that isn't one of my favorite things either."

"I'm holding you to your promise."

He told her about the book he had found at Benny Ryan's and asked her, "Have you ever seen anything like that?"

"No, do you think it was John's?"

"I'm not sure, but it may be a big part of the reason for his murder." Suddenly, he was tired. Fatigued not only from the day, but also by the emotional merry-go-round he had been riding since he bent over John's body on that wooded lane.

She sat quiet, listening to him. After a few minutes, she said, "I can't believe a book is important enough to . . ." She glanced around the room, hesitant to continue. ". . . kill someone over."

"I know I've said this before, but if you remember anything that John may have said about it, please call."

Jillian stepped toward him and he took her into his arms again. She turned her face up and they kissed.

"It's going to work out, Eddie. I just know it."

"We'll make it work, Jill. However, before we can do anything, I need to catch John's killer. Once that's behind us, we can think about us. I promise."

They kissed again and then she took him by the shoulders and turned him toward the door. "Now get out of here before we do something foolish."

25

The storm had turned nasty, a murderous mixture of snow, sleet, and freezing rain. It was miserable, and every road into Massachusetts was a mess. The caller had said nothing about his coming alone, so Traynor brought Max with him. They were both packing hardware, which was risky. Possession of a firearm without a Massachusetts Firearms Owner Identification Card carried a minimum year in jail plus a fine. Traynor was a licensed investigator in New Hampshire and as such had a permit to carry a concealed weapon. However, there was no guarantee the locals would accept either in the Bay State. Nevertheless, for all Traynor knew they were walking into a potential gunfight and he wanted them to be ready.

The storm was another good reason to bring Max along. It was the type of weather where it was nice to be in the large four-wheel-drive Excursion. His Taurus would have been sliding all over on the slick pavement.

"How much trouble are you expecting?" Max asked.

"I don't know. Nevertheless, it's best that we follow the rules of a gunfight."

"There are rules for a gunfight?"

"There are twenty-three to be exact. However, rules one and two are the most important. Rule number one states: bring a gun. In fact, bring at least two and one of them should be a long gun."

"And rule number two is?"

"That's where you come in. Rule number two is: bring all your friends and all their guns."

As they pulled off the interstate and turned toward Lawrence, Traynor took out the forty-four magnum revolver he had brought. Max looked at him and said, "That's some serious hardware. What happened to your nine-millimeter?"

"Rule number twenty-two: Do not attend a gunfight with a handgun whose caliber does not begin with a four. Nine-millimeters are just under a thirty-six caliber—not enough gun. Forty-four caliber turns out to be between eleven and twelve millimeters."

Max shook his head as they turned off the road and entered a huge vacant parking lot. Max parked about a hundred yards from the old ruin, and they sat in the truck and watched the sleet pound against the windshield, reluctant to step out into the cold. "This isn't getting it done; we better check this out," Traynor said. Max nodded. Traynor smiled; there were times when Max was as loquacious as a corpse. Max reached under the seat and pulled out the largest handgun Traynor had ever seen. It made his magnum look tiny. "What in hell is that—a cannon?"

Max grinned. "It's a Smith and Wesson Model 500. You might call it a fifty magnum . . . it meets the requirement of rule twenty-two."

"Must kick like a mule."

"Actually, it has less recoil than that forty-four you're packing."

They sat and watched the sleet pound against the windshield. Traynor did not know what went through Max's mind, but he hoped he would talk him into staying in the warm, dry vehicle a little longer. However, Max turned off the motor and exited the large SUV. Ed realized that he had no alternative but to follow and left the warmth and sanctuary of the Excursion. When he opened the door and stepped out, the full force of the rain, snow, and sleet mix slammed into him. Traynor was still wearing the clothing he had worn to take Jill to dinner and when he stepped into ankle-deep slush he cursed as icy water filled his shoes. A chill ran through him. More than anything else he could think of, there was nothing he hated more than having cold, wet feet.

He heard Max sloshing through the semi-frozen mash beside him. When he glanced to his left, he saw that Max was not any happier with the weather conditions than he was. He resisted the impulse to hunch his shoulders against the elements and made a conscious effort to keep his head up as they walked across the old parking lot, scanning the area for signs of ambush.

Its original owners had abandoned the mill over twenty years ago, letting it fall into disrepair. Its current condition was so bad that its only function was to provide inadequate shelter for drug addicts and the homeless. It had burnt at least twice, the fires most likely set by indigent residents trying to stay warm. It had all the aesthetics of the bombed-out buildings shown in old newsreels of Europe during the World War II blitz. The parking area was a maze of deep potholes and made walking slow and treacherous. If the craters in the asphalt had not made conditions dangerous enough, the thin layer of freezing water made the pavement more slippery. Max and Traynor walked like a couple of cows crossing a frozen pond. Though it seemed like an hour, it only took them a few minutes to reach an opening in the brick wall. They paused before entering and saw that the interior was so dark that Traynor wondered if they would ever find a path through the debris. "I'll be back," Max said, doing his best Schwarzenegger imitation.

"Four million comedians out of work and who do I get? Max Schwarzenegger."

In moments, Max was back at Traynor's side holding two flashlights. "Take this," he said.

Traynor took the light, switched it on, aimed the beam inside the derelict factory, and then stepped inside. As decrepit as the building looked from the outside, the inside was worse. Traynor shined his flashlight around, inspecting the room before them. Droplets of water flashed through the light beam as they fell from the ceiling. Off to one side lay a black spot left by a campfire, and dry human feces littered another corner. The pungent odor of burnt wood mixed with human waste was cutting. Fallen timbers and refuse filled the main floor. If anyone wanted to set up an ambush, it was an ideal location. Using the flashlight was risky. However, when he saw the maze they would have to navigate, Traynor knew it was a better alternative than stumbling around in the dark.

Dead, stubby stalks of large unidentified weeds poked through cracks in the concrete floor and, in the lamp's harsh light, looked like stunted trees. The sickly plants were evidence that Mother Nature was working hard to turn the destruction man had left into something she could recognize.

Traynor entered first. Inside the ruin, progress was no easier than it was in the frozen parking area outside. The floor was reminiscent of a World War I no-man's-land; only rather than hidden explosives and booby traps, they had to watch for deep holes and fissures created when the concrete superheated and split during the fires. The potential for twisting or breaking an ankle was a detriment to rapid movement through the rubble. Like two infantrymen feeling their way across a minefield, they moved deeper into the labyrinth.

Traynor motioned for Max to watch the left while he observed the right. He saw loathsome, filthy objects eerily suspended in the layer of sooty ice covering the deck. He knew the scummy half-frozen water and dirt that coated the ice was wreaking havoc on his shoes and made a mental note to throw them out as soon as he got home. Traynor mused that the thoughts that run through one's mind during stressful situations are often strangely mundane.

"Not exactly a place I'd pick for a meeting," Max whispered.

Traynor glanced at his watch, tilting the face so he could read the hands. "It does seem to be lacking in amenities. We're early. Let's check this dump out. I want to be sure we're alone. If this place is clean we'll meet them in the parking lot."

"One thing this place will never be is clean."

The wind gusted, driving sleet through the busted windows. They came to an old, dark stairway running along the back wall. Traynor waited as Max worked his way around the other side and joined him. "Something ain't right here," he said. He was not sure Max heard him. Dripping water and wind all but drowned out any attempt at normal conversation. It was not until he saw Max's quizzical look that Traynor realized he felt the same way. Traynor didn't know why he felt that he had to elaborate, but he did. Maybe it was Max's reluctance to speak.

"In weather like this there should be street people in here. As bad as this place is, it's better than spending the night outside," Traynor said.

Freezing rain plastered Max's long hair to his head and dark smudges of carbon streaked across his face, making him look like some water-borne ogre rising to the surface. Traynor thought that if he had not come there with him, Max would have scared the crap out of him. "You go down and I'll go up," Max said.

As Traynor slowly climbed down the stairs, he kept one hand on the old metal banister so he wouldn't slip on the ice that coated the concrete steps. At the bottom of the stairs, he found a solid metal door and shined the flashlight on it. What the harsh glare revealed baffled him. The door was new, obviously installed after the fires. He was curious about what could be in such a dump that warranted this much protection. He studied the door and saw that it was secured with a shiny new padlock. He retreated up the stairs and waited for Max. When he saw him descending the stairs, he motioned to him.

Max pointed over his shoulder with his thumb, toward the top of the stairs. "Nothing up there but the sky."

"You got a set of bolt cutters?" Traynor asked.

"Yeah, out in the truck. Why?" Max looked curious.

"Go get them. There's a heavy security door down there with a new padlock on it. What do you suppose someone would lock up in a ruin like this?"

Traynor stayed put while Max went to the truck. The building was getting to him. Every time the wind gusted, the broken timbers and hanging rafters swayed in the wind like sea grass moving in a riptide. Rubble clanged as it beat together, and creaking wood made it sound as if the building was about to fall in. Sleet hit the walls, sounding like millions of shotgun pellets chattering on the broken glass and old brick. He heard something scratching in the corner and turned toward it, directing the light into the corner. A pair of angry ruby-red dots reflected the beam. He moved the beam slightly and could see into the shadows behind the red spots. The dark shape moved and the biggest sewer rat he had ever encountered revealed itself. The situation definitely lent itself to exaggeration, but he would later swear it was as big as a barnyard cat. It scrambled toward the rear of the building, in the direction of the nearby Merrimack River, and disappeared into the safety of the night. Ed gladly let it go about its business.

It seemed like forever before Max finally returned carrying a pair of long-handled bolt cutters, and they went down to the security door. Once again, something struck him as being strange. The cement around the bottom of the stairs was dry and this level was sheltered from the wind, a perfect haven for the homeless, yet it was empty of any signs of their presence. Whatever was behind the door might explain why the homeless were not staying here.

Traynor stepped aside as Max cut the lock. He slowly pushed the door open, stepped inside, and swept his light around. He found a light switch next to the door and flipped it. The room lit up as bright as any modern factory floor. They found themselves standing in a very sophisticated and well-provisioned drug lab. The walls were lined with barrels of chemicals for use in refining and cutting drugs from their pure state to street.

Max whistled.

"No shit," Traynor said. "This place reminds me of the Escobar plant."

"How's that?"

"Nothing here is the way it looks."

Traynor spied another door in the far wall, marched over to it, and tried the knob. It was unlocked and he stepped into a smaller room. He wondered if whoever owned this place felt comfortable that the condition of the upper floors and the heavy steel door would be enough security. The room was rectangular and he estimated its dimensions were ten by twenty feet. Something in the far corner of the room caught his eye. He found yet another light switch, snapped it on, and jumped back in surprise, slamming into Max.

"What the fuck?" Max exclaimed.

A man's body, or what remained of one, was strapped to the top of what appeared to be a stone altar. Whoever he was, he had his chest cut open from his breastbone to his groin, a horrible way to die. Dried blood splatter covered the wall and floor like a horrific abstract painting, but what made it even more macabre was the mask of pain frozen on his face. What Traynor believed to be a human heart was on the floor beside the altar. Blood had pooled inside the chest cavity turning it into a human basin. However, Traynor didn't think the mutilation was what had killed him. His torturers had cut his throat so deeply that he had nearly been decapitated and then pulled his tongue through the jagged opening. Traynor turned his head away.

Max hissed through clenched teeth. "Jesus. I've heard of this, but I've never seen it."

"What are you talking about?"

"Look at his tongue. They call it a Colombian Necktie."

Traynor turned back to the body. *This is how John should have looked if the Escobar brothers had killed him.* He recalled the Derry bodies that he and Buck had found years ago and the similarities were obvious. "This," he said, "is Carlo Escobar's work."

He nudged Max and motioned for him to back out of the room. The last thing they needed to do was leave evidence of having been there. No sooner had they reentered the lab than they heard someone descending the stairs. Traynor pulled his handgun and faced the entrance. Max aimed his revolver in the same direction and stepped to the other side of the room. They waited for whoever approached.

"Mr. Traynor? I know you are armed; please do not shoot. I'm coming in." Gisela Martin stepped out of the darkness, followed by two hulking Hispanics with automatic weapons. She wore an unbuttoned and obviously expensive leather jacket, a tight blue skirt that accentuated her hips, and high boots which pulled Traynor's eyes to her legs. He caught himself and forced his eyes to concentrate on her face. She was accompanied by two tall, muscular men; each of them held a Glock pistol in one hand and a briefcase in the other.

Her appearance was too much of a coincidence for his taste. "So it *was* you who phoned," he said.

"Yes, Carlo asked me to deliver a message."

She opened her purse and took out a gold cigarette case. She offered the case to Traynor. "Would you like a cigarette?"

"No thanks, I gave it up years ago."

"A wise decision, it's truly a nasty habit." She took out a cigarette and lit it with her gold-plated lighter; even her addictions traveled first class. She inhaled the smoke and swept the lab with her eyes. She took in everything, missing nothing. "Very nice," she said. "I've never been down here before—I never would have expected anything this elaborate."

"It's obvious that great minds think alike," Traynor said. "Unless you're planning on a war, maybe we can all put our weapons down?"

She made a motion with her hand and the two goons lowered their weapons. Max and he did likewise. It was an uneasy truce and everyone kept their firearms in their hands—just in case.

Gisela walked along the lab benches. She trailed her finger across the surface, glanced at it like a military officer inspecting barracks for dust and smiled. "It's amazing. I had no idea Carlo was running an operation this sophisticated right up the street from us."

Traynor suppressed a smile. He doubted that she'd never before visited this drug lab—she was too high up in the Escobar organization to have been excluded. Now that he thought about it this place made perfect sense. Carlo was not stupid enough to process the drugs in his coffee processing plant.

The two bodyguards followed her every footstep. "What's back there?" she pointed to the door in the far wall.

Again Traynor believed she knew exactly what was there. Still he answered, "A body."

"A body?" She gave him the impression that finding bodies was an everyday occurrence for her.

"You might want to forego looking at him. It isn't pretty."

Gisela crossed the room, stepped around Traynor, and leaned into the door. For several seconds she studied the corpse. She showed no more concern than she would if she was inspecting a pound of ground beef at the supermarket. Still, Traynor could not help but note how beautiful she looked standing in that door, her arms folded as she smoked her cigarette. She stepped back from the door and snatched a tarp from a pile in the corner. She handed it to the bodyguards and spoke in rapid-fire Spanish. The only word Traynor understood was *cortar*, Spanish for cut. The two goons placed the briefcases by her feet and walked inside the torture chamber to, he assumed, take the body away.

Gisela stood beside the lab bench and said nothing as she finished her cigarette. The slit in the side of her skirt parted and exposed a shapely thigh. She studied Traynor through the spiraling cigarette smoke before jerking her thumb over her shoulder toward the small room. "It's Eduardo. I don't think you're capable of doing something like that. I assume you just found him?"

"I sure as hell didn't do it. I wouldn't do that to an animal, let alone a human being."

"It reminds me of an ancient ritual back in Colombia. The Mayans sacrificed humans, to the god Chac, by cutting them open and removing the heart while they were still alive."

"They cut their throats like that too?" Traynor asked.

"That," she said, "is a modern innovation." She dropped the cigarette to the floor and ground it out. "Mr. Traynor, Carlo has given me the duty of making you an offer."

"I heard he was out of the country. Is he back?"

Her snide smile told him that Escobar had never left; nevertheless, she espoused the company line. "I'm not at liberty to tell you that. I was told to tell you that he and Eduardo had nothing to do with your brother's unfortunate accident. It would have been bad business for them to eliminate the only person who might know where their money is."

"So I've been told—by both Carlo and you. I will admit that makes perfect sense to me—enough so that I actually believe you. You could have told me that over the phone."

"Carlo is a man of the old world; he prefers face-to-face communication."

"Oh, then why isn't he here?"

"Surely you wouldn't expect your superiors to be messengers. He gave the job to me, it's part of what I do for him."

"So it's just another of your many duties as his Director of Special Projects?"

"Exactly, now let's get to the point, shall we?" She leaned back against the stainless-steel table, emphasizing her full bust. "As we discussed, a large amount of money has disappeared. Your brother was one of several people we suspect of knowing about that money's whereabouts."

"Well, Ms. Martin, so far you haven't told me anything I didn't know. Do you have knowledge of who it was helping him?"

"No. If we did, I doubt Carlo would be looking to make a deal with you."

"What you say we cut to the chase and you tell me what Carlo wants?"

"I thought it was evident? He knows your reputation as an investigator and wants to hire you to find his money."

"You can tell Carlo no deal. I won't work for him. I could give a damn about the money. I want my brother's killer. If I find the money in the process, so be it. I assure you if that should happen, I'll contact Carlo and make whatever arrangements are necessary to turn it over to him. I want no part of money earned from other people's misery."

"I've been instructed to offer you a 10 percent fee—which is the real reason that we are meeting in person. Should you accept Carlo's offer, I am prepared to pay you half of the money right now . . . right here."

Traynor noted that each of the thugs held a briefcase. That stopped him. If the missing money were truly in the range of three million dollars, he'd earn something in the neighborhood of three hundred thousand— and that was a nice neighborhood to be in. It was very tempting. He surprised himself when he said, "Tell Carlo to use the money for a nice funeral for his brother."

She lit another cigarette. "You won't reconsider?"

"No, I got enough on my conscience without taking your boss's blood money. You tell him if I come across his cash, I'll call him."

She walked to the door and turned back to him. "I hope you know who you're dealing with. We are not minor criminals from *Cow* Hampshire. This affair is much bigger than you know."

"Oh, I know how big it is. If I had any doubts . . ." he pointed over his shoulder toward the back room with his thumb, "finding that took them away."

The two goons came out of the room with Eduardo wrapped in the white tarp. They paused for a second as if waiting for instructions. When Gisela stepped aside and nodded, they carried the body out of the lab. She ground the second cigarette out on the floor and said, "Carlo is not going to be happy about your answer."

"Well, you can tell Carlo that I'll put him at the top of my Christmas card list, if that'll make him feel better."

She wrapped her coat around her torso and said, "If you should discover Carlo's money and don't return it, I'm certain our next meeting will not be as cordial." She picked up the briefcases and followed her henchmen out of the lab.

Traynor waited until he heard their steps cease pounding on the steps. He and Max remained in place until the building went quiet. Max let out an explosive gust of breath. "I can't believe how much money you just turned down," he said.

"My reputation would never recover from taking that asshole's blood money."

"I never would have thought it was worth that much."

"What, finding John's killer?"

"Nope, your reputation. Three hundred K is a lot of dough."

"Let's get out of here."

They got to the parking lot in time to see Gisela get into a limo. They stayed close to the building as the car spun its tires on the parking lot, throwing a frigid mix of slushy snow and water from its rear tires. It fishtailed, then slowly gained traction and left the mill yard. Traynor was pleased to see she had enough good sense not to take the Viper out of the garage on a night like this.

Max watched the limo disappear and then said, "You know, you got to admire a woman who will ride in a limo with a mutilated body."

"I wouldn't be the least surprised to learn she did it to him."

Max looked at him to see if he was joking. He was not.

They got out of the driving sleet and into Max's truck. Max started the motor and they waited a few minutes for the defroster to warm them and to melt the ice from the windshield. Max shifted into gear and asked, "How long do you think it would take you to earn that much dough?"

"A long time, maybe twenty years—provided they're exceptional years."

Max slowly turned the truck around on the ice that had formed below the slush and crept out of the parking lot.

26

Monday morning started the same way the weekend ended. Traynor tuned in to a local radio station and listened to the weather. A cheery voice said, ". . .snow changing to freezing rain during the afternoon . . ." *Wonderful*, Traynor thought. The news broadcast was full of reports of accidents on every major highway. An eighteen-wheeler was jackknifed in the northbound lane of I-95; two cars were off the road on 101 and three more on I-93 south. Route 4 to Concord was a nightmare; overall, it was a typical winter day commute in the Boston suburbs.

By the time he walked into the office it was after ten and the forecast was accurate. The snow had already changed to freezing rain. The meteorologists had forecasted a break in the weather for that evening. Once the precipitation ended, it was going into the deep freeze—temperatures plummeting into the low twenties, with sustained wind speeds of up to twenty-five miles per hour along with gusts that could hit fifty miles per hour. Traynor wondered what it would be like to spend the holidays in a warm climate, some place like Buenos Aires or Sydney.

He made his way across the parking lot, feeling like a hockey coach crossing the rink in street shoes. He slid across the frozen pavement, afraid to pick his feet up, and still almost fell on his butt a couple of times. By the time he was inside, he was counting the days until summer. It was depressing, the weather was lousy, and it was not even December. It would be three months until the Red Sox went to spring training. He found it hard to believe that only a week ago it had been seventy degrees.

He was surprised to find the door to the office locked. He patted his pockets to locate his keys and then unlocked the door. Susan was not at her desk when he entered the office. She was most likely at the nearby diner getting coffee. Glad that she gave him a reprieve from her lecturing him about his lack of self-preservation, he walked into his office, dropped his overcoat into the guest chair, and sat behind his desk. He leafed through four days of mail and phone messages until he smelled Susan's perfume. She placed a cup of coffee on his desk and said, "To what do I owe the pleasure of your company?"

"It's too cold and the roads are too damned treacherous for me to be running all over the state."

"Really? The weather hasn't held you back the past couple of days."

He leaned back in his chair and watched her as she picked up his coat, draped it around a hanger, and suspended it from the hook on the back of the door. She sat down and laid some papers on the desk. "While I have you here, I need you to sign these invoices so we can collect some of the money that's owed us."

The way she said "owed us" told him the bank account was getting low. He had been ignoring his administrative duties of late. Running a business can be like taking a crap—the job is not complete until the paperwork is over. He smiled and said, "I'll take care of it."

She got up, started for the door, and then stopped. "I probably shouldn't say anything until you've finished, but Charley called. He and Max have John's car. The police called them to tow it to the impound lot, but the roads were too bad to get it there so they have it at their garage. They thought you might want to look at it and used the road conditions and the fact that they were straight out as an excuse for not delivering it."

"Great. I promise to finish this paperwork before I go over there."

After Susan was gone, he swiveled his chair around and stared at the freezing rain and sleet slamming against the windows. With each gust of the wind, the frozen mash clicked against the glass and stuck to it. It was a cold, winter sound, similar to hundreds of small pebbles hitting against a window, and it never failed to give him chills. He sighed. There are only three ways to cope with a New England winter: relocate south to a warmer climate, shoot yourself, or accept it. The first option was improbable and the second was out of the question, today anyhow. He resigned himself to the fact that he would have to deal with the snow, ice, and frigid temperatures until mid-March and turned back to the paperwork on the desk.

Once he finished, he phoned Charley, who must have been waiting for the call, as he answered on the first ring. "Charley, Ed."

"Have you been trying to get through long?"

"No, this was my first try."

"You always were the lucky one. Damned phone's been ringing off the hook all morning."

That put a damper on his vision of Charley sitting there waiting for him to call.

"We'll make a bundle on tows this morning," Charley said. "I love the first ice and snow of the season. All the idiots think they can still run seventy-five, eighty miles an hour. Oh well, their bad luck is our good. I suppose you're calling about John's heap."

"As a matter of fact, I am. Where'd they find it?"

"It was in the parking lot at the Rockingham Mall in Salem . . . just a couple of blocks from your sister-in-law's apartment."

"Does it look like it may have been broken into?"

"No. It's in great shape. Once the cops are finished looking it over, I'll probably drive it to the impound lot."

"It doesn't look as if someone went through it looking for drugs or anything?"

"No, if they did search it, they didn't leave any visible evidence of it. That's not easy to do if you're trying to find something hidden. Anyway, it'll be tomorrow or the day after before anyone will call, looking for it. The county mounties and state police have their hands full pulling idiots off the road."

"Charley, do me a favor, will you."

"What you need?"

"Take that car apart."

"Are you serious? Don't you cops get antsy about someone messing with evidence—you know, chain of custody and all that shit?"

"I'm as serious as having your wife find out you've got herpes treatments listed in your medical records. Go through the whole car, pull the seats, open the rocker panels, look at any place John could have hidden something."

"Cripes, Ed, we're backed up as it is. I ain't got anybody to pull off my cash work."

"So don't pull anyone off anything. I'd prefer it if Max did it anyway. I'm good for the labor cost."

Charley picked up the urgency in his voice. "It might help if we knew what we were looking for. You know—kind of narrow down the search."

"I doubt we'll find the missing money there, but there could be something that will give me a workable lead."

The line seemed to go dead.

"You still there, Charley?"

"Yeah, just trying to think how big three million bucks is."

"Well, it'll be large . . . let's hope it's not in one-dollar bills."

Charley chuckled and said, "Hell even if it's in hundreds we're still looking at thirty thousand bills. We're on it," and then Traynor was listening to a dial tone.

It took a couple of hours to finish up at the office. Traynor wanted to get back on Susan's good side, so he finished signing all the invoices and returned all his phone calls. By the time he was ready to go to Greenville, it had warmed enough that the rain was no longer freezing. Still, the roads were wet and, staying off the main roads, it took him twenty minutes to drive to the body shop.

He walked into Max and Charley's garage. Neither of them was in the shop, so he asked one of the people working on a Dodge with a crumpled fender where he could find them. The guy pointed to the rear of the building, where the detail shop was located. Traynor stepped through the door and almost tripped over the hood of John's car. Max had parts spread all over the room; anything that he could possibly remove from a car was there. The seats were sitting in the middle of the wash bay and the trunk lid was leaning against the wall beside the hood. Traynor saw Max's bulk inside the car and heard the loud chatter of an air gun. Max was leaning forward, concentrating on removing the screws that held the door in place. Ed reached in and tapped him on the back. He turned and smiled.

"You find anything?"

"No. If he was hiding something, it ain't here now."

"The trunk was empty?"

"Yeah, nothing in it—not so much as a spare tire."

"How'd you get into the trunk?"

"Pulled the back seat out and went in that way."

"Thanks, Max."

He wandered back through the shop and into the cluttered office. Charley was banging away on the keyboard of his computer. Ed poured a coffee from the ever-full forty-cup electric urn and sipped on it until Charley finished what he was doing. He spun around and started when he saw Traynor standing there. "I don't think there's three cents in that car, let alone three million bucks," he said.

Traynor sat down across the desk from him and drank the coffee. His mind spun. If he had taken that much money, he would not want to let it out of his sight, and John was less trusting than he was. He would not let the money, and/or his access to it, such as bank passbooks, out of his grasp. Who would John trust enough to give them a key to his car? Then again, if the money had been in the car, the killer may have taken the keys from John when he killed him.

"Charley?"

"Yeah?"

"I forgot to ask Max how he got the car door opened."

"I don't know. I guess the doors were unlocked when the cops found it. Fuckin' lucky the car wasn't stolen if you ask me."

Traynor doubted John would leave his car unsecured. Someone knew where that car was parked and got there first, someone with the key. Maybe that someone had intentionally left the doors unlocked, hoping that, as Charley had insinuated, somebody would steal it. Ed drained the coffee and rinsed the mug in the sink beside the urn. "Tell Max to put it back together. I don't think what we're looking for is in there."

Charley grunted and then said, "Oh, by the way, we found this stuff in his glove box."

Traynor took the small box he held and quickly pawed through it. There was an owner manual for the car and several envelopes. One of them was of particular interest, a rental agreement for a cabin on Governor's Drive in Raymond. "You got a map of Raymond?"

"Yeah, I do. What are you looking for in Raymond? I grew up there."

"I need directions to Governor's Drive."

"You don't have a GPS?"

"A what?"

"A Global Positioning System . . ."

Charley looked at Traynor for a moment and then said, "Sorry, I had a weak moment and forgot that you're a technophobe. Cell phone and desktop computer are about your limit."

"That's only because Susan taught me how to do the fundamental things. So how do I get there?"

"That's easy enough. It's on the eastern shore of Governor's Lake. Go out 101 to exit five. Go right, off the ramp, to Route 27, then left to Harriman Drive. Follow Harriman until you get to Lakeview Road. Go left and follow Lakewood, it turns into Governor's Drive. It's a piece of cake."

"Right, suppose you could write that down for me?"

Charley grinned. "For a guy who was a state cop for twenty years, you don't know a lot about the area."

"I never left the main roads much."

"Sure, I'll dump it into the computer and get you a map."

In a moment Charley handed Traynor a map and said, "Ed, if you're gonna survive in a modern world you need to get up-to-date. Stop by the mall and buy a GPS. Come by here and I'll teach you how to use it."

"Yeah, I know but I still prefer my DeLorme *New Hampshire Atlas and Gazetteer*."

Traynor drove out of Greenville, heading for the Rockingham County seat in Brentwood. He called Buck on his direct line and invited him for coffee. He said he would meet him at Skip's Restaurant in Epping.

Buck was already there when Traynor arrived. He waved to him from a booth in the back of the dining room. Every cop in the seacoast area knew the restaurant; it was one of the more popular police hang-outs, strategically located between the Rockingham County Sheriff's Department and the Epping State Police Barracks. At any given hour of the day, you could find Buck's deputies, state police, or Epping cops sitting in the booths. Traynor would not be surprised to learn that more than 25 percent of the place's revenue came from cops. He slid into the booth. Buck pushed a mug of coffee at him, and he took a drink. Buck's face was drawn and his eyes rimmed with red. Traynor could not recall having ever seen him look as old as he did that day. "You look tired," he said.

He had never told Buck that he thought the job of county sheriff had to be the absolute pits. The very nature of police work places officers in conflict with most people they meet, and the county sheriff is an elected position. Traynor hated to think about the tightrope that a sheriff had to walk. On one hand, he took an oath to enforce the law. Yet, on the other, if he made too many waves he could very well lose the next election. It must feel like being a kernel of corn on a millstone, helplessly waiting for two relentless forces to crush you. When the time had come for them to select second careers, Traynor believed that he had made the better choice.

"This has been the weekend from hell," Buck said, without even saying hello. "This storm has kept us running from one end of the county to the other since Sunday. At one time or another, half of the county has lost power. I've had every one of my guys on duty for thirty-six straight hours."

Buck sipped his coffee then turned his attention to Traynor. "What about you? On the phone you sounded as if it was urgent for us to meet."

"It is. You remember what was in John's personal effects?"

"Pretty much, there was his wallet and an envelope with an airline ticket in it . . . yeah, I remember. Why?"

"When you let me look at them, I didn't see any car keys. Did you?"

He took a minute. From the look on his face, Traynor knew he was running a picture of the crime scene through his mind. "Now that you mention it, I don't recall seeing any either."

Traynor knew he was right. Either John had lost the keys on the way to the crime scene, or the killer had taken them. That dog that had been chasing his tail for two days just got a little closer to catching it.

"I talked to his wife the other day," Buck said.

"Oh? She didn't mention it." He thought it was odd Jill had not said something while they were together. He dismissed the thought; she probably took it for granted that he had assumed the cops had interviewed her.

"I hated to bother her," Buck said, "but you know how it is. In a case like this, you have to talk to everyone. Even the people you know didn't do it. She seemed preoccupied if you ask me." He paused for another drink of his coffee, and then said, "I guess if I was looking to bury my spouse, I'd be a little spacey too."

A flag went up in Traynor's head. If, as statistics proved, there was a 90 percent chance that a spouse or someone who knew John killed him, what were those odds if there were two? His head began to whirl. He dismissed the notion that Jillian was in any way capable of shooting

John. However, Consuela might be an altogether different story. Was she capable? The bum in Fremont had mentioned hearing a Spanish accent. On the other hand, if she had killed John and had the money, why was Humberto running all over the state beating up and killing people? As close as those two seemed to be, one would assume they were in this thing together.

He finished his coffee and chewed the fat with Buck for about fifteen minutes. Buck's radio squawked and he listened as the dispatcher put out a call for him. "I got to go." He grinned, and the fatigue seemed to fall from his face, but only for a second; it came right back. "Thanks for calling, Ed. I needed a break. Get the tab, would you?"

"You act as if I'm the one with a steady source of income." Traynor smiled. "Sure, no problem, I'll get it." He motioned for a refill on his coffee and waited until Buck was in his car and out of the parking lot. It was time for him to have another talk with Humberto and his partner, Theo. This time he wanted to even the odds, and he called Max on his cell and told him he would pick him up around 7:00 p.m. However, before he went after them, he had another stop to make. Governor's Lake was only a few miles west of Epping.

27

Charley's computer-generated map saved Traynor from getting lost as it led him to Governor's Drive. He parked in front of a small lakeside cottage, walked toward the front porch, and peered through the door's glass portal, seeking any sign of occupancy. It appeared to be empty. However, peering through the window he saw several signs of recent occupancy, such as a coffee mug sitting on a small table in what he assumed to be the kitchen. He stepped off the porch and walked along the side of the building toward the lakeshore.

The cottage sat in a copse of trees where it would be cool in the summer and sheltered from the wind in winter. It was near the water and offered a terrific view of the lake. It was a place where a person could spend a lot of time kicking back watching the swimmers, jet skiers, and boaters. On that November day, however, the lake was quiet, and the water looked black and cold although the surface had not yet frozen. Traynor circled the building, checking it out. Plastic covered most of the windows, and the side door was secured with a sturdy lock. He began walking back to the front of the building. He turned the corner and pulled up short.

An old man stood by the porch. "Can I help you?" He wore a plaid shirt, work pants, and heavy boots. His full head of snow-white hair made Traynor think about his own, which was receding, and for a brief moment Ed was envious. The old man was big and, although he appeared to be in his seventies, the years had not turned his middle to flab. Traynor wouldn't be surprised to learn he could outwork most men half his age. His broad shoulders came from years of physical labor and not from pumping iron in a local gym.

Traynor held out his hand. "I'm Ed Traynor."

He took the proffered hand in a strong grip. It was the grip of a man who would stand for no foolishness and take no guff. He said, "Jim Parrish. I own this place." He motioned to a larger adjacent house. "I live next door."

"My brother rented this cabin last month," Traynor handed him the rental agreement.

"I recognized the name. You got some ID?"

Traynor gave him a business card and showed his investigator's license. Parrish looked at the picture for a moment then held it up and compared it to Traynor. "Don't know why they bother with these damned pictures," he announced. "They never look like the real people." He must have thought the resemblance was close enough and handed it back. Not to be rushed, he read the card. "Says here you're a private investigator? Can't say I've ever met one before. Seen a bunch on TV, though."

"Well, don't be fooled by those shows. The job is nowhere near that glamorous or profitable."

"Now that we're old friends, Ed, what can I do for you?"

"My brother had an accident last week and I'm trying to backtrack his activities."

"What kind of accident?"

Though his body appeared relaxed, Parrish's voice was full of suspicion, and Traynor knew he was still wary. He believed that old-timers like Parrish had heard so much bullshit over the years that they could spot it a mile away. Traynor told him the truth. "He was murdered."

"Hey, was he the fellow they found shot over in Fremont?"

"Yeah, that was him."

"So, are you here for his stuff?"

"Stuff? What kind of stuff?"

"He left some clothes and whatnot. I don't have another renter until spring so I just left it inside." He wore a key ring clipped to his belt; the retractable chain ran into his pocket. He pulled out the ring and flipped through the keys until he found the one he wanted. "When I hadn't seen nor heard for him for three or four days, I went ahead and winterized the place, put plastic over some of the windows and what all. I figured it wouldn't hurt and when he came back the place would be warmer. These old windows ain't much good once it turns cold. I'll bet when the wind blows the curtains in there are straight out." He paused, looked at Traynor for a moment, and then said, "I imagine I can seal up the rest of them now."

He opened the door and stepped to one side, allowing Traynor to precede him into the cabin. Traynor was duly impressed the interior was nice. Parrish obviously was one of a swiftly diminishing group of people, those who worked hard for what they had and took pride in it. Traynor complimented him on the place.

"I probably should change these locks now. Your brother never did return the keys. Be awfully hard to tell who has them now."

The small house was typical of seasonal cottages, never designed for year-round occupancy. It had a small kitchenette and dining area nestled alongside a single bedroom. Most of the cabin was a sitting room that faced west toward the lake, the outside wall was completely windowed, and the plastic he had used to seal them obscured the view. It was, however, evident to Traynor that in summer, the vista out the uncovered bay windows facing the lake would be terrific, especially sunsets. It would be a great getaway, if not for the fact that either side of the cottage was within ten feet of the adjacent buildings. That was one reason why Traynor had never wanted a lakeside cabin; they were like living in the city with a flood in your backyard. The kitchen contained a gas cook stove and in the living room there was a small wood burner for heat, so it would be somewhat inhabitable in the off-season.

Parrish stepped into the bedroom and came out with a suitcase. "I thought it was strange that he never came back for his stuff, especially since it was all packed up like he was getting ready to go on a trip."

Traynor took the suitcase and thanked him. The airplane tickets he had found in John's effects came to mind. The itinerary had read Manchester to Chicago O'Hare and from O'Hare to Buenos Aires, Argentina. He was damned certain John had not been planning a vacation trip. Although he had heard that Patagonia is beautiful and the countries south of the equator were going into summer, the Argentine economy was in shambles and the political situation unstable. No, he knew why South America, especially Argentina, held so much appeal for John—it has never had an extradition treaty with the United States. Depending on who was in power, relations between most South American countries and the United States were in a constant state of flux. Today they might be our friends and allies; tomorrow they might be our enemy. One thing had always been welcome there though—the American dollar, and it seemed John had come into possession of a great deal of those.

He popped the suitcase open and quickly searched it. Parrish misinterpreted his action and he tensed. "It's all there," he said. There was indignation in his voice and his posture was defensive.

"I'm sorry. I didn't mean to imply anything is missing. It's just that it's easier to look at it in here than in the car."

Parrish nodded, stoically accepting the apology. Traynor unzipped a compartment and found a small notebook. Notebooks kept turning up wherever he followed John's trail. He opened it and flipped through the pages, stopping when he read an address, phone number, and a name, Jeffrey Saucier, followed by another phone number. He entered the first number into his cell phone and pressed send. Someone answered on the second ring, "First Manchester."

"Jeffrey Saucier, please."

"I'm sorry, sir, but Mr. Saucier is not in."

"Will he be in later?"

The voice hesitated. "Actually, sir, as of last Friday Mr. Saucier is no longer with us. Is there some way in which I might be of assistance?"

"No, thank you, my business with Mr. Saucier is of a personal nature. You wouldn't by any chance have a number where I can reach him, would you?"

"I'm afraid that is against our policy—we are restricted from giving out personal information about our current and past employees." The man hung up but not before he made his sales pitch. "Have a good day and remember First Manchester is the bank that cares."

"Yeah, sure it is." Traynor pushed the end button on his phone, breaking the connection. Another piece of the puzzle fell into place. If he were a prosecuting attorney, he would have little difficulty building a case against John for the robbery of Carlo and Eduardo, and Traynor would have bet the bank that Mr. Jeffrey Saucier was going to be hard to find. John had probably paid him a nice piece of change to get the money somewhere safe—like Switzerland or the Cayman Islands. It looked as if he had underestimated his brother. He *had* planned this caper out, right down to screwing his partners and taking the money for himself. He closed the suitcase and thanked Parrish.

"I'm sorry to hear about your brother."

Traynor thanked him for the sentiment, but thought, *you're the first person who seems even a bit remorseful about John's death.*

Once he was in the car, he called Susan and had her go on the Internet and do a reverse search on the second phone number. In three minutes, Susan verified that the address he'd found in the notebook was that of Jeffrey Saucier.

Bedford is a nice town. Parts are upscale, but on average, it's a middle-class town bordered by Goffstown and Manchester to the north and Merrimack to its south. Saucier lived in a typical middle-income subdivision, nothing fancy. Traynor did not let that detract him; now that Saucier had had a sudden windfall, he would be stupid to upgrade too much. Traynor pulled into the driveway and parked behind a three-year-old BMW. An obese, balding man came out of his garage, carrying two suitcases. If this was Jeffrey, it was obvious that he was about to embark on a trip. Unless Traynor was mistaken, like John's, his trip was on a one-way ticket. He got out and said, "Jeffrey Saucier?"

The big man stopped, dead in his tracks. It was windy and cold, yet his shirt was soaked with sweat and he looked as if he would run as soon as Traynor spoke. "My name is Ed Traynor. We need to talk."

"I was just on my way to the airport . . ."

"Jeffrey, you either talk to me for fifteen minutes or I make a phone call and you talk to the state police for a few hours, or more." The mention of the authorities scared Saucier, and he dropped the suitcases in the driveway and seemed to deflate, as much as someone who tips the scale at over three hundred pounds can. He said, "Let's go inside, out of the cold."

They walked into the split-level, and if Traynor had any doubts that Saucier was planning a prolonged trip, they immediately dissolved. Protective white cloths covered the furniture, and the temperature was not much warmer than the outdoors; the thermostats must have been set low, probably no higher than forty-five or fifty degrees. Obviously, only a fool would pay to heat a house he might never see again. Traynor figured he would lay low somewhere for a few weeks, maybe a month, and then make a call to a real estate agent and sell the place, furniture and all.

"How can I help you, Mister Traynor, was it?"

"Look, Jeffrey, let's cut to the chase, okay? First, you have a more than passing acquaintance with the name Traynor. Second, you got a plane to catch, and third, I have a murder to solve."

"Murder? I don't know anything about any murder."

"I'll be the judge of that. I'm John Traynor's brother and I find it hard to believe you failed to make the connection. After all, John financed this little getaway you're about to take, didn't he?"

Jeffrey looked like a man who had just learned he was skinny-dipping in a piranha-infested river. "I don't know what you're talking about."

"Have it your way." Traynor took out his cell phone and touched the screen with his thumb. The external speaker blared out the irritating sound of a dial tone. He entered a three-digit number and after a single ring, a staccato voice came over the phone's external speaker. "9-1-1, what is your emergency?"

Saucier's face paled. He threw up his arms in surrender and Traynor disconnected the call.

"What do you want to know?" Saucier asked.

"Everything."

28

Traynor stood like a silent sentinel and let Saucier talk to his heart's content.

"John called me last week. He told me the business deal he'd been working on had been a great success. He said he'd rented a cottage and we set up a meeting for later in the week.

"I was nervous about being seen with him, but John said not to worry. He told me that the property owner was an independent sort, the kind who believed in live and let live. As long as John took care of the cabin and did not have any wild parties, the old man would honor his privacy.

"When I got there, John was really wired. Dealing with him was scary. He must have seen my headlights and watched me drive along the narrow lane, because he met me in the driveway. He stood off to one side, out of the car's lights, holding a handgun, and looked like he was ready to use it. Without saying a word, he led me into the cabin. I was scared to death. The minute I set eyes on John I knew he was bad news. He had this turbulent look in his eyes and seemed to be looking in all directions at once—as if he was watching for someone. I didn't know who else might be inside the cabin. John sensed my mood and said, 'Don't worry, we're the only ones here.' However, my earlier premonition was right and it wasn't long before I learned that he ran with some bad dudes.

"Once we were inside and I sat at the table, I apologized for the delay in getting to him. I said, 'I'm sorry it took me so long to get here. But, one can't be too careful in these matters.'

"All he said was, 'Yeah sure.' John looked strung out, obviously in a state of sleep deprivation, and he looked desperate. He jumped at every sound, no matter how small.

"He walked into the back room and brought out the valises, placing all but one of them on the floor. The other he placed on the table. When I opened it and saw the cash inside, my heart raced. I thought I'd have a heart attack; I'd never seen that much cash outside of a bank vault in my life—and he had five more bags just like it! 'My God, how much is in here?' I asked.

"Suddenly, John was cold as ice. He said, 'All total, $3,278,040. I need to get it someplace safe, preferably out of the country.' John told me that he'd spent two days waiting for me without once leaving the cottage. He passed time by counting the money, six times in all, and each time he came up with the same number. He said he was fucking rich!

"I wanted him to know that moving that much cash was no small task and told him, 'That isn't going to be easy.'

"He wasn't fazed a bit, he just shrugged. 'I never thought it would be. But, that's how you're going to earn your money. It's what you do, isn't it?' We cut a quick deal.

"Everything over three million was to be mine, provided I succeeded in getting the cash out of the country and into a safe bank somewhere offshore, like the Cayman Islands.

"I'm good at what I do. That's why John called me. Without bragging, I can say I'm as good as my reputation. It took me two days to deliver on my part of the bargain. The first day I opened ten or twelve accounts, using different names and the employee numbers of different tellers. Once I had the cash safely in the vault, I consolidated everything into two accounts in the Bahamas and then moved it to a single account in the Cayman Islands. The rest was easy. I purged all records in the local bank.

"I knew the transactions would show up during an audit, so I gave notice and quit. I was hoping to be out of here before anyone figured out something wasn't right.

"During the two days it took me to launder his money, John stayed in the cabin. He called me at least once every hour to ask what was happening. No doubt worried about how trustworthy I was. Truthfully, if I'd wanted to, I could've ripped John off as easily as he'd ripped off whoever he got the money from. Nevertheless, I have my ethics and I delivered the passbooks and codes to him. The next time I heard anything about him was when I read about his murder in the *Union Leader*. Now, I've got to leave or I'll never catch my plane."

Saucier finished his tale and sat nervously, awaiting Traynor's reply.

Traynor said, "Jeffrey, you and I got altogether different ideas about what ethics are."

Traynor watched Saucier drive away. As was becoming the norm for this case, he had another decision to make. Should he call the police and turn Saucier in or just let him go? He opted to let him go. As nervous as he was, the ulcers he would most certainly develop would be more punishment than incarceration. Besides, as Saucier had said, it would most likely show up in an audit. No one lost any money, other than the Escobars and the cartel, and it was the bank's problem. Let what will happen, happen.

29

Saucier's story, along with the tale Robby had told him, made it obvious to Traynor that Humberto had held back something. Traynor also believed that he and Max had no chance in hell of ever finding Humberto and Theo without help. The only person Traynor knew who seemed privy to their movement was his so-called sister-in-law, Consuela. He called The Sexy Fox; she was onstage and could not come to the phone. He hung up without leaving a message. Next, he called Max and left a message for him to meet at the strip club. Then he drove to Massachusetts.

The nor'easter had moved offshore, taking the clouds with it and leaving a clear wintry night behind. Temperatures had plummeted into the teens, and the moon was full and lit the snow like a spotlight as he drove to the club. He saw Max's truck and parked beside it, directly in front of the door. Max got out and waited by the entrance.

The bouncer started to protest about the vehicles blocking the door—until he got a look at Max. Whenever he saw Max get out of a vehicle, no matter how large, it reminded Traynor of a dragon coming out of its den, rearing back and stretching its wings. The bouncer took one look at him and decided to let him park wherever he wanted.

Max pushed his way into the club, leaving Traynor to come up with the five-dollar-a-head cover charge. He didn't mind. If he had to reimburse Max for travel, the gas bill alone for the Excursion would bankrupt him. At the current price of gasoline, a trip to the pump had to cost over a hundred dollars. Traynor decided that he could pick up a bunch of cover charges and still pay less than what it cost to fill Max's gas tank.

Once in the club, they stood to the side, away from the flow of traffic, letting their eyes adjust to the smoky interior. "I thought it was against the law to smoke in public places in Massachusetts?" Max shouted, trying to be heard over the raucous rock music. Traynor noticed that his old friend, Alana, was onstage, gyrating to the beat of a rock song from the late sixties. She wore nothing but a garter on her left leg, where she stuffed her dollar bills, and a pair of platform shoes. She grinded her pelvis at a guy who looked as if he were better suited to peering at an accounting ledger than a woman's crotch. The customer shoved a bill into the garter, and she deftly strutted away. Without missing a beat, she danced around some arrogant ass who sat with his feet crossed and propped up on the edge of the stage. Normally, Traynor wouldn't have given him more than a glance—but the jerk's silver-toed western boots caught his eye. Even in the smoke-filled room, he recognized those cowboy boots. A few nights ago, he had met them in the parking lot of the steakhouse. If this was Theo, then Humberto couldn't be far away. Traynor motioned Max to a table, along the wall, away from the stage, but with a good view of the show and Theo.

A server came over and asked, "What you having? After five o'clock there's a two-drink minimum . . . each."

"A couple of Buds," Traynor said.

She left to get their drinks.

He and Max sat back, their eyes scanning the building. After a few minutes, Traynor leaned forward so Max could hear him. He watched Theo out of the corner of his eye. He didn't know whether Theo would recognize him or not. It had been dark in the restaurant's parking lot and Humberto was the one who had gotten closest—still, Traynor did not want the asshole recognizing him—not yet. He pointed to Theo and told Max, "Humberto's tag-team partner, he's hell with those boots."

Max nodded and stared at Theo. Traynor knew Max was memorizing his features for future reference. The music stopped, Alana left the stage, and the house lights came up. When the music stopped and the illumination in the room increased, the level of noise dropped so that normal conversation was possible. Theo decided to take advantage of the break in the entertainment and got up. Traynor's eyes followed him as he wove a path through the crowd. He paused shortly by their table and looked at Traynor as if he were trying to decide whether he knew him.

Traynor nodded and turned his face away, concentrating on his beer. He noted that Theo had a large bent nose, which had been broken a time or two. Traynor hoped he would get an opportunity to break it for him again. Traynor was usually easygoing, but when someone stomped him into the pavement he liked to get even—truthfully, he liked to get ahead. He watched Theo circle the stage and head for the far corner of the room, where a red sign glowed through the smoky fog. He was going to the men's room.

Unlike the old man at Governor's Lake, Theo looked as if he spent a lot of time in a weight room. Traynor believed that if he were going to take him, it would have to be by surprise, and quick. He couldn't allow Theo to get his hands on him; he wouldn't have a snowball's chance in hell if it came down to a wrestling match. On the other hand, if he hit fast and hit hard—very hard—there should be no problem.

When Theo disappeared inside the men's room, Traynor got up. "Damned beer is full of vitamin pee."

Max stood up too.

"Where are you going? I'm not a woman. I don't need company to go to the restroom."

Traynor's attempt at humor missed the mark. Max said, "Somebody has to make sure you aren't disturbed while you're taking a leak."

Traynor opened his mouth, raised a finger as if he'd finally gotten the point, and smiled. "Good idea."

Traynor circumvented the stage with Max following in his wake. They sauntered down the narrow hall to the entrance to the men's room. Max stood to one side and folded his arms across his chest. When he stood like that his arms looked as big as trees. Traynor opened the men's room door and stepped inside.

Theo stood before a urinal. He was one of those assholes who unfasten their pants at the urinal, trying to convince everyone they are so well endowed that their organ would not fit through their fly. He thrust his hips forward, aiming toward the porcelain pisser. He was so arrogant that he urinated without holding his tool with his hand. His fists rested on his hips.

A quick glance showed there were no other occupants in the room and Traynor was confident that no one was getting by Max. He walked over and stood behind Theo.

"Hello, Theo. Do you remember me?"

Theo turned his head, trying to see who was talking, and Traynor saw his eyes widen. Theo made a mental connection and seemed to remember him. Fortunately for Traynor, it had taken him too long.

"You should never have fucked with a bull, Theo . . . because when you do, sooner or later, you get gored. You had your fun the other night. Now it's time for me to have mine."

For a brief second, a confused look crossed Theo's face. Then Traynor jumped up and kicked him in the small of his back, driving him into the urinal. He grabbed him by the hair and slammed his face into the Sloan valve. His nose burst, and blood spurted across the wall. Traynor kept a tight grip on his hair, smashed his face into the valve again, and then swung him around.

They pirouetted across the restroom like a couple of ballroom dancers, Theo's penis hanging limp and spraying urine as they spun. Traynor swung him around, slammed his face into the cinder-block wall, and pinned him against it, avoiding his piss. "I hope you remember me, because I sure as hell remember you," he said as he drove his fist into Theo's kidneys.

Theo tried to answer, but his face was a mess, his nose and several of his front teeth broken. When he spoke all that came out was unintelligible gibberish. Bloody sputum poured from his mouth, sliming the puke-green paint on the wall. It sounded as if he were talking through a bowl of cold, semi-hardened oatmeal.

Traynor rammed his right knee into Theo's kidney and felt all fight leave him as Theo went limp. He released him and stepped back as he slid to the floor. He landed on his knees then rolled onto his side and lay still for a few seconds gasping for air; frothy red bubbles appeared in his mouth. He moaned and rolled onto his back and lay still.

Sprawled on the filthy floor, Theo did not look as tough as he had in the parking lot. He was a mess: his mouth was open, and a steady stream of discharge dribbled out, mixing with the urine that dammed against his cheek. Traynor saw the jagged edges of broken teeth. All the arrogance he had seen in Theo's face moments earlier was gone. Checking his clothes to see if he had gotten any body fluids on him, Traynor was especially careful to look for blood. For all he knew, Theo's lifestyle made him an ideal candidate for HIV.

Traynor took a second to check his appearance in a dirty mirror. He looked okay. He washed his hands and turned to leave, thought better of it, and then walked over to Theo. He kicked him in the ribs, delivering the coup de grace. Traynor felt something in Theo's side give under the toe of his heavy work boot. When the semiconscious man cried out, he smiled, feeling the score was even. He knew he had broken at least one rib.

Being careful not to put his hands in the mess in which Theo laid, Traynor grabbed him by the collar and pulled him into an empty stall. He turned his head in disgust. The toilet was either plugged or nobody had flushed it in a while. Crammed solid, it contained a sickening stew made of toilet paper, puke, piss, and shit. Trying not to look inside the bowl, he raised the seat and grabbed Theo by his shirt. It wasn't easy, but he got him turned around and dropped him seat-first into the mess.

Traynor looked with pride at his handiwork. Theo sat in the toilet with his pants down. His knees angled up with his head resting between them, his face inches above the putrid waste.

Traynor's adrenaline rush dissipated as quickly as it had flared up and he calmed down. He turned away, closing the stall behind him, and washed his hands. Traynor opened the door to a small closet and saw a sign that said, *Closed for Maintenance*. He walked out of the men's room and hung the sign on the door. "Everything come out all right?" Max asked.

"Splendid, simply splendid. Unfortunately Theo is in no shape to give us any information. Let's see if we can find his partner. Those two punks are like snakes and travel as a pair; Humberto's got to be here somewhere."

When they returned to the table and sat down to enjoy the show, an Asian girl was gyrating her hips onstage. Traynor wasn't worried about Theo making an appearance. In the shape he was in, both physically and hygienically, as soon as he walked out of the restroom the on-duty bouncer would escort him to the parking lot.

As it turned out it didn't matter. They were only sitting for five minutes when Humberto came strutting out of the back room with Consuela hanging on his right arm. Traynor's first impression was that her period of grieving was very short and she and Humberto were a lot closer than any friends he knew.

Under the table, he nudged Max's foot. Max turned and looked at Humberto. When Traynor nodded, indicating this was their man, Max flew out of his seat.

Humberto still had a big gauze bandage over his nose, which must have made it difficult for him to smoke the cigarette he held. Consuela must have said something funny because he guffawed and wrapped his arm tightly around her. She pecked him on the cheek and ran to the back room, probably to get ready for her next set. Humberto paused and looked at the empty seat where his partner had been sitting fifteen minutes before. In the dark, smoke-filled room, he didn't see Traynor and Max until it was too late.

Before Humberto could react, Max used one hand to pull his arm back and up between his shoulders and grabbed his belt with the other. Humberto's macho image caught hell that night. He looked like a Tennessee walker when Max high-stepped him through the startled crowd and out the exit door to the freezing parking lot. In the event anyone wanted to come to Humberto's aid, Traynor pulled his nine-millimeter pistol and held it against his leg. The effort was wasted; either no one noticed the weapon or Humberto was not as popular as Traynor had assumed. It looked like the Puerto Rican thug was going to be on his own.

Once outside, Max spun Humberto around and slammed him face-first into the side of the building. Humberto hit with a smack that sounded wet, and Traynor winced as Humberto's already broken nose smeared the frozen cinder block wall with blood. The blood trickled slowly down the frigid wall and froze against the cold cinder blocks. He dropped to his knees, curled into a fetal position, and tried to burrow into the snow to get away from the giant who assaulted him.

Max had no compassion. He grabbed his helpless charge by the collar of his fancy silk shirt, ripped it along the seams, then yanked him off the ground, and flipped him over as easily as if he were a pancake. Snow flew up in a cloud when he slammed Humberto onto his back.

Max quickly frisked him, looking for weapons. He tossed Traynor a thirty-eight special and a nasty-looking knife. Then he pulled Humberto to his feet and smacked him back against the wall. Humberto's head snapped back with a hollow clunk and Max pulled him forward and then pushed him against the wall once more, harder than the first time. Had Traynor not been there, he would not have believed it was possible to slam anyone into a wall that hard. Finally, Max delivered the *estocada*, the final blow, and hit him in the stomach so hard Traynor thought that Max's fist had to hit Humberto's spine. If Humberto had any fight left in him, that punch sent it running back to Puerto Rico. It took a few seconds for him to straighten up and lean against the building. The gauze bandage had come loose, hung from his cheek by a single piece of adhesive tape, and blew in the wind like a pennant.

Assured that he had Humberto's full attention, Max stepped aside, keeping him pinned against the cold cinder block wall with one hand. "There you go, Eddie. I think he'll pay attention now."

Humberto's eyes, although glazed with pain, still managed to communicate his hate. Traynor had no tolerance left for him and was not about to listen to any more bullshit. He said, "You don't learn, do you?"

Humberto swallowed and Traynor knew he was building a bloody clam to spit in his face, but Max slid his hand up and grasped him by the throat, squeezing any such thoughts out of his mind. Humberto's eyes bulged as the huge hand pressed against his esophagus, slowly constricting it. "If anything but words comes out of your food trap," Max said through clenched teeth, "I'm going to break what's left of your ugly face."

Humberto tried to swallow and Max released his grip enough to allow him to do so. Humberto's eyes darted from side to side, looking for help.

"Don't waste your time looking for your buddy Theo," Traynor said. "He's kind of indisposed right now." All hope went out of Humberto. Suddenly he became scared, as if he was a grammar school kid trapped in a dead-end alley by the neighborhood bully.

Max eased more pressure from his throat, and Humberto held his hands up in surrender. "What you guys want?" Max had stressed his larynx and his voice rasped when he spoke. Traynor was impressed. If he had taken the abuse Max had just handed out, he would be unable to talk for days.

"I want to know why you killed Benny Ryan," Traynor said.

Suddenly Humberto looked like a trapped wild animal. It confirmed Robby's identification of him and Theo as the people he had seen leaving Benny's house. Still, he tried to lie his way out of it. "I don't know what you're talking about."

"Don't fuck with us, Humberto." Traynor cocked his middle finger against his thumb and flicked it forward, hitting him on his broken nose. Traynor felt instant gratification when the Puerto Rican hood cried out. Humberto tried to bend over, but Max kept him pinned against the wall. He started crying, tears rolling down his cheeks.

Traynor said, "We got a witness who saw you leaving the scene. I'd imagine tomorrow, the day after at most, the New Hampshire State Police are going to be filing extradition papers with Massachusetts. Then, of course, the interstate flight might bring the feds in. You see, the guy who can ID you scares real easy, and he's more afraid of doing time for a murder he didn't commit than he is of you."

"You going to turn me in?"

"I'm not after Benny's killer, okay? I want my brother's killer. Now what did Benny have that you wanted bad enough to kill him for?"

"We didn't go there to kill the guy, okay? It was an accident. Hell, he was worth more alive than dead. Theo pushed him while we were trying to get information out of him. He rolled off the fucking bed and landed funny." He slapped himself on the side of his neck. "Right here."

Traynor poked him in the forehead with a finger. "Humberto, Humberto. Why do you have to do everything the hard way? You still haven't answered my question. What did Benny have that you were looking for?"

When Humberto looked at them, he saw no mercy on either Max's or Traynor's face; his shoulders sagged and he looked like he was about to cry. When Max tightened his grip, he started to talk like a six-year-old sitting on Santa's lap.

"I don't know where to start," he confessed.

"Start with Benny Ryan," Traynor said. "What was his role in all of this?"

"Like I said, we never meant to—"

"Yeah, yeah, we know you didn't mean to kill him. At this point what you meant to do is not relevant—he *was* killed."

"Yeah, but it was never supposed to go that far."

Traynor was tired of his skirting around the issue. "Okay, I accept that you guys didn't want Benny dead. So tell us how it went down—why you went there in the first place. If you keep pussyfooting around I'm going to let Max go berserk on you."

Humberto's eyes widened and Ed knew they had his full attention once again.

"Okay, we got to Ryan's house early, like around six in the morning. When we walked in—you know Benny was as stupid as John was smart."

For some reason Traynor questioned that statement. He had never thought of John as being smart, not in the way one usually thinks of people being smart. He was clever, as many criminals can be, but when it came to realizing that his life could only end one way, he was stupid.

"Ryan didn't even lock his doors when he went to sleep," Humberto said. "We were in his room before he knew it. At first, he acted tough, like he wasn't gonna tell us anything. Theo smacked him a couple of times and he spilled his guts—he was soft."

Humberto glanced from Traynor to Max, trying to determine whether his words were having any effect on them. He didn't seem to realize that, like Benny, he too was spilling his guts and wanted to please them. "I don't know why John hung out with that coward," Humberto said, "he had no loyalty—he was a punk."

Traynor remembered how Benny had rolled over on John twenty years ago and agreed with Humberto's assessment. "So, what did he tell you?" Humberto went quiet. Traynor nodded at Max who tightened his grip on Humberto's shirt. Traynor said, "Man, you're starting to piss me off again—by now you should know that isn't smart. I'm getting weary of having to pull everything out of you. It's late, I'm tired, and I'm cold; not a good combination, Humberto. Either you start talking or I'm going to lose my temper again—and you know that's not gonna be good for your health." He cocked his middle finger against his thumb again and popped him on the broken nose once more.

He yelped in pain and said, "Okay! Okay! Jesus, man, don't hurt me no more!"

"Then get on with it."

"Benny said that John came over one night, about three nights earlier. Benny was on some shit and was high, but not so high that he didn't get scared. By then, the word was out that somebody had ripped the Escobars off and they were looking for whoever done it. They wanted them bad too."

"How bad?"

"Bad enough to offer us a reward of 10 percent of whatever was recovered."

Traynor let that sink in for a second. Carlo had made the same offer to him that he had made to the entire world. Either way, three hundred thousand was a more than sufficient reason for anyone, let alone a bottom-feeder like Benny, to roll over on a friend.

Humberto said, "Benny told us that when he told John that he'd heard the take was over three million bucks, John got really uptight." Humberto grinned, as if he had just remembered the punch line to a joke. The grin must have pulled the skin on his face taut because it quickly turned into a grimace of pain. "John must have shit a razor blade. There's no way I'd trust Benny with that much money at stake and John didn't trust nobody, no how. It was common knowledge that Benny had a loose mouth and he'd fuck over his own mother to make a quick buck.

"Theo started to get worked up, really pissed, and he asked if John had left any money there. Benny said no, all John left with him was some fucking book.

"When we asked him where the book was, he said he'd destroyed it. Theo didn't believe him and punched him. Like I already tol' you, Benny rolled over the bed and landed on the side of his head—like this."

For a second time, Humberto tried cocking his head to show them how Ryan had landed. "It was scary, man, you should'a heard it when he hit. SNAP! When I heard that, I knew his goddamned neck was broke. We panicked and got out of there quick."

His story finished, Humberto calmed down and the adrenaline rush that had been sustaining him abated. He began to shiver and shake in the cold. His eyes beseeched them as he pleaded, "Hey, guys, I'm freezing my *cojones* off—can we go inside?"

"In a minute," Traynor said. "I have a couple more questions." He didn't want to disclose that he had the book, so he pursued that subject. "You and Theo don't strike me as readers. What kind of book? What's so important about it?"

"It's one of them books that ain't got no words printed in it . . . you know, the kind you write in."

"A journal? You were looking for someone's journal?"

"Yeah, we were looking for someone's goddamned journal. Shit, man, that book may be worth more than the money to whoever has it. It's a list of every pusher in New England plus more."

"Who's book was it?" Traynor inquired.

"There's a rat bastard in Carlo's organization who kept a record of everything, even where the bodies are buried."

Traynor looked at him, recalling that Charley had said almost the same exact thing.

Humberto must have seen that he was confused because he added, "Really. In that book there's a map showing where Carlo has buried his opposition. Someone stole it from the rat bastard, and Carlo learned about it. He'll pay plenty to get that back. In the hands of the right people, like the district attorney, that book represents a life sentence for Carlo and his brother."

"You still haven't told me whose book it was. Who sent you after it?"

Humberto's eyes moved from side to side. Traynor knew he was inter-rogating one scared man. "You got one more chance, Humberto. You better tell me who owns that book."

"The book belongs to someone with big-time connections."

"A name, Humberto, I want a goddamned name."

"Gisela Martin . . ."

30

The hostess led Carlo Escobar to a private room in the back of the most upscale restaurant in Lawrence. Carlo was nervous and wary. Never before had the cartel sent anyone as important as Federico Treviño to see him. It didn't bode well. The only thing that gave him hope of surviving this meeting was the choice of location, a public restaurant. Nevertheless, nothing was certain.

He entered the room and saw Treviño sitting with Reyes Aguayo, a known cartel enforcer. Carlo knew that the situation was fraught with danger and that he probably had no more than one chance of convincing these men that he could recoup his recent losses and come out of this situation alive.

Treviño saw Escobar and stood up. He walked around the table with open arms and said, "Ahh, Carlo, I am so happy that you could meet with us on such short notice."

Carlo was tense and stiff as they embraced, patting each other on the back. Treviño said, "Relax, *compadre*, this is a social visit."

Carlo forced his body to relax and let Treviño guide him to a chair beside the one he had vacated when Escobar had arrived. As he settled in, Escobar eyed Aguayo. Treviño was higher up in the cartel, but if Carlo were in danger, Aguayo would be the one to dispense the organization's most often used form of justice.

"Have some wine," Treviño said. "It is a very good vintage."

While Treviño poured, Carlo wondered where a man whose family had always been *peóns* had learned about anything as alien as a wine's vintage. He kept his thoughts to himself and raised his glass in toast. "*¡Salud!*"

"I have taken the liberty to order for all of us," Treviño said. "In the meantime, we have important matters to discuss."

Escobar maintained eye contact with the *jefe* as he placed his glass on the table. He began to sweat and hoped that the two men did not notice it. He nodded.

"It has been brought to our attention that you have had a . . . shall we call it a business setback?"

"I am working on a resolution to that as we speak, *Padron*—"

Treviño held his hand up and Carlo stopped talking. "We have absolute faith in you and your abilities, Carlo. Whether or not you will come good for what you owe us does not concern us. You have a much more pressing problem."

Involuntarily, Carlo's brow furrowed. He waited to hear the rest of what the representatives of the cartel had to say.

"You have in your midst a *traidora* . . ."

Involuntarily, Carlo's head snapped back. "I believe that I have already dealt with Eduardo."

Treviño placed a hand on Carlo's left arm. "Listen to me, Carlo. I said *traidora* not *traidor*."

"I don't understand . . . there is only one woman that knows anything about our business—and I trust her implicitly."

"Would this woman be Gisela Martin?"

Escobar's stomach sank and then he felt his face flush with anger.

31.

Carlo was sitting at his desk when Gisela arrived for work. As soon as she had removed her coat, he called her to his office. She sat before his desk and said, "You have something for me to do?"

"What do you know about these people?" He handed her a sheet of notebook paper on which were three names: Humberto Baerga, Theo Cruz, and Consuela Puente.

Gisela read the names, hoping that she did not give herself away. "How is the woman involved?"

"The Puente woman was married to John Traynor. She and Baerga have been fucking one another since they learned how boys are different from girls. They grew up in the same shit hole in Puerto Rico. I find all of this very interesting, do you not?"

He waited for her to respond.

"Yes," Gisela said, "if John Traynor stole our money, she would know about it. Baerga may also be involved."

"Oh, I have no doubt that the two men are in this up to their eyes." Without a glance, Carlo dropped the paper onto his desk and said, "I want you to bring her to me."

"Is that wise? What if we are seen bringing her here?"

"No, it isn't wise. That's why you will call me once you have her and I will give you instruction as to where you are to bring her."

Gisela stood and turned to the door.

"Gisela . . ."

She turned back. "Yes, Carlo?"

"Don't you want to know where to find her?"

Her stomach turned. "I was going to ask you once I have arranged for some men to assist."

"Well, let's save some time. She lives in Lawrence." He handed her another piece of paper on which he had written an address. Without as much as a glance, she put the piece of paper in her pocket. "That is her home address. She works at The Sexy Fox. She's a stripper. The two *hombres* are known to hang out there also. Take care of them."

Martin turned to the door.

"Gisela . . ."

She looked at him over her shoulder. "*Si.*"

"Aren't you forgetting something?"

She turned and looked quizzical.

"The paper with the names—or are you already familiar with them?"

She walked back to his desk, took the paper, and left his office. On her way to the elevator, she grabbed her coat from the hanger where she had placed it and put it on. She stood before the elevator and looked toward Carlo's office.

When the elevator arrived and she was on her way down to the first floor, Carlo opened the door that led into a conference room that was adjacent to his office and Federico Treviño and Reyes Aguayo entered.

There were no customers in The Sexy Fox when Gisela and her entourage walked inside. The bartender was behind the bar, busy wiping glasses and filling the reefers with beer. He wore his ever-present Grateful Dead T-shirt and smoked his ever-present cigarette, firmly gripped by his lips. When they opened the door, the mid-morning light illuminated the room and a blast of cold air swept into the room. Gisela Martin gave him a scathing look and asked, "We're looking for Humberto Baerga and Theo Cruz—are they here?"

Her escorts stood off to either side of her and made no effort to hide the fact that they were carrying pistols. The barman quickly decided that whatever Humberto and Theo were involved in, he wanted no part of it. "In the back," he said, "there's an employee break room. They'll be having coffee with some of the ladies."

Gisela doubted that any woman who worked in this dump warranted the title of *lady*. She nodded to the gunsels and they followed the bartender's nod to a doorless opening that led backstage. Gisela lit a cigarette and looked at the room, hoping to find a table with a chair that she felt was clean enough to sit in.

In short time, her men returned, herding Humberto and Theo before them. They pushed the two minor hoods after Gisela as she strode across the room to a table as far away from the bar as possible. Once they arrived at the table, Gisela sat down and said to the two gunsels, "Leave us, we'll talk alone."

One of the bodyguards gave her a quizzical look and she said, "Nothing will happen." She turned to Humberto and Theo who sat across from her. "Isn't that right?"

Theo and Humberto nodded their heads and she said to her men, "Wait over by the bar."

When they were alone, Gisela turned her attention to the two men sitting across from her. She saw their ravaged faces and asked, "What happened to you?"

"We got into a fight," Humberto said.

Gisela studied them for a few seconds and decided not to push the issue. "Have you two idiots found my journal yet?"

Even in the dimly lit room, Humberto's face looked pale. "No."

"The situation has changed," Gisela said. "I don't know how he found out about you two, but Carlo gave me your names this morning with instructions to bring you to him."

Hearing her news scared them and they looked at each other. Humberto said, "What should we do?"

"It's time for us to take some action. Carlo also wants me to bring your cousin, Consuela, to him," Gisela said to Humberto.

"Consuela? Her only involvement in this is that she married that pig, Traynor."

"Are you sure of that?" Gisela asked.

"Positive."

Gisela turned to Theo and looked closely at his face. It was a wreck. "It must have been one hell of a fight."

He didn't reply and she turned to Humberto who also showed signs of having had a rough time. "Who worked you two over? Did Ed Traynor do it?"

From the sheepish look on Theo's face she knew she had hit the mark. She dropped her cigarette to the floor and ground it out with her foot. "Jesus Christ, you two are completely useless."

Humberto ignored her scathing remarks. Under normal circumstances, he would have slapped any woman who spoke to him in that manner. However, this woman had the Escobar organization behind her. He gave the armed muscle at the bar a tentative look and asked, "What are you going to do about us?"

"Nothing. I'm going to find Consuela and take her to Carlo."

"What about them?" Humberto asked, nodding toward the bar.

"I'll take care of them. Carlo will tell me where to take Consuela once I have her. I, in turn, will call you. Today we end the Escobar control of the organization and we take over." She looked at each of them in turn.

"Come ready to kill anyone who tries to get in our way—and don't fuck things up."

She stood up and walked to the exit, motioning to the two gunsels as she passed them.

Consuela Puente-Traynor was still in her nightgown when she entered the kitchen of her small single-bedroom apartment. She had worked until the club closed at two in the morning and her eyes burned from lack of sleep. She turned the gas burner on under a kettle of water. She walked to the bathroom, inspected her bloodshot eyes in the mirror, poured some micellar water, and washed her face. Once she had removed the remnants of the previous night's makeup, she patted her face dry. The kettle started whistling, and she walked to the kitchen and turned off the burner. She took a tea bag out of the cabinet, dropped it into a cup, and poured the boiling water in.

There was a knock at her door and she went to answer, calling, "I'll be right there, Humberto." She raced into the bedroom and grabbed a robe before answering the door. Expecting to see her cousin when she released the dead bolt, she took off the recently repaired security chain and opened the door. Consuela was surprised to see a very well-dressed woman standing in the threshold. The woman's expensive clothes looked out of place in the dim, dirty hallway.

"Consuela?" The woman asked.

"Yes."

"If it's not too much of an imposition, would you come with us, please?"

Consuela immediately noticed the Colombian dialect in the woman's Spanish and she slammed the door and slid the chain home. Before she could turn the knob on the dead bolt, the door burst inward and ripped the chain out of its mooring. Two big men rushed in before the woman.

Consuela backed up and struggled to stop her backward momentum before she fell. The first of the gangsters grabbed her arm holding her upright. His grip was so strong that she knew her arm was going to bruise.

"What do you want?" she asked.

The woman told the man to release her. She turned to Consuela and said, "My name is Gisela. My employer wishes to speak with you."

"I have to go to work."

"I'm afraid you have no say in the matter and your job will have to wait."

Consuela heard noise outside of the apartment and looked over Gisela's shoulder. Her neighbor across the hall, Señora Martinez, peered out. The man closest to the door turned and stared at her, and the old woman quickly disappeared inside her apartment. Her dead bolt clicked and the chain rattled as the old woman locked her door.

"I have to get dressed," Consuela said. She turned to her bedroom and grabbed the door.

"Leave it open," Gisela said. "We know what you do for a living. Every night you take off your clothes in front of a room full of men. Men watching you put them on shouldn't be any different. Now hurry up. My employer is waiting and he is not a patient man."

"What about the old woman? She saw us," the thug named Armando asked.

"She will say nothing. If she does, we know where she lives, now don't we?"

Gisela's cell phone rang. "Yes, Carlo."

She listened for several seconds and said, "Yes, we have her."

Again she listened and then said, "Yes, I know where the mill is." A pause. "The key is in a box hidden in the rubble." Another pause, "We'll take her there."

32

Traynor sat at the kitchen table, sipping on a bourbon and ginger, and turned another page in the journal. This new wealth of information brought a number of questions to Traynor's mind. Something didn't seem right. He thought of his interactions with Gisela and wondered if she had the nerve to betray Carlo. Was the journal intended to be turned over to the law or somebody else? The most intriguing question was: Since Gisela knew Humberto and Theo, it was entirely possible that she also knew that John had ripped them off. Could she be doing an end around? Maybe she had killed John, now had the money, and intended to keep it all for herself. He couldn't help but smile at that thought . . . it seemed as if everyone was screwing Humberto and Theo. Early on he had thought that there was more to Gisela than what she revealed; now he realized that Charley's assessment was correct—she was as ruthless as she was devious.

The map in the journal was of a meadow near a landfill in Hillsborough County, and Humberto was right. It showed where the Escobars had buried all the bodies. It was going to take a long time to search the site; if the journal was accurate, there were more than twenty victims of Carlo's wrath buried there. He tossed the book aside. If Carlo learned that he had it, he would do anything to keep the authorities from getting their hands on it and it would not be long before he came for it. Traynor knew by all rights, he should have turned it over to the cops and at some point he would, just not then, not while it was still of use. It was bait, his only foolproof means of bringing Carlo out in the open. As for the ethics of keeping evidence of the murders from the police, he wouldn't lose any sleep over that. If the book was credible, and he had every reason to believe it was, not a single body in that field was anyone to mourn. They were trash when they were alive and, ironic as it may seem, Carlo had made them garbage when they were dead, and in doing so had possibly done society a favor. Traynor would sleep just fine.

He started to see light at the end of the tunnel. As crazy as it seemed at the time, he was starting to feel as if things were racing toward a conclusion. He was sure about the *why* behind John's death; however, it was *who* that still eluded him. Nonetheless, he felt certain it would not dodge him much longer. There was something rolling around in his subconscious, like the BB you tried to put into the hole in a kid's game, and it was just a matter of time before he matched it up with the right hole and it fell into place. Then he would finally put an end to this and get on with his life.

Traynor settled back and let his mind drift, hoping something would overcome the barriers. The only thing that happened was the phone rang. It was an old friend; he had tickets to a hockey game and wanted to know if he wanted to go. Traynor loved ice hockey.

The Manchester Monarchs, an affiliate of the Los Angeles Kings NHL team, took it to the Providence Bruins, affiliated with the Boston Bruins, by a score of six to four in a well-played game. After the game, Traynor and his friend stopped off at a local bar for a beer or two. They were talking hockey and enjoying a relaxing evening when Traynor's cell phone rang.

"Hello?"

"Eddie?"

"Susan?" He became concerned. Susan never called this late. "Are you all right?"

"I'm fine, but I just got a strange phone call."

She and Bob were okay; his heart stopped pounding. "Define strange for me."

"A Ms. Martin called the office a couple of hours ago and the service just forwarded it to me—I will be inquiring into why it took so long in the morning. The woman said that you have something that belongs to her and she has your sister-in-law. I immediately called Jillian and she's at home. This woman is obviously mistaken about having your sister-in-law, unless she's talking about the stripper. I didn't know what to do so I told Jillian about the call, just in case someone was going after her. What's going on?"

"It's complicated; trust me until I put a handle on this mess, then I'll explain it all to you."

"She left a number; I did a reverse search on the number, and it's a cell phone."

"Give it to me." She read the number and he scribbled it on a napkin. He excused himself to his friend, telling him something had come up and he had to leave. Traynor thanked him for the great night and crossed Elm Street to the Convention Center parking lot. He jogged to his car and drove onto the street before he got enough signal to call the number. Carlo Escobar answered.

"I have your sister-in-law, Consuela."

"Okay."

"I believe that you have something of importance to me."

Traynor tried to string him along as best he could. "I told you, I don't know what my brother did with the money."

"I'm not talking about the money and you know it."

There were times when Traynor would admit that he might not be the sharpest tack on the bulletin board; however, this wasn't one of them. Slowly but surely things started to make sense to him. Escobar must have discovered there was a turncoat in his organization and the identity of the insider who had compiled the information in the journal. All he needed to do now was figure out what Carlo's game was. Of one thing he was certain: the drug lord was one ruthless and cold son of a bitch. There was no doubt in his mind that he would kill Consuela without a second's hesitation.

"Suppose," he said, "you tell me what you want and stop playing twenty-one questions."

"All right, if you must insist on playing dumb, go ahead. But I know you have the journal."

"What makes you think I've even the slightest clue what you're talking about?"

Escobar must have taken the phone from his ear and held it out so Traynor could hear Consuela pleading as she cried out in pain.

"Come to the mill, where you met Gisela the other night, and bring the book."

"I don't have any goddamned journal."

"You have one hour to find it and bring it here, or we kill her." The circuit was broken.

He called Max as he sped down the highway to his apartment in Portsmouth and filled him in on what was going down. They agreed to meet in South Lawrence and this time Max promised to bring all of his guns.

33

C onsuela sat on the metal stool and studied the brilliantly lit room. When her captors brought her through the filthy, burned-out building, she envisioned her dead body lying in the filth and squalor. She knew that there was no way on Earth she was leaving this room alive. Her only recourse was to tell these people as little as possible.

Two immaculately dressed men entered the room whom she had never seen before, followed by Carlo Escobar. Escobar reminded her of the roosters that used to strut around the streets of her home in Puerto Rico—only this rooster was infinitely more dangerous. However, what caught her attention the most was the look of abject fear on Gisela Martin's face when she saw Escobar's companions.

Escobar walked between the stainless-steel tables and stood before her. His eyes scanned her body and made her feel as if they were going to rape and ravage her. "Is it Señorita Puente or Señora Traynor?"

Consuela glared at him but made no effort to answer.

A sudden as a cobra strike, Carlo slapped her so hard that she rocked back and almost fell off her perch on the stool. "When I ask you a question, *puta*, I expect an answer!"

Consuela's mouth filled with the coppery taste of blood and, in an act of defiance, she spit a bloody wad of sputum at his feet. "The next time I will spit in your face, *cabrón!*"

Carlo turned to Gisela and the two henchmen. "Take her in the back and hang her on the chains near the altar."

Consuela slid off the stool before the men could grab her. Defiantly she turned and walked unassisted to the door at the back of the room. Once inside she stopped and waited for someone to turn on the lights. One of the men reached around her and flicked the switch. The first thing that she noticed was the stains on the wall and immediately knew what had made them . . . human blood. She then saw the manacles and chains that fastened to a stone altar centered against the far wall. She spun around, intending to leave the room, which she was certain was a torture chamber, but was grabbed and dragged to the restraints. In seconds, the men chained and hoisted her until she could only reach the floor by extending her toes downward. Carlo entered the room and motioned for them to leave.

As soon as the goons were gone, Carlo closed the door and took a knife out of his pocket. He pressed a button and the twelve-inch blade opened with a sharp *SNAP*. "Now, *puta*, we shall see just how brave you are."

Consuela's heart raced and she struggled to free herself from the manacles that secured her to the ceiling beam.

———

Humberto and Theo darted across the parking lot and were standing with their backs against the blackened bricks of the wall. Humberto motioned to Theo and followed him inside. They stopped, astonished by the degree of devastation they confronted. "Why would anyone bring somebody to this place?" Humberto asked.

Theo, his mouth still sore from the beating he'd taken in the men's room of The Sexy Fox, shrugged his shoulders. He moved forward, deeper into the rubble. They were halfway across the mill floor when they heard the sound of someone running. Believing they'd been led into a trap, Humberto and Theo spun around, scanning the area with pistols.

A rifle barked and the right side of Theo's head exploded, and his body dropped like a sack of wet oats.

Humberto spun, looking for both the source of the shot and a place where he could take cover. He started forward and a high-powered bullet tore through his chest. He did a pirouette, blindly firing his pistol in whatever direction he was facing, hoping to hit the sniper. Another bullet slammed into his torso and he fell onto his back. His last thought was: *They're right—you don't hear the one that gets you. . . .*

Gisela heard the gunfire above and knew that if she didn't do something, she too was about to die.

Carlo appeared from the back room and walked over to Aguayo. He held his hand out as if the cartel assassin had something for him. Aguayo opened his overcoat and took out a sawed-off shotgun, which he handed to Carlo.

Gisela fumbled with her bag and stopped when Carlo snapped, "*ALTA!*"

Escobar gripped the shotgun in his right hand and asked, "Why, Gisela? I took you off the worst street in Bogotá. I saved you from a life as a street whore who ate her meals off a pile of garbage in the dump."

Her eyes narrowed and her face twisted into a mask of loathing. "All so you could make me your personal *puta!*"

Carlo looked hurt. "I always treated you with respect."

"Hah," she spat out the words, "only when you wanted something, or if it suited you. You have no idea how many times I wanted to cut off your *cojones* and feed them to you!"

Carlo's face reddened with anger and, with no warning, he grabbed the front grip of the shotgun with his left hand and pulled the trigger with his right.

Gisela's breasts took the full force of the blast and she staggered back, fell to a sitting position, and toppled onto her left side—dead before she hit the floor.

Carlo turned to Treviño and said, "At least her face was not destroyed— we can have an open coffin at her funeral. Now if you'll excuse me, *amigos*, I have more work to do." As he turned, he asked Treviño and Aguayo, "If it isn't too much of a bother, could you finish up in here?"

"It'll be our pleasure," Treviño replied. The cartel representatives took pistols out of their coat pockets and shot both of Gisela's men.

"If there is anything that I cannot abide," Carlo said, "it's disloyalty."

34

Max met Traynor in the parking lot of a vocational high school in North Andover, Massachusetts, where they could leave their vehicles out of sight. They walked three quarters of a mile through open fields and snow to the old mill. As they entered the ruins, they found Humberto and Theo lying on the filthy, sooty ice. They had had a couple of lousy days. The beatings Max and Traynor had inflicted on them were bad, and Ed almost felt remorse over having been so harsh in dealing with the two minor hoods—almost. The big difference between what he had done and what these other people had done was that he did what he'd done out of rage: when Max and he finished with them, they were alive. Whoever had done this did it because they enjoyed it.

Traynor squatted down beside Humberto and placed two fingers against his neck. There was no pulse and his body was already cooling. He guessed he had been dead at least an hour. The stakes in this game were getting high. Traynor had brought two pistols and checked to make sure they each had a round in the chamber and that the safeties were off. Max carried a twelve-gauge pump shotgun and led the way to the stairs.

Traynor sensed the attack before he saw it. Muzzle flashes lit up the inside of the ruin and the sound of gunfire echoed off the walls. Bullets clanged off the rusted steel beams that littered the area and ricocheted into the night. Max and Traynor dove into the filth and rubble seeking refuge from the onslaught. Max rolled to his left and came up blasting with his shotgun. The boom of the twelve gauge was deafening and its muzzle flashes lit up the darkness like bolts of lightning. Traynor heard a muffled grunt and knew Max had scored a hit.

Hoping to find a better place to take cover, Traynor scrambled onto his hands and knees and tried to move closer. It was not easy; he kept sliding on the frozen surface. A figure rose up, aiming a gun in Max's direction, and Traynor fired three shots at the black silhouette. He heard the distinctive *POW-WHOP* of a nine-millimeter slug leaving the pistol and hitting a body, immediately followed by a grunt of pain. The gunman fell into a pile of old sheet metal and burnt timber.

Max fired again and shifted to a new position. The night was alive with the sound of bullets hitting metal with dull clanks, and the mill reverberated with the sound of gunfire. Max jumped up and fired. Traynor heard another anguished cry.

Max crawled to the gunman's left and circled behind him.

The hood fired blindly, the heavy slugs from his semiautomatic clanging off metal. He shifted and fired a volley over Traynor's head.

Suddenly, Max loomed up beside their assailant and fired the shotgun. The gunman seemed to fold in the middle and he staggered back a couple of steps before falling into a bloody heap. His partners noted Max's position and turned their attention to him. However, like a ghost, Max had already disappeared into the darkness. Concentrating on the places where he had seen their muzzle flashes, Traynor emptied his pistol, shoved it in his belt, and grabbed the other. Their assailants must have realized their ambush was a failure and decided to take off. Traynor heard footsteps running away across the parking lot.

Max reappeared from the rubble. Dirt and gunpowder residue covered his face; he looked wild. Unsure if the ambush was over or if their running was a ploy to get them to lower their guard, he and Traynor moved forward slowly, searching the rest of the rubble. They found the bodies of two ambushers; everyone else had fled the area. Max turned to the door and a dark car flashed by as it raced away, its rear end fishtailing on the loose gravel and broken asphalt that littered the surface of the abandoned parking lot. They watched the car disappear, heading into the city, and turned their attention back to their surroundings. There was a soft glow of light in the stairwell. The lights were on in the lab.

"Let's check out the lower level," Traynor said. "We better be quick about it; someone is sure to have called the cops about all the shooting."

Max stood at the bottom of the stairs. He was staring into the lab. He looked up at Traynor and said, "I don't think we got to worry about cops."

"Oh?"

"There was shooting going on long before we got here. If the cops aren't here now, then they're in no rush. I think they've been bought off or they'd be crawling all over us."

"Unfortunately, we didn't pay them off. The ones who got away may be on a cell phone right now, telling them it's all right to hit this place now."

As soon as he stepped inside the lab, Traynor saw one of Gisela's goons lying on the floor. There were two nasty looking holes in his chest. He was not curious enough to check his pulse and stepped around him, finding the other bodyguard about fifteen feet away. Obviously, someone had taken exception to the way Gisela was running things.

They found her last. Even the carnage left by a shotgun blast to her chest could not completely hide her beauty. If you ignored the bloody mess of bone and meat where her breasts used to be, she was as elegant in death as she was in life. She was impeccably dressed in an expensive pair of black leather pants and a jacket that was so bloody and gore-splattered Traynor knew she would not want to wear it to her funeral.

Traynor looked around and saw no sign of Consuela. Max walked into the back room where they had found Eduardo. When he called, Traynor knew, without looking, that Consuela had not fared any better than Gisela. He walked to the door. As he stepped into the room, he thought of it as an execution chamber.

Consuela's nude body hung above the same altar that Eduardo had died on, blood still dripping off her feet and bare legs, and, like Eduardo, her chest cut open and her heart removed. Her torso and the surface of the altar were a quagmire of blood. Her head tilted and rested at an odd angle, her eyes were half-open. The tips of her toes were in a puddle of congealing blood beneath her feet, her clothing was piled in a corner, and her bag was nearby with its contents spread across the concrete floor. Lying against the wall was a set of keys with a big round fob on which the initials *CT* were engraved. Traynor stopped dead. It was as if the world had gone into freeze-frame.

For several seconds he drew a blank. All he knew was that he had seen those keys, or a matching set somewhere.

Max whistled and said, "Man, I could use a cup of coffee, or something a lot stronger."

That was it! The word *coffee* triggered it. Traynor had the missing bit of information that had been rolling around in the back of his mind. It finally made itself known and he knew who killed John.

"Let's get out of here," he said.

They left the ruins and were in the field between the mill and the high school when the first police car rolled into the parking lot, its lights splitting the darkness.

35

The next morning, Traynor was listless. Knowing the identity of John's killer had taken all of the drive out of him. Hindsight is a great thing. Now that it had come together, he could see the trail of evidence. It had been there all along and he either hadn't seen it or didn't want to see it. He drove to the killer's home.

She buzzed him in and stood at the door. "You're out and about early."

"Yeah, I couldn't sleep last night. I had a lot on my mind."

Jillian stepped aside and let him in. He walked into the kitchen and sat at the table.

"Coffee?" she asked.

"I'll get it."

"Thanks, I got to get the girls off to school."

"Go ahead, don't worry about me." He poured a cup from the coffee pot and opened the cupboard. The key chain was still there. He picked it up and studied it, turning it in his hand. It had a fob identical to the one he had seen beside Consuela's body. The only difference between the two was the initials; on this one they were *JT.* The last time he saw this particular key ring, he had assumed the initials stood for Jillian Traynor. Now he knew he had been mistaken and a simple test would show whether they stood for John or for Jillian Traynor. He wanted to give Jillian the benefit of the doubt; the last thing he wanted to do was falsely accuse her, damaging their relationship. Maybe John had gotten both of the women he had married similar key chains; that would have been like him. Traynor hoped he was wrong but was sure that the next hour would tell him the truth.

The girls came out, their faces still flushed from sleep, and he felt as if his heart was about to break. He hoped against hope their mother was innocent of the murder. After the loss of their father, he was not sure that he was tough enough to take their mother away too. Uncle Ed would be the ogre who turned their tiny world upside down. In the midst of all his internal wrangling, he realized Christmas was just over a month away. What kind of holiday would the girls have?

He kept busy by reading Jillian's copy of the *Boston Herald* and thumbed through the news, no mention of finding bodies at the old mill in Lawrence. It would make the evening editions; the Lawrence paper, *The Eagle Tribune*, was one of the few evening papers still publishing. Guaranteed it would be front page on this afternoon's edition. He flipped to the sports pages and noted that all the area winter sports teams were in first place. That had not happened since the mid-eighties; all was well with New England sports fans.

Jill had gathered the girls and put them in the bath together, trying to save time and effort. He heard them squealing with delight and smiled at their youthful innocence. He heard Jillian say, "Julia! Get back here!" Suddenly, a pink bundle of soft, wet, soap-scented girl rounded the corner at a dead run and leapt into his arms. She was as naked as the day she was born and with that innocence very little ones have, she grinned an impish smile. She knew she was not supposed to be running around in the buff. Nevertheless, Julia was a free spirit and hated wearing clothes. He had always thought of her as his little wood sprite and right then, sitting on his lap, she looked the part.

Jillian came around the corner with fire in her eyes. She saw Julia nestled into his chest, curled against him with her thumb in her mouth, looking as contented as she had ever seen anyone. Traynor smiled at Jill, was at ease, and didn't mind the water from the child's body soaking through his shirt and trousers.

The anger left Jillian's face and she smiled. "Come on, Imp, we got to get you ready for preschool." Julia kissed him on the cheek and he saw the sparkle in her eyes; she knew she had both her mother and her uncle wrapped around her finger, and they both loved it. In fifteen minutes, the girls were dressed and eating breakfast to the raucous sounds of their favorite cartoon. Traynor watched SpongeBob SquarePants for fifteen minutes and wondered: *Whatever happened to Wile E. Coyote and the Road Runner?*

At seven forty-five, Carrie left to catch the school bus and he was finished with the *Herald*. Jillian bundled Julia up in a heavy coat and said, "I have to drive her to preschool. You want to come?"

"Sure." Under normal circumstances, he would have offered to use his car but he needed one more answer and there was only one way to get it. He pulled on his overcoat, glad that his shirt had dried after Julia's wet hug. He followed Jillian to the door and said, "You got your keys?"

She pulled her hand from her pocket and jingled a set of keys. "Always."

Even though it felt like his stomach dropped through the floor, he smiled at her as he flipped the locking mechanism so the door would lock behind him. He followed her down to her car. They stepped out into the crisp November sunshine in time to see Carrie wave as she boarded the yellow and black school bus. Traynor waved back, still uncertain whether her mother was going to be there when she got home.

They didn't talk much on the drive to Julia's preschool. The traffic was light, and Traynor wondered if Jillian had guessed why he'd come over so early in the day. When they stopped in the schoolyard, Julia bounced across the back of the car seat and kissed them each in turn. She opened the door and hopped out of the car; it took all of her strength to close it. She gave a happy wave and darted off toward a group of little girls who swarmed around a woman, who appeared to be in her mid-fifties. The kids scampered about like kittens with a suspended ball of yarn. "That's Mrs. Clark," Jillian said. "The kids love her."

"It looks like it."

"You eat breakfast?" she asked.

"No. Drive over to Bickford's, I'll buy."

"You don't have to buy. I can afford it."

"I know. You can afford it served on your own sterling silver service."

She looked at him. The look on her face told him that if she hadn't known he knew she was involved in John's death she did then.

Bickford's was a local chain and they served up a good breakfast. Traynor requested a booth in the back away from everyone else—a place where they could talk privately. Jillian ordered a ham and cheese omelet. It sounded good so he ordered the same. She sipped on her coffee and said, "How long have you known?"

"Since yesterday I had my suspicions. But, I wasn't sure until a half hour ago."

She thought for a moment and then said, "Those damned keys. Ed, you have to believe me when I say that there was a time when I loved him and was willing to forgive him for anything. But he was no good—I put up with a lot from him, but when I learned about Connie—"

"You knew about Consuela?"

"Yes. I assume you've met her."

"Oh, yes. I'm afraid I have some more bad news for you."

"You're not going to tell me—"

"That Consuela's dead? Yes, I am. Obviously she took your little secret to the grave."

"We were going to split the money."

"You have the money?"

"I have the bank books. I got the pass codes to the accounts from the son of a bitch's car after we shot him. Somehow, he got somebody to set up an account offshore, in the Cayman Islands. Can you imagine? He was so low he was going to run off and leave my girls with nothing! I wasn't about to let him get away with that. He hurt us too many times. I couldn't let him do it again."

"How long have you known about him and Consuela?"

"About six months ago she called me. She wanted to assure me that the girls would always be welcome to visit with her. She promised to keep her job and any other bad influences away while they were there. I told her I had no idea what she was talking about. I told her that she had the wrong number. She insisted that she had the correct number and then called me by name. Then she told me she was married to John. I told her I was too."

He thought back to the last time he had seen Consuela alive and realized she missed her calling; she should have been an actor. Anyone who could look as surprised and distraught as she had when learning of her husband's bigamy had some real talent. "So when did you two decide to kill him?"

"In October, we decided it was time to do something about him. We met and had dinner together. She was really a good person, in spite of what she did for a living and some of the people with whom she associated. We decided to keep everything quiet because we knew he was up to some sort of dirty deal but were not sure exactly what it was. When Humberto told Connie about their scheme to rip off the Escobar brothers, we knew it was time for us to act."

"Wait a minute. Are you saying that you waited to act until *after* he stole the Escobars' money?"

"No. All we knew was they were planning the job—not when they were going to do it. We were surprised when Consuela got word that they'd done the job and that John had double-crossed his partners."

"Okay, go on."

"Humberto later learned that John had a connection at a local bank—"

"Jeffrey Saucier."

"Is that his name? It's evident that you've learned a lot about this. Anyhow, John paid someone, whom I gather was Saucier, to set up an offshore account in the Cayman Islands and move the money into it.

That's where it'll stay until my girls are old enough to use it. Nobody is taking that money; even if I go to prison for the rest of my life, my girls are going to be taken care of."

Their food came and Traynor picked at the omelet, his appetite gone. Jillian was not faring any better. "So what do we do now?" she asked.

She had asked the three-million-dollar question: what *did* he do now?

Traynor placed his fork in his plate and motioned for the server to bring their check. "What did you do with the gun?"

"I didn't know what to do with it, so I put it in a plastic bag and buried it behind the apartment. I've read the cops always look real close at the spouse of a murder victim. I was afraid they'd show up with a search warrant and find it. In fact, I was sure they were on to something when your friend Buck talked with me. For some reason, I got the impression he was going easy on me."

Traynor believed that she was right; if Buck wasn't his friend he might have pressed her harder, maybe even pushed for a warrant, and Jillian would have been in custody days ago. He left a tip on the table and said, "You seem to have lost your appetite."

"I'm scared, Ed. Please don't misunderstand me, I know what I did was wrong and I'll have to pay for it. I'm not afraid for myself. Shit, after all these years of being married to John, what can prison do to me? What really scares me is thinking about what will happen to the girls when I go to jail."

Jillian always had a knack for posing tough questions. If they were lucky, the girls might be able to stay with Maureen, in Nashua. However, foster care was more like it. As far as Traynor knew, Jillian's only living relative was her mother who lived on a fixed income in a seniors-only condominium in Florida. Even under less trying circumstances, it was almost impossible for out-of-state relatives to get custody from the New Hampshire Department of Health and Human Services.

He stood up and grabbed the check. "Let's go."

Neither of them spoke while he paid the bill and they drove back to Jillian's apartment. He kept trying to figure a way out of the mess Jill was in and could not shake the feeling that somewhere in hell John was laughing at him. He could visualize the smug look that surely covered his face as he watched his older brother struggle with yet another of his never-ending messes.

Once they were inside her apartment, Traynor grabbed the keys from the cupboard and put them in his pocket. "Do you remember where you buried the gun?"

"Yes."

"Take me there."

They went to the basement and Jillian led him to a wooden toolbox with a broken hasp. She opened the box and over her shoulder, Traynor saw it held the maintenance man's tools. He grabbed a pointed shovel and Jillian led him to the back of the building and out the back door. A patch of woods separated the apartment complex from the street that ran behind it and she led him past a line of dumpsters and into the trees. They followed a small path.

As they walked, a gentle breeze blew and leaves swirled along the trail in front of them. If an eighteen-wheeler hadn't roared past, Traynor would have thought they were miles from civilization. The track was about half as wide as the lane in which he had stood on when this whole thing started. An involuntary shudder ran through his body. He thought John's ghost must be around. Traynor was not into psychic phenomena, but he believed the dead stayed around, at least for a while. Most people in his profession reject anything they can't inspect with their five senses. Nevertheless, he thought there were many more paranormal activities going on than 90 percent of people realize; their lives have become too busy and they were too numb to sense it. All that morning, he felt that John was nearby. His mother once said that everyone must go through a life review when he or she stands before the heavenly gates. They see how they hurt everyone they ever encountered. Traynor knew that while his life review would be bad, he wondered what it had been like for John when he had faced that judge.

Jillian stopped about a hundred yards into the woods. She had picked a good spot. Even with the leaves gone from most of the trees, they were out of sight of anyone who might look out of their window. She pointed to a large rock a little over ten feet off the trail. "There," she announced, "at the base of that rock."

He walked to the boulder, which towered over him and touched the shovel to the ground. "Here?"

She motioned to her left. He took a step in that direction. She motioned him farther. He took two more paces and she nodded. He touched the shovel to the ground again. "Here?"

"I think so. It was dark when I buried it."

Traynor took the shovel and lightly pushed it into the ground. It immediately hit something hard, which in New England usually means a rock. He looked at Jillian, noting how fragile and helpless she looked against the gray background of the leafless trees. For the first time he realized just how much of a burden her life with John had been. The reserve of strength upon which she must have relied to get this far seemed to have finally exhausted itself.

"How deep did you bury it?"

"Not very, I was in a rush."

Not wanting to damage the weapon, he scraped along the surface with the side of the shovel rather than dig with the point. In seconds, he revealed a piece of black plastic, set the shovel aside, grabbed the end, and tugged. The pistol was in the bag and came out of its grave easily.

Jillian and Traynor walked back along the path leading to the apartment building and he put his arm around her. He felt her trembling and, more than anything else, wanted to be her hero again; to ride in on his white horse and save her from the villain, all the while comforting her as much as he could. He said, "Don't worry, Jill. It's almost over now."

Tears trickled from the corner of her eyes. "What's really pathetic about this entire mess is that right up until he died, he never once thought he was doing anything wrong. Should I call and turn myself in?"

He did not answer her for a few seconds. Before deciding on a course of action, he needed to think over what their options were. On the walk back to the apartment he said, "Before you call anyone, I want to know exactly how it all went down."

When they got inside, she told him the story.

36

Jill sat beside him, her hands in her lap, and she twirled her fingers, never raising her eyes from the floor. "I hadn't heard from John for a week. Then, unexpectedly, he called. He said he had to go away for a while and he wanted to see the girls before he did. I knew he was probably taking off for good. If Connie and I were going to do what we planned, it had to be then. I called her at the club and told her what was going on. She told me she'd come over right away and would call me when she was in position. We knew one of us had to follow and grab him.

"I had to find someone to watch the girls, so I called my friend Carla, and arranged for her to take the girls for the night. Fortunately, she lives close by and I was able to drop the kids off and get back before he arrived.

"He got here a bit after seven and as usual came through the door like God's gift to the world. I tried to act as if things were normal, but it wasn't easy. I mean, how are you supposed to act around someone who has betrayed you so badly that you're going to kill him?

"He didn't seem upset that the girls were gone, or angry with me for not telling him they were at Carla's for the night. Still, he stayed until just before nine-thirty. The asshole even tried to get me to go to bed with him. He probably thought I'd appreciate having him crawl over me for his usual five minutes before he came—and went. I turned him down by lying to him, begging off by telling him that it was my time of the month. The truth of the matter is that I decided a long time ago that he wasn't going to treat me like some weekend whore he'd picked up in a bar—we hadn't had sex together in over a year.

"When he left, I called Connie's cell phone. She was waiting nearby, picked me up, and we followed him.

"I think he wanted to avoid the early holiday shopping crowd so he waited until just before closing to visit the travel agency. I can only imagine the look that must have been on the travel agent's face as he outlined his itinerary to her. If it had been me, I would have told him to come back in the morning. However, knowing John, he couldn't have cared less what she wanted—everything was always about him. I could see him in my mind's eye. He'd planned everything out carefully and no insignificant pissant of a travel agent was about to throw his plans off. I visualized him glancing at his watch making the agent think she was tying up a very important person.

"Connie hid in the doorway of a vacant shop and saw John walk out of the travel agency. He stood there for several seconds, checking out the mall. He and about seven other people had the place to themselves. He smirked and shoved an envelope into the inside pocket of his coat; we assumed that it contained his plane tickets and itinerary. Having purchased them seemed to give him a sense of security. He turned away and while his back was turned, Connie darted out an exit. She wanted to get back to the car before he got out of the building.

"John left the mall and shrugged his shoulders against the chilly temperature. He walked across the dimly lit parking area to the remote corner where he had parked.

"Not wanting him to see me, I had waited in the car Connie had borrowed. If he spotted either of us, our plan wouldn't work. I slouched down in the seat so he wouldn't see me through the windshield. The car's side windows were tinted and in the dark he couldn't see inside through them, even though we could see him. Connie started the motor.

"I was glad Connie had chosen to borrow the old Impala; it held John's attention. When we backed out of our parking spot, he paid more attention to the car than who was in it. It was, as John would have called it, *cherry*, not a scratch on it.

"I don't have to tell you that John had a thing about old cars. He stopped and watched the '64 Chevy Impala Super Sport 409/425. For a brief second, he looked uncertain, almost nervous. Enough so that Connie thought he would run. He seemed to relax and breathe easier when she slowly drove away from him. He waited until she turned down one of the parking aisles and then continued walking to his car.

"Connie pulled into a parking space directly in front of his car and turned the motor off. When John heard the car pull in, he seemed to tense up, and we hoped he wouldn't bolt before we had a chance to grab him. John paused, his hand digging in his pants pocket for something, probably his keys. I hoped he would assume that anyone making a hit would not be so stupid as to drive a car as recognizable as the Chevy. He kept an eye on the car as his hand fumbled in his pocket, trying to get his keys out.

"John turned his head away from the Impala, concentrating on getting his door unlocked, and didn't see Connie get out. For a few seconds, he seemed to forget about everything. Before he knew it, she stood beside him. John spun around, ready to defend himself, and froze.

"Connie aimed the gun at John's face. She was a foot shorter than John and had to point the gun upward to make sure he saw it. With her free hand, she made a stop sign, like a traffic cop halting traffic. She stepped close to him.

"John looked shocked and, when he saw it was Connie, he ignored the gun. I assume he didn't think she'd use it. Most likely, he was considering a way to bullshit his way around her.

"Connie was tougher than he'd thought and she didn't waiver. She kept the gun aimed at his head and didn't let it deviate, for even a second. She motioned for John to turn around. I heard her say, 'Turn around, Juan.'

"John tried to reason with her and while his attention was on her I slipped out of the car. We only had the one gun, but I had a carving knife that I took from my kitchen.

"Connie told him again to turn around.

"I think he intended to run, hoping she would not have the courage to shoot him. When he turned and saw me standing there with the knife pointed at his stomach, he stopped . . . surprise and shock on his face. Connie took advantage of his momentary paralysis, pulled his hands behind his back, and securely wrapped his wrists with duct tape. Once she was sure his hands were secure, she stepped in front of him, tore off a piece of tape, and covered his mouth. Then she used the gun to push him toward the rear of the Impala. She said nothing while opening the trunk. Once again, she motioned with the gun, another mute order—this one directing John to get in the trunk.

"John looked at us, apparently still uncertain whether or not to run for it. He glanced around the parking lot, hoping to see someone who might scare her off, no luck. The only people in the parking area were the three of us. Walking out of the mall after closing, which had seemed like such a smart move fifteen minutes ago, was probably the stupidest thing he'd ever done. Parking the car in a secluded part of the lot was also dumb, so foolish it cost him his life. He always thought that he was so smart. The truth is that most of the time he was brainless. He must have decided the odds were against him escaping without being shot and crawled in the trunk, complying with Connie's command.

"Once he was safely locked in the trunk, I got into his car and searched it. At first I had no idea what I was looking for . . . other than something that would tell us where the money was. I found the passbooks in the glove box.

"I left his car unlocked, hoping it would be stolen, which turned out to be wishful thinking. I got in Connie's car. She was as nervous as I was.

She gripped the steering wheel so tight that her knuckles were white. Her coal black hair was shiny and her face soaked with perspiration. We drove out of the mall parking lot."

Traynor interrupted her tale and asked, "Why didn't you cover your faces?"

"We didn't care if he knew it was us—in fact we wanted him to know it was us."

"What if someone else saw you?"

"At that moment I didn't care. For years, he'd been manipulating me. I believe he thought he could convince me to help him—not this time.

"We turned the radio up and faded the speakers to the back so John wouldn't overhear our conversation. I don't know why we bothered, it didn't matter what he heard; before long he'd know exactly what we had in mind for him and why.

"We pulled out of the mall and took Route 28. Connie used back roads to get us to our destination. We took Route 111 to Danville then 111A to Fremont. She looked at me and asked if I was okay.

"I stared straight ahead and nodded. I hoped the resolve I felt showed in my face. I wanted to see this thing through.

"Connie concentrated on her driving and asked where my girls were. I knew she was making conversation, we were both nervous. It isn't every day you kill your husband. I told her that I got a friend to take them for the night.

"She gave me a nervous look and asked if I thought that was wise.

"I told her it was not a problem. The friend was close enough to the girls that they called her 'aunt.'

"Connie lit a cigarette and rolled the window down so the smoke wouldn't bother me. She must have sensed my nervousness because she asked me if I was sure that I wanted to go through with our plan.

"At that stage of the game, I wasn't about to turn back, so I said, 'Yes.' It's funny, even after all that happened, I can still forgive him for all the pain he caused me. But, I can't forgive him for deserting his children and leaving them with nothing. I think about all the years of mental and physical abuse. Of how John used the girls and me as if we were his pets, something he could pay attention to when he wanted to and ignore when he didn't. Ed, he was no damned good. I'd known it for years but stupid female pride made me keep trying to turn him into a father and husband of whom we could be proud. There was something rotten inside John, some selfish and hate-filled spirit that drove him to play with people until he hurt them beyond repair. Whatever that something was it had surely come from the deepest parts of hell and I was going to get it out of our lives and send it back, even if it meant John had to go with it.

"Connie must have had some reservations about my part in the plan. She asked me if I had thought about what would happen to the girls if we were caught.

"That was the one question about which I'd spent long hours worrying. When I'd learned that John had ripped off the Escobar brothers, I knew I had an answer to my dilemma. I assured her that everything would be okay. I believed that once we had the money we'd be home free. Before anyone knew it, we'd be gone. I reached over and placed my hand on Connie's arm and asked her if she only wanted one million. I told her that I was willing to split it down the middle.

"Ed, I don't know how well you knew her, but she wasn't a greedy person. Quite the contrary, she was a very giving and caring woman. She put me at ease by saying she could live very well on one million. She told me that I had two daughters to think about and that it would be expensive to hide out because it could be years before the Escobars stopped looking for the money . . . if they'd ever stop.

"The conversation died away and we rode in silence until Connie turned onto a wooded road. There were widely spaced houses on either side of the road; many of them had started out as mobile homes and been modified into weird mixtures of metal and wood. We passed a narrow lane, did a U-turn in a driveway, and returned to the road. She shut the car off and said, 'Last chance to call it off.'

"At that point I was dedicated and told her that all I wanted to do was get it over with.

"We got out of the car, quietly closing the doors so as not to wake any of the neighborhood's residents. We opened the trunk and stared at him.

He looked pathetic, lying there, blinking his eyes as he looked up into the moonlight. I motioned for him to get out.

"It was difficult for John to get out of the trunk, a task made even more difficult since neither of us helped him. He finally got out and stood on wobbly legs. I don't know why, but I pulled the tape off his mouth . . . maybe I wanted to give him a final chance to say something that would redeem him. Rather than that, he looked back and forth between us and tried to talk us out of our plan. He got that suckhole smile he always used to get around me. There were many times when I'd fall for it, but not this time.

"He looked around and saw that where we had taken him was way the hell out in the willy-wags. I think it was then, for the first time, that he really understood his predicament. He started to negotiate, offering us a share of the money.

"Connie pushed him toward the narrow lane leading into the woods. The night had turned cold, below freezing. It felt as if true November weather had finally arrived.

"The lane quickly turned into a trail for ATVs and motorbikes and John began to seriously bargain for his life, offering us one-third of the money.

"Connie told him to shut his mouth and walk. The tension made her accent stronger.

"John continued to plead with us and upped his offer to a million each.

"We walked until we were about a quarter mile from the car. Connie pushed him and he stumbled, falling to his knees. By this time, he had obviously figured out what our intentions were . . . that we were not trying to scare him and had a deadlier intent. He started begging and his voice rose; for the first time in my life, I saw John scared, truly scared. That's when he told us that he had passbooks with the codes to some accounts and if we let him go he'd give them to us.

"His face fell when I reached inside my coat and took the passbooks out and said, 'Are you talking about these?'

"Then he started crying and pleading with us. His groveling only enraged me more. I told him: 'Fuck you.' I took the gun from Connie.

"His eyes glistened with tears and horror, his head was bowed, and he never took his eyes off the ground. You know, if he'd only looked at me, into my eyes, I might have thought about sparing his life. But, he didn't, not once."

Jill wiped at the tears running down her cheeks. She looked at Traynor, her face flushed from crying. "I think for the first time the realization that I was about to kill the father of my children hit me—it was too late; at that point there was no turning back.

"He was blubbering like a baby and he changed course, trying to reason with me. Finally, he did look at me and smile, only this time it didn't make me weak in the knees. If I was angry, that unconscious arrogance pissed me off even more. He wasn't going to wheedle his way out this time. I told him not to give me anymore of his bullshit. That I knew he was going to abandon our girls, as if they were garbage. I told him that I might have been able to forgive him for all he'd done to me, but not for what he was going to do to them.

"Once again, he began to plead. All our life together he'd manipulated me, and I'd had my fill of it. He was such an ass! Even looking down the barrel of a gun, he wouldn't accept the reality of his situation. I guess he still had delusions that he'd be able to talk us out of it.

"Connie saved me having to talk to him, telling John that he was a bastard and would never change.

"I looked around and didn't think we were far enough away from the road. I saw a house through the trees with a light on. I told him to get on his feet—we could talk as we walked.

"He seemed to feel he had been given a ray of hope and struggled to his feet.

"We heard a door slam at one of the houses and I pushed John farther down the road. The moon illuminated the ground enough for us to see where we were going. We came to a place where a large mud puddle stood in the road. John started caterwauling like a scared kid. His mouth was running a mile a minute, but saying all the wrong things. Ten years ago, I would've bought his crap. However, now I'm older and wiser. All his whining did was make me more determined and grated on my nerves.

"We had walked about a hundred yards and I told him that we had gone far enough.

"I placed the pistol against the side of his head and said, 'Goodbye, John.'"

Jillian looked at Traynor, tears rolling down her cheeks.

"Is that when you shot him?" he asked.

"As mad as I was, I still couldn't do it, Ed. I looked at Connie and she knew it too. She reached over and took the gun.

"John must have felt relieved. He smiled at Connie, trying to soften her. However, she was strong, Ed, a lot more than me. I'll never forget his last words; even at the end I don't think he understood how rotten he was. When she pressed the gun against his head, he cried, 'C'mon girls, let's work this out. I ain't done nothing bad enough to deserve this?'

"If he didn't know what he'd done by then, he never would, and with the last words he'd ever hear, I told him so. Connie pulled the trigger and stepped back as he fell face down in the muddy water.

"I stared at him in the moonlight, the dark water turning even darker with his blood. After a few seconds, his body stopped twitching. We watched until he went still. Then when he didn't move for a few minutes, Connie said, 'Let's get out of here.'

"As we walked out of the woods neither of us looked back."

She sat quietly. "We had to do it, Ed. He would never have changed into someone of whom we could be proud. He'd keep right on hurting and using everyone he knew."

Jill sat on the couch, her elbows on her knees, hunched forward. Her eyes locked on the floor in front of her. She had kept them averted from him during the entire confession. When she finished her tale, she sighed and sat back on the couch. When she finally looked at Traynor, tears and mascara tracks covered her cheeks.

"So, Ed, what happens now?"

Traynor knew that there was no way he could turn her in, not for doing what half the people in New Hampshire wanted to do. John's funeral was going to be small, so small that Ed doubted he even had enough living friends to serve as pallbearers. Traynor made up his mind that he wouldn't be able to send this woman away from her girls—or from him. He gathered her in his arms and held her close. *Besides*, he rationalized, *the person who had pulled the trigger was dead; Jillian was an accomplice, but not a killer.*

He felt her body shake as she cried and whispered to her, "Don't you worry, Babe. I'll take care of you—for the rest of your life."

37

Traynor's headlights reflected off the fog, highlighting what little snow remained after two days of rain and mist. He drove along a sparsely populated section of state highway 102 east of Derry. As was usual for eleven o'clock at night, he had the road all to himself.

He saw the sign announcing Blackmane's Gun Shop and turned off the highway. Slowly, he drove along the narrow dirt road that led to Fred's shop. In Traynor's business, it paid to know a good gunsmith, and Fred Blackmane was one of the best. When your life depended on firearms as much as Traynor's had for years, you quickly learn the lethal consequences of shoddy work. Nothing gets the quality message across quicker than when a handgun misfires or a rifle blows up in your face when you need it most.

Fred probably would have done more business if his place was in town, but he was a perfectionist and wanted certain things for his business. He was also a smart businessman, who is more than willing to give a little to get what he seeks. One thing he wanted to avoid was fighting with the city council and anyone who felt firearms were of the devil's making. A little peace and quiet was one reason he opened his shop on the boundary between Derry and Chester, just across the Chester line. The other was because the structure, formerly the office of a construction company, came with an old sand and gravel pit. Fred remodeled the office building into a store/shop combination and built a couple of fantastic shooting ranges, one for rifles, and another for pistols, out of the old pit. The location was perfect for the meeting Traynor had arranged. Although if things went south, he wasn't sure how Fred would react to him using his business for a killing ground. He would cross that bridge with Fred when they came to it.

About fifty feet in from the road, the surface turned to dirt and widened into a parking lot. Traynor backed the Taurus close to the trees, where it would be invisible from the highway. He opened the trunk and took out a Beretta Model 1201 FP twelve-gauge, full-choke, autoloader shotgun and a box of double aught shot. He took a handful of shells from the box and fed them into the shotgun until it would take no more. Federal law limits how many shells could be loaded in a hunting weapon, but Fred knew Traynor was a former cop and altered his. He had pulled the plug out of the magazine allowing the gun to hold its full capacity, six shells in the magazine and another in the chamber. It was a great weapon for a close-up fight; it had an eighteen-inch barrel and was lightweight, only six and a third pounds when fully loaded, which made it easy to handle. Nevertheless, it was lethal at short range, and Traynor figured he would be working close tonight. Once the shotgun was loaded, he checked the load in his nine-millimeter pistol and set out to make sure the area was clear.

On one hand, he was thankful for the fog; on the other, he cursed it. The heavy damp haze made it easy to hide, but what worked for him, worked for his opponent as well. He checked out the back of the building to ensure Carlo hadn't gotten the same idea and decided to show up early. Seeing that he had the place all to himself, Traynor relaxed. Then he heard a vehicle turn off the road. As it came closer, it slowed down. He stayed behind the building and watched the glow of the headlights die out. Gravel crunched as the vehicle drove over the frozen surface of the dirt road and made him think about his situation. He realized that he was a fool for coming here alone and waited as the vehicle circled the building. He raised the shotgun, ready to blast anyone in the vehicle.

The nose of Max's Excursion rounded the corner and he lowered the twelve-gauge as the Ford stopped in front of him. The motor died and Traynor stood in the sudden silence listening to its motor tick in the cold fog. The doors opened and Max and Charley stepped out, each carrying a rifle. "You didn't think we were going to let you face these guys alone, did you?" Max announced.

Truthfully, Traynor was damned glad to see them. A little insurance sure is a nice thing—especially in a gunfight.

Charley piped in. "You don't expect Escobar to come alone, do you?"

Traynor smiled. "What? You think I just crawled out from under a cabbage leaf. No, I'm certain he'll have some troops with him. Nevertheless, you guys have done enough already. This isn't your fight."

Max ground out a cigar and said, "Ain't you the one who said the second rule of a gunfight is to bring all your friends and their guns?"

Traynor grinned. "Yeah, I suppose I was."

"Well, here we are, all your friends—both of us."

Traynor laughed. Nevertheless, Max was right. He had a lot of acquaintances but so few friends that he could count them on one hand.

"Okay, Max, you take the left side of the drive and Charley take the right. And guys . . . don't shoot each other, okay?"

Max smiled, and Charley got a worried look on his face. "Don't worry, doofus," Max said, "I'll show you where to hide and which direction to shoot."

The three men circled the store and Traynor sat on the steps of the farmer's porch that ran along the front of the gun shop. If Carlo followed his instructions, he would be along any minute. When he'd called Escobar from Jillian's apartment, Traynor told him that if he wanted his money, he'd be there at midnight. He sputtered about the book and Traynor lied, claiming ignorance. All he had was John's bank account books. He could have them in return for leaving John's family alone. He agreed to Traynor's conditions. However, experience had left Traynor with little or no faith in his fellow man, nor did he believe a word Escobar said.

If Carlo came there thinking he was going to rely on him keeping his word, he was not the sharpest crayon in the box. Traynor had been around Escobar's kind for years and knew them for what they were: parasites thriving and living off the fear of their victims. They had no loyalty to anyone, not even their own families. Every morning they asked, "What have you done for me today?" and if the answer was "nothing," you could be dead by sundown.

Gisela Martin was ample proof of that—at least she was all the evidence Traynor needed. He was certain that she was a classic example of how Escobar dealt with problem employees. That was the only reason for her execution that Traynor could think of. It goes to show good looks, a great pair of legs, and a six-figure sports car will only take a woman so far.

As for Consuela, Humberto, Theo, and John, they grabbed a tiger by the tail and found themselves unable to let go. As a result, all of them, with the possible exception of John, became what the military would consider acceptable losses, collateral damage if you will.

Gisela must have believed that Humberto and Theo got the book when they killed Benny. By the time she figured out that she was wrong, it was too late. Carlo had caught on to her little swindle.

As soon as John's wives killed him, Traynor had become the proverbial fly in the ointment. He found the book and stumbled, albeit after the event, into Carlo's ambush. He didn't think the Lawrence cops had figured out who was who at the old mill yet. They were probably trying to track down where the twelve-gauge shotgun shells and nine-millimeter casings came from. Of one thing he was certain, someone on the Lawrence police, it was more than likely that it was more than one, had to be on the take. It was improbable that nobody called the cops until after he and Max stumbled into the shootout. The cops held back, which led Traynor to believe it was someone well up the chain of command—whoever that person may be is for the cops in Massachusetts to figure out . . . odds were that the name or names were in Gisela's journal. He heard another vehicle approach and made a final check of his guns. When he was satisfied that everything was in order, Traynor sat back to wait.

The car flashed by the drive and then the red glow of brake lights lit up the thickening fog. The land around the gun shop was mostly flood plain and, in the winter, got a lot of fog. It developed when the air got colder than the ground, or maybe it was the other way around. The result was always the same—a heavy, ground-hugging mist. There are days when it never lifts; that day had been one of them.

There was a small country road about twenty yards past Fred's drive. Traynor heard the car slow down. If he were Carlo, he'd let a couple of gunmen out there with instructions to circle back through the woods. He didn't hear any doors open, but then, if they were careful, he might not. The car backed up until it passed the driveway, stopped on the road for a couple of seconds, as if its occupants were trying to determine if they were in the right place, and then turned into the drive.

Traynor stayed put and waited for the car to stop. As it approached, the driver put the headlights on high beam and Traynor shielded his eyes against the glare. He cursed, knowing the lights would ruin his night vision. Which, he was certain, was what they intended.

The car stopped thirty feet short of him. Traynor kept his left hand over his eyes, trying to block the light. The doors opened and three men got out, one to his right and two on his left. He figured that there was a fourth, maybe more, and that they were in the woods near Max.

"You fellows want to kill those lights?" he asked. "I don't think we want any unexpected guests." In the brilliant glare of the halogen lamps, he could not tell if anyone had heard him or not, but after a few seconds, the lights went out.

Carlo stepped around the guy on the left and said, "Good evening, Mr. Traynor."

"Why bring the armed entourage, Carlo? I thought this was supposed to be just you and me."

"What can I say? I'm cautious by nature."

"Is that what you call it? I call it being a lying coward."

Carlo tensed at the insult. Traynor decided to fire another shot across his bow. "I was sorry to hear about the deaths of your brother and your assistant. I guess it's hard to get good help these days."

His head jerked as if Traynor had punched him. "Unfortunately, those things happen in this business."

"I'm sure, but killing a beautiful woman just seems like such a waste. What happened? Did she become too ambitious?"

"Sometimes people become too greedy and they try to move up too fast."

"Yeah, I guess that's how this whole thing started. Ambition, I mean."

"Ambition is something I can understand. But, disloyalty, now that is an entirely different matter."

"So, Gisela was selling you out. I figured as much."

"Yes, it's a sad thing when someone you have taken out of the filthiest bordello in Bogotá, someone to whom you gave every opportunity, decides to cross over. But then we both know what it's like to be unappreciated, don't we Mr. Traynor."

Traynor continued the banter, thankful for the time, which allowed him to recover his night vision. "I guess you might say that. I'm intrigued though, how long have you known about the drug lab in the old mill?"

"I've known about that for a long time—after all I paid for it to be built. If you recall, it was I who had Gisela call you and arrange the meeting the first time you visited there."

"Did you know your brother's body was in there?"

"Ah, you are clever. My brother, much like yours, was not to be trusted. You see, like Gisela, he too was involved in negotiations with certain parties . . . parties who didn't have my best interest at heart."

"So you killed him and made it look as if he'd been sacrificed to some pagan god."

"You're as smart as I thought. Nevertheless, it was business and Eduardo knew that. I mean after all, what does a brother's murder matter? Especially if he's only a half brother."

"Tie up one last loose end for me. Where did the Puerto Rican three-some fit into this?"

"They were acquainted with your brother, who by the way proved to be very resourceful. I still haven't found the property I want. The money, however, while important, is of secondary value. I can always make that up. That is, provided Gisela's book doesn't get into the wrong hands."

"Ah," Traynor said, "now we get to the heart of the matter."

Carlo must have decided to dispense with the social niceties. "So in spite of your denial, I will ask you again. Did you bring the book?"

Traynor patted his left side. "Okay, I'll fess up. I got it—it's in my car. I didn't want it to get lost or damaged, so it's been by my side all week."

"So it was you who found it, not those two bumbling fuckheads?"

"You could say that."

Throughout the conversation Carlo had been standing with his left arm bent around his back. Traynor knew when that arm came into view, it would be brandishing a weapon. He slowly placed his hand on the shotgun, his finger on the trigger. Hoping Carlo would not notice, he clicked the safety off and pulled it a few inches closer.

It didn't work. Carlo noticed the shotgun for the first time. He seemed less sure of himself. Nobody wants to face a twelve gauge up close; it is possibly the deadliest weapon on Earth inside forty feet. He turned his head as if checking the area and asked, "Were you trustworthy? Did you come alone?"

"Nope, but then I never thought you would either. My father raised a fool, not a babbling idiot. If I were a gambler, I'd bet even money that right about now there are a few rifles aimed at you."

He grinned as malicious a grin as Traynor had ever seen and said, "I thought as much."

Traynor heard a twig snap in the woods to his right. It took all of his willpower to keep from looking in that direction, but it probably saved his life. Carlo pulled his arm around and whipped an assault weapon toward him. The trees erupted with muzzle flashes. Max and Charley opened fire; the sharp barks of their rifles filled the air. Carlo's two bodyguards were down on the ground, their blood flowing across the snow-covered hardpan surface, looking black in the parking lot lights.

Traynor rolled off the step inches ahead of the stream of bullets from Carlo's machine gun. The slugs ripped through the wood where he had been sitting a millisecond earlier, showering him with splinters. He rolled over, came to his knees, and fired the twelve-gauge. He heard Carlo grunt as his legs took several pellets of double aught buck. The bulk of the blast hit the car, shattering one of the headlights. Traynor rolled again, presenting the Colombian with a moving target as he tried to bring the assault rifle to bear. A shot came from the woods and the passenger side window of Carlo's car disintegrated.

Carlo's magazine ran empty and he threw the weapon aside and ran for the safety of the building. With a glance, Traynor checked Carlo's men and saw they were still down and at least one was dead, his body heat rising into the night, creating a cloud of steam in the cold air. He saw blood in the sand and snow where Carlo had stood and followed it around the side of the building.

Two more shots ripped through the woods and Traynor heard the sound of someone running through the trees. There was another shot. *POW! WHOP!* He heard the unmistakable sound of a high-velocity bullet hitting a flesh-and-blood target. He heard Charley call out, "Did you get him?"

Max answered, "Yeah."

It was finally down to the real nitty-gritty; only Carlo was left. Traynor circled the building, following the blood trail in the snow. Carlo, however, never hesitated. He continued circling the building, just ahead. Traynor knew that he had one of two things on his mind. To either get behind him or . . . he heard a car engine start. Carlo was getting away! He ceased being cautious and ran for the Taurus.

Traynor heard the Mercedes's tires spin, making a whirling noise as Escobar backed the car out of the drive, weaving side to side as he tried to make himself a difficult target for Max and Charley. Traynor's friends stepped out of their concealment, firing bullets into the car. The transmission whined as Carlo accelerated to speeds higher than the reverse gear had been engineered to handle. Steam drifted from under the hood and the single headlamp seemed a bit out of alignment. The 560SL hit the paved surface of the highway. Its tires bit into the pavement, burning rubber and squealing. Carlo locked the brakes, rammed the car into drive, and spun out heading east.

Traynor ran to the parking lot and hollered for Max and Charley to stop firing. He vaulted over the bodies of Carlo's men and ran to the Taurus. He fished the keys from his pocket and dropped the shotgun as he got inside the car. His fingers were cold and reluctant to take orders from his brain as he fumbled with the keys, trying to get the correct one into the ignition. He cursed his clumsiness. Just when he thought he'd never find the elusive slot, it slid home. He twisted it and the motor rumbled to life. It sounded as if someone had awakened an angry dragon.

People were always asking Traynor why he kept the old Ford when he could easily afford something newer, maybe even an SUV. What many of them did not know was that he had a lot of money under the hood of the battered Ford. Charley's cousin, Peter, was a NASCAR mechanic during the racing season. In winter, when racing was at a lull, he came home for a couple of months and did selected jobs for Charley. Like Charley and his computers, he was a magician with a set of wrenches and loved nothing better than to fine-tune high-performance motors. Last year, Traynor gave him three grand and Peter dropped a racing engine in the Taurus. Traynor was not a motor head, nor had he ever been; he couldn't tell you the horsepower or the cubic-inch displacement of the motor, but he did know one thing—there were not many cars on the street that could outrun it.

He sped around the trees and into the driveway, the rear end fish-tailing in the sand and gravel that Fred had spread on the snow-packed road. The tires threw a cloud of snow, dirt, and debris behind him as he urged the car off the snowy surface of the gun shop's access road and onto the paved highway. The rear tires chirped as they hit the pavement and he pushed the accelerator all the way down. The car sat in place for a full second, the tires spinning ferociously. The inside of the Ford filled with the acrid smell of burnt rubber and smoke. The screeching was so loud it must have awakened everyone within a five-mile radius. Finally, the tires gained traction. He felt the acceleration push his body back into the seat as the raw horsepower he had unleashed shoved the car forward. He had no idea how much motor Carlo had in the Mercedes, but he knew the Colombian needed a lot more than a stock motor if he hoped to get away.

Route 102 was a twisted, curvy strip of two-lane asphalt running across the southern tier of the state. Between Nashua and Derry, it was quite straight and over the years had developed into a string of mini-malls and stores. However, once past the Derry roundabout and Beaver Lake, all that ends. The dwellings on either side of the road turned into widely spaced homes, scattered farms, and small businesses. Through that section, the road twisted and turned like a snake with its head cut off. Through Chester, there were stretches where it was mostly woods and a few gravel and sand pits. The speed limit was forty-five with reduced speeds on the sharper curves. Traynor hit eighty in no time and overtook Carlo in less than two miles, just as they climbed the long grade that led to the crossroads in Chester. They were lucky no one crossed the inter-section; there would have been no way they could have stopped if there was. Traynor edged up behind Carlo and bumped the back of the 560SL.

They shot through the intersection, both cars leaving the surface of the road, sailing through the air for almost thirty feet. The Benz hit down first, sparks and pieces of exhaust system flying out from under it. Traynor slammed down right behind it, his head snapping as the Taurus bottomed out. He heard a horrible scraping and felt the Ford's under-carriage slam the road. The Ford shook violently and he felt something roll along beneath the floor and then heard a loud banging. The engine's roar increased tenfold, sounding like a rocket on takeoff. He glanced in the rearview mirror and saw sparks and something shiny fly up and disappear into the fog. *Scratch that muffler,* he thought. The Chester Fire Department building flashed by and they were back on the twisting road.

He was close enough to Carlo to see the drug lord's eyes shining in his rearview mirror; they were like two penlights as he struggled to stay ahead of his pursuit. Traynor could see his head darting back and forth, as he rocked like a little kid, trying to urge another mile per hour out of the car. Traynor had his lights on high beam and left them there, hoping to blind him. They used the entire road, cutting across lanes as they tried to straighten out the twisting curves. Each time they approached a sharp bend in the road Traynor prayed they would not meet the one fool who was out on a foggy night. A couple of times, Carlo seemed to lose his nerve and tried to brake, but Traynor did not let him slow down. He knew this road and had a specific destination in mind. Each time his quarry tried to decrease his speed he bumped the Benz, forcing Carlo to keep the insane pace.

They whipped around a curve and missed a pickup truck by mere inches. The driver laid on his horn, the claxon's sound Dopplering away as he flashed by. They had shot by the Chevy truck at ninety miles per hour, and Traynor got a glimpse of the driver's face in his headlights as he shot past; all he noted was the fear in the whites of the man's huge eyes. Traynor glanced in his rearview mirror and saw the driver's arm come out the window, his middle finger raised, and red brake lights quickly disappearing in the fog—most likely cursing up a storm.

Traynor continued to herd Carlo, pushing him to speeds the drug kingpin didn't want to hit. Ed stayed on his ass until he saw what he was looking for. Traynor almost missed the sign in the fog. Carlo did miss it. It showed a nasty S curve and posted the speed limit as thirty-five. In the middle of the curve, a small bridge crossed the Exeter River and the road cut back. At that particular place, the Exeter is not much of a river, maybe twenty to thirty feet across, but there was a fast current and the only reason the surface was not frozen was the rapidly moving water.

Carlo straightened out the S and smashed through the guardrails. The Mercedes's hood flew up and smashed against the windshield as it vaulted across the river. The nose dipped and the car slammed into the far bank, the front end smashed into a granite boulder, and the rear end crashed down into the water and mud. The impact was so powerful that the car's frame twisted, the windshield and back windows exploded, and the motor burst free of its mounts and tore through the firewall, pushing Carlo and the front seat into the back seat, in turn forcing it into the trunk. For a moment, it seemed that the current would grab the car and pull it into the middle of the river. However, the sedan settled into the shallows with a resounding splash.

When Traynor saw the warning sign, he rammed both feet onto the brake pedal. There were a few seconds where the antilock brakes made him hope that he was straight with God. Like most people who grew up on conventional brakes, Traynor liked the sudden snap that drove you into the harness straps as the wheels locked and the comforting sound of the tires wailing and screeching. With antilocks, you got neither. The harness locked but it felt as if the car was still accelerating, until the brakes finally grabbed and the Ford slid to a stop, spinning around and ending up sideways, across both lanes. The Taurus rocked up onto two wheels and held there for a second before dropping back down on all four wheels. Traynor backed the car into the eastbound lane and pulled onto the shoulder.

He saw a light come on in an upstairs window of a house across the road, the shades went up, and a head appeared. Someone peered out, trying to see what had happened and a man shouted, "Jesus Christ, Margie, some fucking idiot just jumped the river in a car! Call 9-1-1!"

Traynor knew he had to move fast. He grabbed a flashlight from the glove box and then ran back to his trunk and opened it. He shined the light inside and frantically pawed and fumbled around for what he felt was an eternity. During the mad dash down Route 102, the trunk's contents were tossed like a salad. The need for urgency seemed to make time speed up and panic started to build in his chest. The light finally rested on the plastic garbage bag. Somehow or another, it had gotten wedged in the spare tire well. He grabbed it and ran across the bridge, following the riverbank until he got to Carlo's car. A cloud of steam from the superheated engine sitting in the cold water hung over the car and he smelled gas, oil, and motor coolant as the fluids ran out of the demolished engine compartment.

He stepped into the freezing cold water and inhaled sharply. Traynor removed the twenty-two revolver from the plastic wrapper and discarded the bag, tossing it out into the current as he waded through the river. He breathed hard as he fought his way along the muddy bottom; somewhere in the mud, his left shoe came off and he lost it in the current. The frigid water was over his knees when he reached Carlo.

Traynor shined the flashlight on him. He was a mess. His chest and legs were pinned under the car's superheated motor, and his torso appeared crushed; at least Traynor assumed it had been. He was unable to see much through the mass of twisted steel that filled the place where his legs should be. The engine was so hot it was cooking Escobar where he lay against it. Water streamed inside the car, hissed, and snapped as it hit the sizzling metal. Traynor reached inside and grabbed Carlo by the hair, pulling his face from where it rested on the hot engine. His left cheek pulled away from his head; the flesh stuck to the searing metal like a frying egg. His head rolled toward Traynor, who saw that his right eye had popped out of the socket and swung from side to side as it dangled against his cheek. Traynor wanted to back away but concentrated on the task.

Sirens warbled in the night, their volume increasing, and Traynor knew he only had minutes. He finally found Carlo's left hand and wrapped it around the pistol's handle. He forced his still pliable index finger into the trigger guard, aimed the pistol out the broken window, and fired a shot into the river. He thanked God that twenty-two pistols didn't resonate loudly.

Confident that Escobar's fingerprints were on the small caliber gun, Traynor threw it into the car behind Carlo. He heard it drop to the floor and then took the book from his inside coat pocket and tossed it behind the body where he hoped the water would not reach it. He placed Carlo's face back on the engine and stepped back. He saw blood on his coat and did not want anyone to come to the wrong conclusion, even if it was the right one. He braced himself and submerged his body in the river, hoping the water would wash away any blood. The water shocked him as he submerged, but he forced himself to stay under for as long as he could stand it, then quickly bolted to his feet and waded to the shore.

He was in his car with the heater blasting when half the cops in New Hampshire arrived.

38

Traynor pushed a piece of omelet around his plate with a fork and looked up when Buck flopped into the booth. He nodded at him. "Hey, Buck."

"Ed."

The waitress placed a cup of coffee in front of Buck.

"You eating today?" she asked.

"Just coffee."

She shrugged and left them alone.

Buck poured cream and added three heaping spoons of sugar to the mug. He stirred his coffee with slow circular strokes, stared at Traynor, and said nothing.

"Okay," Traynor said, "obviously something is on your mind . . . out with it."

"She did it."

"She?"

"Jillian . . . she killed John, didn't she?"

Traynor hoped his expression did not give anything away. "State police say Escobar did it," he answered.

"State police got it wrong. And, unless I'm entirely off base, you're an accessory—albeit, after the fact."

Traynor leaned back in the booth. "What leads you to these conclusions?"

"A number of things: first," he raised his index finger, "John was an ass. He was dumping her and taking a powder."

"That's on the record. Lots of guys are asses, doesn't mean their wives killed them."

"Let me go on." He raised a second finger. "Manchester PD is still trying to get to the bottom of that rip-off a week or so before John was killed. A lot of money was taken and has since disappeared. I think John was involved."

"You still got nothing but speculation, Buck."

"Okay, let's go on." He raised his third finger. "The Mass State Police found a marriage certificate. Seems one John Traynor married a Consuela Puente last June. Mrs. Traynor, née Puente, was a stripper at a joint in Tyngsboro. The Lawrence cops found her murdered in a drug lab by the Merrimack River. There were other bodies there too . . . all losers and dealers, so we won't go there."

"I still don't see how Jillian ties into all this."

"Okay, here's what took me over the top." He raised a fourth finger. "Anybody who has known you for more than a day knows how you feel about Jillian and those girls. In fact, I believe you'd do anything—and I mean anything—for them."

"Come on, Buck. They found the murder weapon in Carlo's car."

"That bothered me too. Law enforcement has been after Escobar for ten years, never got close; he was too friggin' smart." He took a drink of coffee. "So I ask you this. Why was he hanging on to a gun used in a hit a week earlier? The other thing I don't understand is why was he in New

Hampshire gunning for you? Unless he thought you knew something about his money."

"We always said criminals were stupid."

Buck paused and then said, "Did I mention that Escobar's fingerprints were on the gun?"

"No, but that should clinch it."

"The prints were from Escobar's left hand."

"Oh?"

"He was right-handed."

"Really?"

"Here's what I think, Ed. I think you baited him . . . got him to come up here where you and your goombahs, Max and Charley, blew the shit out of his flunkies. Carlo got away and you chased him. He jumped the road and you planted the gun."

"You missed your calling, Buck-oh. You should be writing scripts for the movies."

Buchanan shook his head. "Come on, Ed, don't be insulting. You were soaking wet when we got to the scene."

"I tried to save him."

"Bullshit. You and I both know that's absolute crap."

Traynor leaned forward. "Okay, so where does all this theorizing leave us?"

"No place." Traynor would have felt better had Buck smiled. There wasn't the slightest hint of one when Buck continued, "The staties in both New Hampshire and Massachusetts are happy. Our boys got a case off the books and the Mass police got rid of the Escobar organization. Hell, even the DEA is happy, a major source of drugs is gone forever."

"Some other scumbag will fill the void," Traynor said.

"No doubt someone will, but in the meantime, there's a lot less shit on the streets."

"So, what are you telling me?"

Buck replied, "I'm telling you that as far as I'm concerned it's a closed book. Everyone is happy and only the bad guys lost. If you can sleep in spite of what you say really went down, I can too." His face turned serious again. "You want to know what I think you should do?"

"If I said no, would it matter?"

"Nope, not in the least, so here it is. John is in the ground, Ed. No matter who put him there, that's where he is. You were never responsible for him or the way he turned out. So, bury him up here too." He tapped the side of his head with his index finger. "Then move on, marry Jillian and raise those girls, but put John behind you forever—both of you." He stood up and threw a ten-dollar bill on the table. "Breakfast is on me." He started walking away.

"Buck?"

Buchanan stopped and turned. "Yeah?"

"Thanks."

"Hey, what are friends for?"

"Next time you have a homicide . . ."

"Yeah?"

"Don't call me, okay?"

"Believe me, after this you'll be the last to know. Hang in there, Eddie."

ACKNOWLEDGEMENTS

This novel started out as an exercise for NaNoWriMo (November is National Novel Writing Month), a forum in which writers take on the challenge of writing fifty thousand words in thirty days. The goal is to write, not edit nor revise. Get the novel on paper. The first result was a work in need of a lot of polishing and correcting.

As usual, thanks are owed to a number of people. First, and foremost, I thank my late wife, Connie. She was my best friend, number one fan, and often my most honest critic. When I ran into a problem, like the time I lost the entire novel when my laptop blew away the file, she was there to prod me on. Over the course of a thirty-six-year marriage, she taught me many lessons, the most important being: your true friends will tell you what you need to hear, not what you want to hear. It's a lesson that has been reinforced many times, usually when I present a chapter of my current novel to my current first reader.

Thanks are owed to Stephen Singer and Merchants Automotive Group of Hooksett, New Hampshire who contacted me to explore the possibility of auctioning off the use of the highest bidder's name; all proceeds went to the BOB BAINES BLARNEY BREAKFAST—the recipient charities are the American Red Cross, the Special Olympics NH and the International Institute of NE.

Special thanks to Patrick Bigg, President of Commercial Property Tax Management, LLC of Manchester, NH, and Maureen Rose Marx for being the high bidders.

Thanks are also owed to Paula Munier, Skye Alexander, and Susan Oleksiw, the members of the first writers group I joined. They gave me honest, constructive criticism (although my first reaction was to get defensive); after giving their feedback some thought, I realized that they were right (not an easy thing for a stubborn Yankee from New England to do) and revised accordingly.

Special thanks are due to Beth Canova, my editor at Skyhorse Publishing. Her feedback and recommendations made this a much better novel.

Finally, there are you, my readers. Without your support, none of this would be possible.

Stockholm, Maine, November 2018